MU

Early react

Simon Davies (CEO TCT) (who has be
progressed)

22 March – "However much I appreciate
yourself must face, I have to share with you the torture of being a
good read! Being left on a precipice with no surety as to the date of the next
instalment is worse than a cliffhanger TV serial. At least you know it's 7 days and
that the Sunday supplement will give clues to what's next. I'm in the garden with
Apricot and Pod waiting … Seriously though, I do love your style and content, so
take whatever time you need to weave your tapestry."

11 April – "I can honestly say that there are few modern authors I have read that
bring characters and scenes together so vividly and with such colour. As a reader
I have total trust that you will look after me. I can't tell you how often I am
disappointed by authors who seem only to write for themselves or some strange
sect. Write on, write on…"

Jeffrey Archer (Novelist) – "This gentle story is beautifully descriptive and you
have a lovely turn of phrase for each of the characters you bring into the story.
Alison, (my PA), read it, and loved it."

Jo-Ann Caulkin (Publisher's representative) – "I started reading this morning and
can't put it down. The story has drawn me in very quickly. It is so exciting when
a book grabs you straightaway and you can't wait to get back to it. It becomes a
parallel world you want to keep jumping back into."

Helen Fearnley (Freelance journalist) – "I've finished it and I think it's just
magical – especially the way you've kept the narrator's voice so consistent. Any
publisher will be mad if he/she doesn't snatch it up!"

Kat Gould (19 year old student) – "Oh My Goodness! I'm hooked to the novel
and couldn't put it down. Your book took over my Sunday afternoon. It was a
fantastic distraction from my original plan … I loved the descriptiveness and I felt
that you had drawn me into your magical world. Although it has quite a serious
element to it, you also made me smile. I felt like I was watching through a window
at a family story unfolding. One of the best things I have read in a while…"

Jennie Gould (Kat's mother) – "I have just finished reading your book and I
am totally in awe of your ability to write in such an amazing and magical way
about such a sensitive subject. The story has taken me on a beautiful journey.
Inspired from the very first sentence, I have read non-stop for 3 hours. Your
ability to create such beautiful descriptions, to weave such magic and joy into
this family is inspiring. There is so much I love about this book – the comedy and
tragedy of family life that you have captured brilliantly. It is fantastic and must be

published for all the world to read. I loved all the characters so much, especially the relationship you created between the children Apricot, Lizzie and Jamie; it hits so many notes of childhood and the relationship between siblings. The mounting tension of the secret served so well in keeping me enthralled and I wanted to find out the truth as much as Apricot did. Of course, I also felt a connection in that I knew the smells, sights and sounds of some of the places you were describing but it is done so well that I know any reader would feel they were actually there with Apricot on their own mission to find out the truth. The fairy tale at the end just takes the reader to a greater high in describing all those emotions as colours of thread, connecting us with the truth and beauty of the world."

First published in this limited edition (January 2008) by
The Book Castle
12 Church Street
Dunstable
Bedfordshire LU5 4RU
www.book-castle.co.uk

Illustrations for title page and 'Window of Far and Wide' by Jackie Astbury

ISBN 978 1 903747 89 6

Printed in Great Britain by Antony Rowe, Chippenham, Wiltshire
Designed and typeset by Tracey Moren, Moren Associates Limited
www.morenassociates.co.uk

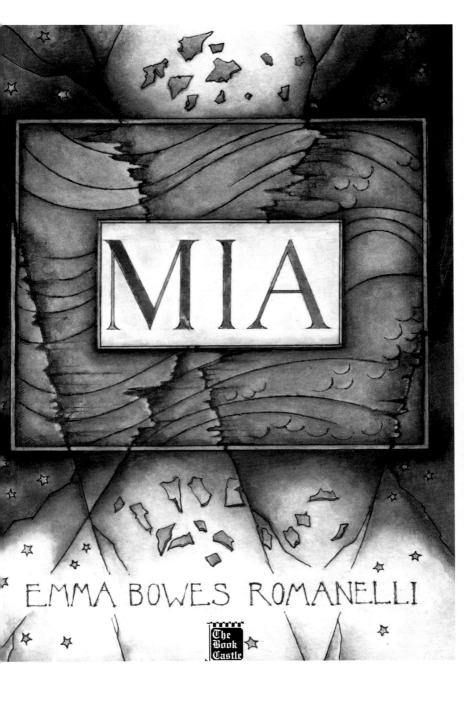

MIA

EMMA BOWES ROMANELLI

The Book Castle

For Lorenzo ...

without whom neither this book nor my life
would ever have come to fruition

Prologue

I knew her name long before they told us that the tiny, beating form that took safe-harbour in my ever-swelling belly was a girl.

'Broad Bean,' Jamie said, 'would suit her best.'

She wouldn't always look like a bean, the nurse had smiled flirtatiously – and, in any case, it wasn't usually the uncle who got to choose.

Lizzie was speaking at The Franklin Science Institute in Philadelphia on the day of the scan, but she texted back immediately to put in her bid. Still, she'd have to wait for an Isadora.

Alex wanted Bea, after his Irish grandmother, who had flashing green eyes and, at 23, had flown single-handedly across the Atlantic.

This wasn't far off being Bean, my joker-brother pointed out, before I sent him off into the corridor to give us room to breath.

And, after all, the conversation was really at an end because I think we all knew deep-down that her name was going to be Mia.

The only question was when we would tell her why...

Chapter One

I can't smell mimosa blossom without being eighteen again – dancing beneath the trees in the long, waving grasses, my knees sticky with cuckoo spit and my head spinning with the newness of it all...

I've recalled that summer often in the ten years that have followed. Where other memories fade and lose their will, those months still live and whirl inside.

You see, we were, all of us, a little different from the outset. Did we know then that our lives would be changed forever, or is it only with the passing years that we begin to understand?

I suppose all I can tell you for sure is that it started with a letter. As to the rest, well, I will take you back to meet me on the day it all began; the day when the rest of our lives arrived on the doorstep. Just waiting to be opened...

Well, here we are, outside a large Edwardian house. It stands in a happy garden square full of other big Edwardian houses. But this one is different. Not just because of the twisty-twiney jasmine vine that tumbles irreverently over the shiny black front door, or because of the fourth chimney stack that stands proud and tall against the skyline despite having long ago lost its relevant fireplace. No, this one is different most of all because this one was ours.

Beresford-Linnels have walked, skipped and clambered up its three stone steps to the door of number 47 Paultons Square for as long as the house can remember. And for now it is us, Paul and Nathalie, Lizzie, Jamie and me, Apricot (Amelia-Anne), who close its smart front door behind us each night, bid The Rest of the World adieu and amble up its many long-ago stairs to bed, to add our dreams for the future to those of generations past...

That's me over there in the square garden, lying on my tummy on the lawn. No, not the one in the sun visor and the purple string bikini.... Just a bit further over there – beyond the lime-tree... Yes that's it! – I'm the girl with the surprisingly large Mexican hat shielding my eyes from the noonday sun. No-one is quite sure where the hat appeared from but it's been hanging on the peg inside the hall cupboard for as long as any of us can remember and there is something rather cheerful about its 'five fruits' trim that felt just the thing for that morning.

It was early May and that day Summer had arrived. The camellias in all their operatic glory had taken their final bow. The cherry blossom had paid its delicate homage to the master printmakers of the Orient. The bountiful clematis was trailing chaotically over the woodshed and the daisies were exploding rebelliously out of the usually primly clipped lawns. A sense of expectation was dancing on the warm wind – it was the day the winter had been waiting for and anything was possible...

At least I hoped it was, as turning water into wine felt like a breeze compared to my current task in hand. You might have spotted all the papers fluttering prettily beside me on the lawn... Oh! so that's where 'The Edict of Nantes' got to... when it comes to escaped papers, a second look is definitely a distinct advantage... Anyway where was I? Yes, those exams. It was three weeks and three days before my A-level history paper and time was definitely of the essence.

It had been Nathalie's suggestion that I tried the garden as a venue for some serious revision – rather, I suspect, because my large, gangling form, sprawled (contemplatively), as it had been over the previous fortnight, across armchair, staircase or sofa, was in untidy conflict with the fundamental dictates of Feng Shui, than because she was convinced by the inspirational powers of Divine Nature. And between you and me, though I had just whiled away a very mellow three hours pondering how and why it is that daisies have those pretty pink tips to the underside of their petals and counting the (dismaying) number of new freckles that seemed to be appearing by the moment on my right forearm, I am not altogether sure that my grasp of the finer points of Charles 1st's foreign policy was any firmer than it had been when I spread my blanket out on the lawn at nine o'clock that morning...

Anyway, for better or worse there I was and, if I remember rightly, it is just about now that Nathalie herself appears on the scene. Yes, here she comes – and she is on the warpath...

"Amelia-Anne!"

I should explain – swiftly – that Nathalie is my mother. Her calling me Amelia-Anne is not a good sign and I suspected that, on this occasion, her

4

use of my (rarely used) 'formal' name might well have something to do with the voluminous, white, bejewelled kaftan which I had rescued from the dark recesses of her vast wardrobe this morning in celebration of the glorious day. At the tone in her voice I was not altogether confident that she was in quite such a celebratory mood...

"Amelia-Anne!" she called again, (merely for effect, as I, along with everyone else this side of the King's Road, had clearly heard her the first time), as she stormed, as thunderingly as her teetering pink mules would allow, down the front steps and across the square to the garden.

I sat up and straightened out the offending article (oops, isn't it surprising how crumpled one can become lying on one's tummy for an hour or two?) and draped myself strategically, if a little uncomfortably, in order to best conceal the mocha-coloured splodge about two-thirds of the way down that I suspected might reveal the final fate of the small piece of Kit-Kat that had mysteriously disappeared about fifteen minutes before. And just in the nick of time...

"Amelia-Anne," she glowered at me over the fence. "Are you going to let me in or not?"

That was the question. So far it wasn't looking like a tempting proposition. There is, you see, only one key allocated (for a gi-normous annual fee) to each household in the square. It is then down to the discretion of each (extremely discerning) resident to decide upon whom they bestow the great honour of entry to this particular little corner of Paradise. At that moment I had the key, and therefore the proverbial 'upper hand'. All of a sudden I was feeling especially discerning.

"I am not going to ask again," she thundered, which I suspected was not entirely truthful, but, conceding that a) she did after all pay for the key in the first place and b) if I didn't co-operate I was likely to be spending the night out there in this (potentially very chilly) little corner of Paradise, I stood up and nodded my acquiescence.

Walking over to the gate whilst concealing the Kit-Kat splodge proved an interesting undertaking. Still, never one to shirk a challenge I gathered the skirt up into a fetching bundle on my right hip and, with the pretty, footloose air of a Victorian milkmaid I danced across the lawn...

"Have you got a stitch?" Nathalie called, from beyond the gate, forgetting for an instant to be 'thundering' in her, slightly puzzled, moment of parental concern.

"No!" I replied crossly, transported with a bump back from my pastoral idyll into the 'here and now', and, in my pique, dropping the bundle of white fabric from my grasp.

Ooops. Nathalie's face resumed its stormy outlook and there was now a definite tinge of pink about her ears.

"It was an accident," I pleaded pathetically (all of a sudden 5 years old instead of 18), as she pushed past me through the now open gate. Without a word (far more scary than all the 'vocal thundering' stuff) she strode over to my hitherto rather dreamy encampment, rolled up my blanket and thrust the papers into the waiting box file. Following meekly behind – and you try looking meek in a vast Mexican hat bedecked with plastic pineapples – I picked up my shoes and resigned myself to my fate.

Nathalie, it's relevant here to explain, is French. She is petite, inordinately neat, dark and beautiful and would not be seen *eating* a Kit-Kat, let alone squashing one down her front. In fact quite how she gave birth to me, a tall, gangly redhead, inordinately chaotic and absolutely guaranteed to maximise any opportunity for 'squashing' has long been a mystery to all – except, fortunately, my father. Perhaps the only thing we have in common is our passion – a potentially explosive recipe for disaster. On this occasion, however, I suspected that meekness was the most tactical approach to an already inflamed situation.

As Nathalie click-clicked her way up the steps and in through the front door I took one last, fond look at the world outside and pulled the door to behind us...

Chapter Two

It's strange to think of it now but the letter must have already been there on the side-table as we passed it in the hallway, its life-changing secrets sealed up with a lick and a stamp. Ordinarily our father would have taken the post with him to the gallery, picking it up from the mat by the door, tutting his mild disapproval at the inevitable junk mail and sorting through the rest in the cab that waited for him outside at 9 am each morning. This particular morning, though, was different.

Our father, I should take this opportunity to explain, has been 'Pod' to us for as long as we can remember. If you were to ask him about his 'affectionate name' he might well tease and say that it is because it is only a few steps away from 'God'. And if he is after your sympathy he will tell you it stands for 'Poor Old Devil'! But it really comes down to the simple fact of his initials; P.O.D. Paul Oliver Daniel. P.O.D. Beresford-Linnel. Phew! Are you still with me?

Well, a very long time ago, Pod was a painter. At 19, he told us, inspired by the light and colour of the Mediterranean, as so many artists before him, he journeyed to Southern France, sat down on a remote, pine-fringed beach and didn't get up again for nearly fifteen years... Somehow during this time he not only painted hundreds of broad, light-drenched canvases but also managed to meet and marry Nathalie and even give birth (in a manner of speaking) to me. When I was three years old and my Grandfather died, (Grandma Beresford-Linnel died before I was born), the family art gallery, 'Beresford's', in Mayfair, needed someone at the helm and so our little family sailed across the sea and made our home at number 47. Goodness, all those years in just a few sentences. Still, there's plenty of time for all the bits in between but for now I just needed to explain all the paintings that lined the entrance hall that morning, and why it was that Pod did not have time to pick up the post as usual...

'Beresford's' has always championed modern art. In the first half of the 20th century it was Matisse, Picasso, Georges Braque and the Fauves. Great-Grandpa Beresford-Linnel had a passion too for Gustav Klimt,

7

Egon Schiele and for the then highly controversial art of the Austrian Secession. Subsequently the gallery remained always a little 'on the edge', giving wall (and floor) space to one or two select contemporary artists each year whilst maintaining its interest in the, now mainstream though no less remarkable, masters of the 20th century.

Well, for years, friends and colleagues had been pressing Pod to show his own work in the contemporary room. Each smiling suggestion had been met, down the years, with a polite but firm "Not in my lifetime" response and the subject was once again closed. Until the next time. And then this. This time it was the suggestion of an old school friend for whom our father had always had a great deal of respect. A former army officer, he had given up everything in order to work voluntarily amongst the abused and abandoned children of war-torn Rwanda. Heading up his own charitable organisation for abused children world-wide, run from his family's estate in Peebleshire, Rob McIntyre had changed the lives and prospects of countless young people, many of whom he followed up personally as their fortunes turned and their hopes and dreams became realities. Rob had a proposition for my father, and one that was to prove impossible to refuse...

And so it was that this week was to see the grand opening of an exhibition. Entitled 'Hope', it was to feature 52 oils on canvas by Paul Beresford-Linnel and all sale proceeds would benefit the immensely worthwhile charity of the same name.

All of which, I realise, only goes part of the way to explaining what 25 of the 'Hope' paintings were doing there in the entrance hall only 6 hours before the doors opened on the exhibition, rather than jostling importantly for prime position on the gallery's newly-painted walls.

Well, cast your mind back to the scene about 30 minutes before Nathalie made her portentous appearance... Did you happen to notice the small, white van that pulled up with a choke outside number 47? That's it, the one emblazoned, with no small degree of pride, 'Andrew Wells – Fine Art Framing and Restoration'. If you had been watching closely you might have seen the burly delivery man swing open the back doors of the van and hoist out, two-by-two, the brightly-coloured canvases, their transcendent Mediterranean light not to be thwarted by multiple layers of bubble wrap. And perhaps if *I* had been watching closely and not been quite so absorbed in my right forearm – '27 freckles and I am *sure* there were only 24 this time yesterday' – I might have noticed him deposit them with an irreverent bump on the lower step and climb back into his van. And I might have registered, as he drove out onto the King's Road to join the queue of traffic shuffling its way down to Sloane Square and beyond, that the reason Pod had left before the post arrived that morning was to ensure that he was at the gallery in good time to receive the final delivery of paintings from the framer. And perhaps I would have had time to run across the lawn, out of the creaking iron gate and over the road to where the little white van and its big burly driver waited none-too-patiently for the black cab ahead to make its opportunist pickup. Even at this late stage I could have suggested that he pulled back into the square, collected his cargo and redelivered it in the twinkling of an eye (or, at least, as fast as the King's Road snake could slither) to the 'delivery' rather than the 'billing' address. I might have. But – regrets and recriminations – I didn't. And so, unfortunately, it was left to Nathalie to discover the paintings sitting gaily out there on the doorstep, challenging the early May sun to match up to their dazzling Mediterranean glory instead of adapting to their newly-acquired smart Mayfair address. Hence, you see, those clickerty-click heels and that clickerty-click tongue. The borrowed gown, it seems, was just the icing-on-the-cake.

Or, you might say, the Kit-Kat-on-the-kaftan...

Still, as if by magic, two harassed phone calls, one grumpy delivery man and five hours later there we all were in our 'in-the-nick-of-time-emptied' entrance hall; Nathalie, Lizzie, Jamie, Jamie's two-foot grass snake 'Toots' and me – dressed to the nines and preparing to make our father proud. Then, five hours and five minutes later, there we all were again, Nathalie, Lizzie, Jamie and me, 'Toots' having been discovered poking out of Jamie's right sleeve and thus dispatched back to his murky glasshouse on the bathroom washstand. In fact, since we're all here and arguably looking our best just at this moment, it might be the perfect opportunity to introduce you, albeit briefly, to the rest of the family...

Lizzie, 'Elizabeth' to no-one except our Great Aunt Emily who refuses to accept any abbreviation for anything on the grounds that it is 'unnecessarily slack', is my sister. She is twelve years old, impossibly intelligent and the most organised person I know. She is also exceedingly pretty, not in the least conceited and unerringly considerate. Sometimes I hate her. But most of the time I love her, as does everyone, though I can never quite shake off the unnerving sense that she is not entirely human...

9

Jamie, on the other hand, is reassuringly of this world. Nine last December, he is 'the baby' of the family and as such is forgiven disproportionately much disproportionately often. Forgive me (for once), I'm still smarting about the minor incident with the Kit-Kat. He is inquisitive to the point of being nosey – which, he asserts, is essential to his work as a Secret Agent – but has a good heart and an irresistible sense of humour which from time-to-time even makes the corners of Pod's mouth turn up, which we don't see terribly often these days.

Perhaps more on that later.

But in the meantime we must get off – the 'curtain' goes up in fifty-two minutes.

And counting. Tick, tock...

PS The letter is still on the hall stand...

Chapter Three

It was one of those evenings unique to early May, after the sludgy grey of a city winter and before the claustrophobic heat of late summer presses itself needily at the doorways of air-conditioned offices in the hope of some reprieve. The sky was cool and blue, the air spirited and clear, as though the world were washed clean, its sins newly forgiven... London shone.

As we swung into Bruton Street from Berkley Square a small crowd was already gathering outside the gallery, loitering happily, intentions clear but loath to leave the small patch of early evening sunshine that slanted down across the street...

"In just another moment or two, perhaps..."

"Ah, isn't that Oliver?"

"So, how was Maastricht?"

"Lovely evening..."

And, ultimately, perhaps prompted by the arrival of our taxicab pulling up eagerly at the sociable kerb;

"'Hope' is something we could all do with more of, wouldn't you say..?"

"And so, finally, the curtain rises on the elusive artist behind the man we all know and love ..."

"Shall we?"

"After you..."

And so on... and in...

Strange how, until I pushed open the heavy glass door that evening, into the familiar light and airy room that fronted Beresford's three 'upstairs' exhibition chambers, it had never struck me as odd that Pod had always been so secretive about his own artistic output. The walls of our home were positively groaning with pictures; original paintings, drawings and lithographs by artists as diverse as Kandinsky and Arthur Rackham, but there was not one by Paul Beresford-Linnel. The impact now of the bright, vibrant canvases, despite the milling crowd who were

11

– I couldn't help notice – fast obscuring much of the view of the paintings they were supposed to have come to see, was, for me, overwhelming. It was as though they shouted out, in their glorious, ringing tones, a whole new dimension to a man, I realised then, I hardly knew. And yet, as I stood there, the life and colour lifting from the walls and seeping into my inner consciousness, something in me stirred.

I moved in closer to a single picture, close enough to see the individual, broad sweeping brushstrokes but not so close as to lose a sense of the scene as a whole. It was a seascape, as were a number of the other pieces in this first room, but something about this one seemed familiar. The image was simple. Almost stark. A solitary yacht, vulnerable and isolated, a white dash of purity against a dark and fathomless sea. And I knew I had seen it before. I peered even closer to the small gilt-framed canvas. There was, as I had expected, my father's signature in the bottom right-hand corner, faint and illegible, but I had seen it enough before on letters and cheques to recognise it as P. O. D. Beresford-Linnel. But then... hang on a mo... there was something else in the same, painterly, hand, caught up – and almost obscured – by the foamy crest of a wave...

"Apricot!" Nathalie hissed, coming up behind me and prodding me squarely between my shoulder blades. "Mingle. Remember, you are here to represent your father. I am relying on you as the eldest to make a good impression."

It has often seemed to me that this 'being the eldest' business is jolly unfair. After all, what say did I ever have in taking on what is, if you do take the trouble to ask me, a preposterously disproportionate amount of responsibility, family-wise, merely by virtue of the fact that I was the first to be squeezed out into this big, wide, unjust world? None, would be my answer. Yet it always falls to me to "set a good example", "make a good impression", *and* clean out the rabbits (which incidentally are actually Jamie's), without so much as an, "...if you wouldn't mind...", "...how much we would appreciate it if you would... ", let alone a crisp, new five pound note or two. Anyway, just at that moment it was particularly galling.

Though I was sorely tempted to hiss back, "I'm busy!" ("Go away!" would, I felt, have followed it up nicely), I was conscious that in terms of my representing Pod she did have a point and I definitely didn't want to draw attention to myself. So, resolving to come back to the little picture at the earliest opportunity, I turned away and entered the happy throng...

And happy it was. Rob gave a passionate and moving speech about his work with the children for whom they were all there that evening. He spoke of the 'Hope' that the exhibition's proceeds would bring to many disadvantaged lives and of the miracles that he had seen take place before his eyes. Grasping Pod's hand firmly, he thanked him for his contribution to the miracles of the future and it was clear, even as he spoke, that there would not be a painting unsold by the end of the night...

And when we held the many light, flimsy slips of paper in our hands at the close of the show, how strange it was to know that though they looked like cheques they were really miracles waiting to happen and that already new Hope was sailing on the wind...

Having played their part, each of the paintings, over the coming week, would be carefully packed and delivered to their respective buyers. I loved to think of them finally taking pride of place on walls around the country, bearing vibrant, colourful testimony to the legacy that they would leave behind. All, that is, but my little sailing-boat. Who had bought that, I wondered, and why was I so drawn to it myself? I wandered back over to the narrow pillar on which the painting was hung and, finally able to take advantage of a moment to myself, I peered closely once again at the mysterious inscription in the corner of the canvas. No, there was no doubt, though what it meant I had no idea. There, just below my father's name, was written:

'Mia'.

Chapter Four

The next morning we were all woken with a bump. Literally. The 'getting up' part of the day has never been my favourite one and frankly it would take something akin to Armageddon to rouse me with any sort of urgency from my cherished torpor. Though this 'bump' was loud, it became rapidly clear that it was not to be followed up by plagues, lakes of fire and brimstone and the like and therefore did not merit undue concern or rash levels of activity. The fact that Nathalie – who is an undeniable meercat (this astonishing little fellow merits a trip to your local zoo if you have never seen one) to my sloth – was already 'on the case' in terms of investigating said 'bump' at source, further removed (if such were possible) any misplaced folly of obligation from my door... Jamie, never light of foot at the best of times, thundered down the attic stairs shortly after – the amount of noise preposterously disproportionate to his size and surely of great disadvantage to a secret agent – though I suspected more out of a burning sense of curiosity than a burning desire to be of any appropriate assistance. Moments later a loud cry from Nathalie and a somewhat weaker response from Lizzie shed further light on the situation, affirming my conviction that not extracting myself from the warm embrace of my duvet was the most intelligent approach to the whole business. Nathalie, however, clearly had a different perspective on things.

"Apricot!" she screeched, as she flung open my bedroom door. "For goodness sake get up! Your sister has had the most terrible accident and an ambulance must be called immediately."

This news effected the desired response. As I mentioned before, I have a great deal of affection for Lizzie, despite the fact that she is perfect, and to hear that she was in some degree of distress – that might even require hospital attention (though Nathalie is rather inclined towards overreaction, particularly where Lizzie is concerned) – was more than enough to see me sever relations with my feather-stuffed friend once and for all.

"What happened?" I inquired anxiously, pulling on my dressing-gown. (Actually it is Pod's dressing-gown but I like the way it wraps so copiously around me and I'm hoping that he will become so familiar with seeing it on me that he forgets altogether that it was his Christmas present from Nathalie's mother last year). Her response left suspended in the air, just to the right of the chest of drawers, as she shot back out of the door, she informed me rather impatiently that Lizzie had inadvertently fallen off the top of the guest room wardrobe. Quite what Lizzie had been doing on top of the guest room wardrobe at 7 o'clock in the morning seemed to be of rather less interest to her than it was to me, so I temporarily suppressed my curiosity in the interest of calling for immediate medical assistance.

Finding the telephone proved to be my first challenge. Always a family somewhat behind the times, we were still acclimatising to the radical invention of the 'walkabout' telephone and as such, factoring in the inevitable hunt, making a phone call that might otherwise take, say, 3 minutes, tended to take 33. Since Jamie had pointed out on his return from school this time the facility to 'call' for your handset via an unnecessarily small, highly obscure button on the 'base-station' should just such an occasion arise, our efficiency rating had improved markedly, but there was still undoubtedly room for improvement. Nathalie, I knew, would have little patience with my plight. It was a strange irony that the more often she admonished us for forgetting to replace the phone on its 'nest' the more obscure the places we found to leave it. On this occasion the helpful ring tone appeared to be coming from somewhere in the linen room, though quite what anyone might have been doing making calls in there was beyond me. The tiny room also housed the hot-water cylinder and as such rivalled Venice in August for swelter-factor. Merely the idea of being in there for more than a 10 second dash to find a clean pair of pants brought me out in beads. Still, the ringer kept ringing and logic or no, it seemed pretty convinced that Venice it was – and this *was* a crisis. Resisting the urge to strip off entirely, I dove in and began rummaging around on the shelves, emerging triumphant, if fevered, 16 seconds later, phone in hand.

Realising that I was not altogether sure what to inform someone on reaching assistance, I stormed back down the stairs to the guest room landing: Our house is built on three floors – four if you count the basement – with the guest room being situated at the top of the first flight of stairs. (Which to my mind makes it the second floor but for some reason estate agents always seem to call this the 'first floor'... anyway, I digress...) So

15

there I am just outside the small, pretty bedroom and there too is my small, pretty sister, half in and half out across the stairway, looking decidedly uncomfortable.

"Should her leg be able to stick out at that alarming angle?" I asked unhelpfully, conscious that were mine at that moment doing so I would be making a darned sight more noise about it than Lizzie was.

"No!" snapped Nathalie, quite reasonably in the circumstances. "I expect it is broken – now get on that telephone!"

I cast what I hoped was a supportive, sisterly kind of look at Lizzie and set about my task. Actually I was quite nervous about my designated role in all this. The last time I had been involved in calling the emergency services I had been 4 years old and a casual friend of mine – who had just learned how to use the telephone 'in the case of an emergency' – thought it would be rather a wheeze to telephone for the fire brigade. Sure enough there they were in a flash, sirens wailing, complete with suits and hats, hoses and all – just like Trumpton! The only problem seemed to be that there was no fire, a fact about which you might imagine they would be jolly pleased. But no, not a bit of it. Polly and I got a stern talking to about abusing the emergency system and wasting valuable time and I vowed never to do anything so irresponsible again. I just hoped they didn't remember me...

Within a reassuringly short time, however, the ambulance-men had arrived and negotiated poor Lizzie onto a stretcher, confirming the fact that she was indeed sporting a badly broken right leg along with the multiple bruises that were already becoming impressively apparent. Of course, Nathalie would accompany her to the hospital – this must, I couldn't help myself note, rather cattily given the circumstances, have been the first time she had been seen outside the house without a full face of make-up since she was 12 years old – but this gave rise to a further complication.

Ironically that very morning Nathalie was due to start a new job. Truth be told, not only was the job a 'new' one, but it was also the first that she had had for over 20 years. Though the idea of her actually admitting to anyone outside the family that she might even have been old enough for employment so long ago was, naturally, unthinkable, in private this made her even more nervous about making the proverbial 'good impression'. Given that not only is she beautiful, intelligent and cultured but that she is also terrifyingly self-disciplined, efficient and organised, I personally felt that all she really needed to do was turn up and close the door behind her, but therein, of course lay 'the rub'. If she was sitting wringing her hands in the A & E department of the Chelsea & Westminster Hospital how could she simultaneously be tripping decoratively into the offices of Messers Pomp and Circumstance in about... 10 minutes... time?! Yikes! There was no doubt about it. Even with her superhuman powers it could not be done.

The prevailing sense of human tragedy was not lost on me. Not only was Lizzie, ballerina extraordinaire, looking at spending no short amount of time legless (as it were) but my mother was having to come to terms, simultaneously, with the fact that, for the first time in her life, she was going to be late. And all because Lizzie fell off the wardrobe. Which reminded me – what on earth had she been doing up there in the first place?!

But clearly this was not the time to make further enquiries, as the ambulance-men, Lizzie, Nathalie and I – closely (and loudly) followed by Jamie – made our way down the stairs, with varying degrees of agility, to the waiting ambulance.

At the front door Nathalie turned to me. "Apricot," she appealed, with an unfamiliar warmth and consideration in her eyes that quite tugged at my heartstrings, "will you telephone Giles for me and explain what has happened? Tell him I am extremely sorry and that I will call him myself the moment Lizzie is more comfortable."

I squeezed her hand. "Of course I will," I reassured her, though even the sound of Giles 'Pomp' Pontsbury's name made the hair stand up on the back of my neck and the daisies droop on the lawn. "And I'll drop Jamie off at Max's for the picnic later on."

"Goodness," she flapped, in a most uncharacteristic manner, "I had forgotten all about the picnic."

"No problemo," I replied, noting her eyes narrow *almost* imperceptibly – she hates me saying that – "everything's in hand."

Though I confess that I might not be the most reassuring person to leave your life and times with whilst you attend to a crisis, beggars, unfortunately, as they say, can't be choosers, and thus she climbed, with her usual poise and elegance, despite still wearing her slippers, into the back of the vehicle. She looked out at Jamie and me anxiously. I gave her what I hoped was a competent sort of smile and tickled Jamie good-naturedly to show just how jolly and 'sorted' we were going to be and the doors were closed behind her...

"Why did you poke me?" Jamie grumbled as the ambulance whizzed off importantly to its destination, about 2 minutes away as the crow flies – or 52 as the traffic crawls.

"I didn't poke you," I replied, equally disgruntled, "that was a tickle."

"Well, it wasn't like Pod's tickles," Jamie retorted. "His don't hurt."

"Well, I am doing my best," I answered him, rather piqued and feeling increasingly like poking him for real, and thus showing him the difference between a true poke and a playful tickle into the bargain. "And Pod isn't here at the moment so you will just have to make do with me."

Our father had opted to stay over in the little studio flat above the gallery after the final, slightly sozzled preview 'guest' had been shown politely to the door. He was doing that more and more often these days – we had all noticed, though none of us liked to dwell upon the possible reasons for his increasing absence. When the thought does manage to sidle in between my defences, Giles Pontsbury perpetually heads the cast list.

Giles Pontsbury was our family lawyer, largely on the strength of his being an old school friend of Pod's, although I have no 'beef' about his professional capabilities. In fact I didn't really have any strong feelings about him one way or the other until *that* drinks party last Christmas...

Chapter Five

We were all feeling jolly excited about that Christmas. Nathalie's parents were coming over to stay for two weeks before embarking for a long-anticipated expedition to New Zealand. They had finally handed the business – Florient, a 'Confiserie' whose jams and naturally flavoured confections were renowned throughout France – over to Nathalie's brother and were looking forward to celebrating their retirement. We had arranged a number of 'Christmassy' things to do all together, and sure enough we had great fun ice-skating on the temporary rink at the Broadgate Centre, dancing into the stalls for the Nutcracker and singing carols by candlelight at the magical Christingle service. All this, however, was to be merely the 'amuse bouche', the ultimate feast for the festive soul to be had on Christmas Eve with a gi-normous fancy-dress drinks party in their honour.

Needless to say, much energy and thought had been instantly set to planning our costumes. Nathalie said we could each choose who we wanted to be, with the only proviso being that we were to make our outfits ourselves. Jamie did the classic Blue Peter thing; with the aid of numerous egg boxes, copious amounts of green paint and a large, extremely dubious, shiny green bedspread that I found (with no minor loss of bodily fluids) buried deep in the linen room, he was a crocodile to the life. Not terribly Christmassy and I suspect the oak-topped kitchen table will forever bear its livid green scar in memory of 'Old Croc', but no one could deny that he would make an impression.

Lizzie's first choice was to go as Galileo, as she was currently in the process of weighing up the importance of his contribution to contemporary astronomy, but, since the task of transforming a pretty, blond, twelve year old girl into the somewhat grizzled (if eminently wise) old fellow depicted in the only picture we could find would, we suspected, prove too great a challenge in the time available – not to mention the fact that it seemed more than likely that most of the guests were unlikely to recognise who she was even should the likeness be an astonishing one – she finally

19

conceded to go as Anna Pavlova. We hoped that the fact that Pavlova was very definitely a brunette would largely pass people by, as Nathalie drew the line at our dying Lizzie's hair black for the occasion, despite the fact that this seemed like a small concession to verisimilitude in comparison to the multiple plastic surgeries required by her preferred option. Anyway her outfit was a straightforward one and would lend a generous amount of angelic beauty to the whole occasion which seemed very apt.

My outfit on the other hand promised to be about as rich and ornate as one might possibly be; all velvet, pearls and the (temporarily adapted) tapestry curtains from the downstairs loo. With my shocking red hair and pale (and interesting) complexion, Good Queen Bess, Nathalie decided for me, seemed the obvious choice. I was rather looking forward to taking on the persona of such a strong, proud, competent woman for the night. There's no denying that should *I* have been the one confronted by Sir Walter Raleigh and his celebrated cape, I am likely to have found the only patch of the large muddy puddle to have remained exposed in which to plant my be-satined size eights. As such, the evening's challenge should undoubtedly prove an interesting one.

Nathalie's own costume, however, and that of our father, were shrouded in secrecy. She was undertaking them both herself, in the small study-room off the second landing and entry was strictly prohibited at all times. Naturally such 'forbidden fruits' just cried out to be...well...peeled? Oh, anyway, you can see where I am heading... Basically we tried every trick in the book to find out what was going on behind those permanently closed doors. Our early tactics were not terribly sophisticated. Jamie even offered to carry her (most intriguing) large carrier bags upstairs for her on her return from the haberdashery department at Peter Jones, which was such an unlikely event in the absence of an ulterior motive that he failed even to make it to the bottom step. Maria, our thrice-weekly housekeeper refused to be bribed and the most we could glean from pressing our ears to the door (far more uncomfortable than you might imagine) when work was actually 'in progress' was that it involved the sewing machine – which wasn't exactly explosive. So we were left to ponder and 'fish' for titbits of information. But Nathalie was adamant – she was having as much fun as we were with all the 'mysterious', 'top-secret' stuff and all she would disclose was that the costumes were very much a 'pair'. For the rest we would just have to wait until The Night.

And before we knew it, as is the wont of Time, there it was. Four...

five...six o'clock; guests were half an hour away, Jamie was green, Lizzie was angelic (what's new?) and I was doing a very good approximation of being regal. (At least, as close as one might reasonably be expected to come whilst voluminously bedecked in the lavatory curtains.) But no Pod.

We had known that his flight back from Germany that day would cut things fairly fine. The Schirn Kunsthalle in Frankfurt were mounting an extensive exhibition of works by Gustav Klimt and Egon Schiele, and, this being his specialist area, Pod had arranged for a number of the paintings to be made available for loan. For the past two weeks he had been at their gallery helping to co-ordinate the final stages of shipment and hanging for their Christmas Eve opening. He was due in at Heathrow at 2 pm and therefore was unlikely to have been home before 5 pm. Still, Nathalie had calculated, there would just be time to bundle him out of his pinstripes and into his mysterious new guise. So where was he?

"There's no need to worry," Nathalie reassured us, though she could not hide completely her own growing concern as the minute hand ticked mercilessly ever closer to the half-hour...and then beyond. The guests began to arrive and soon our narrow 'up and down' house was positively bulging. Everyone was there, from Tinky-Winky to Tutankhamen; Marilyn Monroe hobnobbing flirtatiously with Jabba-the-Hut, whilst Robin Hood attempted to 'un-snag' his tights from St George's rather-too-prominent spurs. But still no Pod. Drinks flowed and Nathalie, as always, was the perfect hostess. The little-used mahogany dining table, as a rule proffering nothing more appetising than a pair of rather ponderous Georgian candlesticks, was positively queasy with delicious fare – and who'd have thought Tarzan had such a penchant for smoked-salmon blinis? Everything was going with a swing.

Except that it wasn't. Chic and elegant she may have been, but Nathalie certainly wasn't in costume and I could see the tension behind her perfect smile. Extracting myself from the attentions of a rather squiffy giant banana proved to be something of a challenge but, on spotting a welcome window of opportunity, I made my apologies and went in search of my anxious mother. With a house the shape of ours, any social occasion naturally ends up spilling out of the main reception rooms. As if floundering in one of my more barmy dreams I squeezed past nuns in the hallway, chanced upon Elvis Presley just coming out of the downstairs loo (hope he didn't mind about the curtains) and mouthed a quick "Hello" to a pair of Supermen who were helping themselves to mugs of coffee in the kitchen, and I suspected were the gay couple from three doors over who had advised Nathalie on her latest bout of interior redecoration. Finally, having exhausted all other options, I wandered up to the third floor landing and her bedroom...

Finding the door slightly ajar, I was just about to push it open when I heard a man's voice from within. "You're not alone anymore," he murmured, "whatever time of night or day, I will always be there." Realising that I had inadvertently stumbled upon an intimate romantic tryst – though they had rather a cheek setting up in my parents' bedroom – I turned softly in the hope of avoiding confrontation. And then she spoke. "How different I feel already," she said. "I wasn't sure how I could carry on. Paul has been so distant for so long now that it is almost as though I no longer have a husband..."

The words were like a huge weight hurtling into my chest. Winded and reeling I processed this latest information. His paramour was Nathalie, my mother! And he, this smooth talking, silken-toned man was, very definitely, not my father. A part of me wanted nothing more than to dive back down the stairs and out into the cold night air... to run and run and never come back. Somehow, though, the very horror that inspired this instinct compelled me to delve further into the vile dark heart of my discovery and I crept still closer to the door. Peering through I made out the two figures sitting on the bed. Locked in a strong embrace he stroked the top of her long, dark, Nathalie hair. She lifted her face to his and he brushed his hand across her cheek tenderly, as if wiping away a tear. Giles Pontsbury! Pod's best friend!

As I stumbled backwards from the door, the couple, startled, got up from the bed but even before they had time to fully turn towards me I was gone. Down the stairs, through the surreal throng and out into the night...

It was about 2am that my father arrived home. We never did find out what their costumes were. It didn't seem to matter any more.

Chapter Six

Resisting the urge to use Nathalie's request to call Giles as an opportunity to tell him exactly what I thought of him was not going to be easy. I had been storing up a wonderfully colourful speech just right for such an occasion. Still, heeding the wise words of Mrs Rainier, the elderly lady who lived next door and in whom I had been confiding my innermost secrets since I was 4 years old – only she is, and will ever be, privy to the fact that I once cheated on my spelling test by writing the most difficult word, 'ceiling', on my left forearm – "My dear, always give people the benefit of the doubt. You will find the world to be a much happier place and sometimes you might even be right..." – I zipped up my petulant lip and went off to find the telephone...

Benefits of the doubt were all very well, but I knew what I had seen, and, when he picked up the other end of the line, the sound of his voice was inextricable from the image of him and my mother locked in each other's arms. Summoning up all my self-control by inwardly reassuring myself that, in the terrible event that all doubt was removed, I would by that time have thought up even more satisfyingly unmentionable things to call him – (I'm not sure that that is how Mrs Rainier would have done it but the key thing was it worked) – I was able, at least, to inform Giles very politely that Nathalie would be late to work. His concern for Lizzie's well-being and his being so utterly understanding about everything seemed to me entirely inappropriate (unless, of course, he was having a torrid and altogether immoral affair with my mother), and I was just about to tell him so when I spotted my self-control making a wild dash for the front door and managed to reign it back just in the nick of time. "Yes, yes, of course, I'll tell her," I assured him calmly and I even managed to squeeze out a "thank you, good-bye," before, very firmly, hanging up. (On the 'nest', just to make sure that he was gone.)

God clearly agreed with me that this idea of Nathalie tripping gaily back and forth to Giles' office every day, batting her eyelids at him across the desk and sorting out his briefs (or whatever), was not good. Quite why Pod didn't put his foot down about the whole thing I had no idea. He must have noticed how often Nathalie was dropping Giles' name into conversation these days and that she was spending an awful lot of time curled up on the window seat in the snug-room purring *almost* inaudibly into the telephone. But then Pod didn't seem to notice anything anymore. Even when he was at home he seemed to be somewhere else at the same time. And it wasn't only I who had noticed. Lizzie, who, thinking about it, lives almost permanently in a parallel universe, had asked me on more than one occasion whether I thought he was all right, and Jamie, taking flagrant advantage of the situation, managed to extract £40 out of him towards a new skateboard without him even turning a hair. Whenever I tried to talk to him about it he would avoid catching my eyes at all, ruffling my hair affectionately just as he had always done and making some sort of excuse to put the conversation to one side. And there the issue remained, on the side-dresser in the drawing-room, the bookcase in the library, the little corner-stand in the entrance hall...

Ah yes, the little corner stand. And look, the letter is still there unopened, addressed to our father in a large, looping hand. The stamp is a foreign one – let's see... it looks like... Italy, yes, that's right. Well, there's nothing curious about that – Pod has correspondence from all over Europe – although why this has come to his home address rather than the gallery.. hmmm?

But for now there are more pressing matters to attend to. And wait! Was this Pod putting his key in the door? So it was. Nathalie had telephoned him from the hospital about Lizzie's fall and he was anxious to know more.

"What happened?" he inquired immediately, spotting me loitering about the entrance hall when he stepped through the door. "All Nathalie said was that Lizzie has had an accident and is waiting to be seen by the emergency doctors."

I filled him in.

"What on earth was she doing on top of the guest-room wardrobe?" he asked, astonished. My faith in my father was restored.

"Quite!' I exclaimed, with immense relief that someone else saw this as a question very much worth pursuing.

"Well," he went on, "knowing Lizzie, there'll be a very good reason behind it." And he chuckled.

All of a sudden I flung my arms around him and held on to him as tightly as could be.

"Hey!" he teased, (windedly), an echo of the amused smile still dancing about his lips. "What was that for?!"

How much there was that lay behind that overwhelming rush of love for my father, brought bubbling to the surface by a brief but wonderful reminder of the real Pod behind the sad and distant impostor that had taken his place of late... In that instant I was then and there and I was 3 years old again; whirling and twirling through the warm Mediterranean air as my Daddy span me ever faster and faster... Until the world was just a green-gold smudge with rainbow streaks and we tumbled, breathless and giggling, onto the parched, crackly lawn, still joined fiercely by both hands.

"I just love you, that's all," I answered simply, and he kissed the top of my head.

And then, curiously, I remembered about the little sailing-boat. "Pod, who bought the small 'sea' picture with the sailing-boat in it?" I asked. Almost as soon as I had said it, I wished I hadn't.

Right there before me the impostor moved back in, reclaiming the territory that was never really his for the taking and banishing the smiley, 'once-upon-a-time' Daddy to a dark and distant realm where the sun never rose and the birds were too afraid to sing...

"It wasn't for sale," he replied bluntly, the smile that he tried to soften his tone with not reflected in his faraway eyes. "Now I'd better get off to the hospital and see what that sister of yours has been getting up to."

Somehow the effort he was making to hold on to the warm, relaxed mood of only moments before made the change still more marked and poignant. But I didn't know where to find him and so I smiled my own half-smile and squeezed his hand. "Take a big kiss to Lizzie for me," I said, "and tell her that she needn't worry about the petri-dishes, I'll put them in the airing cupboard at the right time if she isn't back." Lizzie was in the process of growing some very dubious looking bacterium on the bathroom windowsill – Nathalie says that if it's dubious looking bacterium that she is interested in then she only has to look under Jamie's bed where one can usually rely upon finding at least two festering old cocoa mugs but, as Lizzie explained patiently, this was a controlled experiment and as such required strictly monitored conditions.

The old Pod ruffled my hair frailly but defiantly and closed the door behind him.

Chapter Seven

As I stood there, once again alone in the entrance hall, how strange that it wasn't Pod or Giles – or even what Lizzie had been doing on the wardrobe – that teased my mind but the little sailboat, so vulnerable amidst its dark and threatening sea. And so familiar. But where had I seen it before? And how curious that of all the paintings this one was not for sale. Remembering having seen a copy of the catalogue on the round 'island' in the kitchen which, though designed as a convenient serving table for all the roast dinners that we never seemed to have, tended rather to act as a convenient 'stopping off' place for anything of the 'paper' persuasion that happened to be passing through. Once a week Nathalie would insist upon the 'round' being cleared, at which point the various chaotic piles were merely transferred to the large coffee table in the snug-room to await further instruction. With a bit of luck the catalogue was still at 'first base', since the coffee table was really a kind of Hades for the printed word: sort of like the place where elephants go to die. Fortune prevailed. The kitchen it was and, extracting it from the random embrace of Jamie's half-term report and last week's invoice from the window cleaner, I took it through into the snug and curled up in the squashy old armchair. I had always loved this chair best of all. It was Pod's chair and it held the faint but unmistakable scent of him – a lemony, musky smell that, now I think of it, quite possibly owes as much to the chair itself as to my father, but, for me, to sit in it was always to be cocooned in security and love.

The 'Hope Paintings', the catalogue informed me, consisted of fifty-two oils-on-canvas by Paul Beresford-Linnel. Painted over a period of ten years, the paintings 'represent for the artist not only his response to the natural beauty of the Mediterranean coastline but the sense of freedom and possibility that characterised that time of his life'.

'Freedom'...'Possibility'... I turned back to the cover, to the bright, animated picture, entitled simply 'Day'. And I could feel it. The broad brushstrokes, casual but at the same time so precisely placed, seemed to yearn beyond their canvas, spirited and alive, though over twenty years had passed since their capture. The light was strong and clear, the scene not of the sea but a landscape, at a point where the hills and the mountains met, where the soft, forested curves conceded to the might of rugged red rock. I could almost breathe the cool, clean air as I followed the narrow shepherds' pass that forged a valley in between and carried me out to the to-be-imagined world beyond...

The tale, as our father told it, was always different to Nathalie's, but we loved them both. Nathalie's was a love story – but then perhaps his was too, in its way... Hers told of a young French girl, growing up among peach trees and olive groves. It talked of fields of sunflowers throwing their golden smiles up and out as far as the eye could see. It recalled the scent of lavender on the wind that buffeted in through her bedroom window and the softness of the salt-laden air. We heard of the glamorously named 'Florient', the family 'confiserie', renowned throughout France, and each time we learned of it we would run our tongues along our lips lusciously and taste anew of its rainbow jars of unctuous fruit confections, still warm from the making. But most of all what we loved to hear about was the handsome prince, who rode into the yard for her one sultry afternoon on a steed that might once have been a heavy legged cart-horse but forever after was to be a wild and splendid stallion with eyes that flashed and a spirit that galloped like the wind. And always we cheered as the noble beast tossed its head proudly and carried the two of them off into the future, where the horizon went on forever and anything was possible...

From Pod we learned about a young man, idealistic and true, with a yearning not for adventure but for sanctuary. He told us how he had arrived in France at nineteen, seeking to rediscover a peace once, for the briefest of moments long-ago, held in his heart and then lost on the wind. He had been drawn too by his longing to paint – to express himself in the universal language of colour and line. So many other artists, he knew, had found their peace and their inspiration around the golden hilltop town of St-Paul and so it was to there that he made his slow and steady way. We laughed to hear about this other father, the one with the soles flapping on his shoes, with straw in his hair after a night spent under the stars and a little stray dog yapping incessantly at his heels. We marvelled at the very idea of setting out on such a journey with no more than a few coins in your pocket, an easel under your arm and hope in your heart. And did he find his peace? we wanted to know, though we knew the answer would always be the same. "It was there, right where I had left it," he would say. "And with it I found your mother and look what that got me into!" Then, in the old days, he would scoop us all up into his arms and we would wriggle and giggle and pretend that we were trying to escape but really we were nuzzling still deeper into his lemony, Daddy smell and knowing that there was nowhere nicer to be. And when we were too big for scooping but loved to hear the story just the same, he would, instead, twinkle at us and ruffle our hair and we knew that we were part of something extraordinary.

As I sat there, the catalogue in my hand telling the story in still another way, I was suddenly aware of how long it was since we had heard Pod's tale. Of course for the exhibition it had been necessary for him to put down on paper the facts, to pinpoint dates and catalogue the pictures according to time and place, but in that sort of account there is no life, no romance, no soul. I glanced down at the rest of the text where it described how Pod had approached Nathalie's parents at 'Florient' for temporary work – "an artist," he had always warned us, smiling, "is never financially appreciated until after his death." And we would try and shake from our minds the image of the newly-dead artist, lying flat out on a grassy bank, the soles of his shoes flapping and coins raining down on him from above. It explained how our father had subsequently been taken on in a 'more permanent capacity', and I smiled to myself in recalling Pod's so much more flamboyant telling of his tale. Never resisting a chuckle at his own wit, he recalled how relieved the family was on his arrival at Florient, astride a gentle-eyed cart-horse (that had cost him two months' fruit picking on a nearby farm and a large painted canvas of the owner's dog). Nathalie's brother, they had explained, was away 'finding himself' for the summer, after which he would take over the running of the business. Until then, they could use an extra pair of hands. Well, Pod would grin, it seems that after those first few months he still hadn't 'found himself' and – since no-one else could find him either! (there the smile would widen still further) – they asked Pod to stay on. And, as the months turned into years, so the little Provençal hillside became his home...

And mine too, I thought – at least for my first three years, when everything was new and strange and wonder-full and when each time I opened my eyes I was surprised to see it all still there waiting for me. Now and again I would remember; not so much a day or a particular occasion but more simply sounds, smells and that extraordinary light that sometimes, even now, illuminates my dreams... I had expected the pictures to bring it all flooding back but somehow they were my father's vision of his world not mine. Instead, though I wasn't sure why, I felt a kind of sadness seeping through me, creeping up my legs, weighing heavily in my tummy and finally reaching my heart with a quiet, sympathetic ache.

Suddenly conscious of the 'here and now' and, more specifically, my responsibility to get Jamie organised and off to Max's, I flicked to the end of the catalogue to find out what I had set out to know. There the exhibition paintings were listed, numbered and priced and I was curious to know where and how my little sailing-boat painting was marked in. 'Mia', that was its name, and I checked the list and checked it again. Sure enough, 52 paintings were catalogued but 'Mia' was not there. In fact there were no pictures there whose dimensions could possibly be those of such a small canvas. So... it had never been intended for sale! And then I remembered when I had seen it before.

Chapter Eight

Actually, I was jumping the gun a bit. What I had, in reality, to call a 'memory', was a collection of random mental 'snapshots' rather than the seamless roll of cinematic film that might have been ideal. The challenge, I foresaw, was to proceed to put this untidy 'pile' into some sort of order; to 'pin them up' on a metaphorical cork board so that I could view the 'remembering' as a whole. This way I could also be sure to eliminate the odd 'rogue' picture that might have crept in – sort of like the snap of the skiing holiday that had found its way nonsensically into the batch of 'Cornwall 1987'. Of one thing I was sure – and this got me off to a flying start – the last time I had seen 'Mia' was before we left France. Since we set out for England three days before my fourth birthday, that narrowed things down 'date-wise' pretty decisively. How strange it was, as I settled deeper into the armchair and took myself back to another time and place, to view this world through the eyes of a three year old child...

As I sat there, so my mind was clambering up onto the high, broad stool that is there specially for me, so that I can stretch my arm up and out just far enough to reach the toothpaste and my favourite red toothbrush. If I stand up on my tip-tip-toes I can even peep out of the big window beyond the washbasin and look out to the sunflower fields beyond. The giant heads are heavy and tired on their drooping stems. Mummy has told me not to be sad because this is the time that they have been waiting for all summer, when each golden smile becomes a thousand tiny seeds that will feed birds and animals and, if I am very good, make a sticky brown seed-cake for our picnic on the hill. And so I'm not sad but just curious to know how God didn't only *make* the flowers but he told them how to make food so that I, and the animals and birds, can grow big and strong – and have cake for tea...

And then, as if by magic, the long-ago Apricot is curled in Mummy's lap, wrapped in something warm and pink and listening to her soft, Mummy voice singing the familiar French lullaby that she told me my Grandma had sung to her, a long, long time ago. The room about us is merely a

30

collection of shadows, indistinct impressions of, perhaps, a lumpy sofa here, a large bookcase there... As she sings I feel my eyelids closing and the beginnings of sleep drawing me out of the room and into the land of dreams... But suddenly, my eyes are fully open again! What's happening? My ears are alert to the sound that has caused Mummy to pause in her song and sit up straighter in her chair! Are there lights outside..? Is it a car..?

The 'here and now' me screwed up her eyes tightly, trying to remember... First nothing, then, from behind the dark, another scene was appearing, like a Polaroid print, its indistinct colours and shapes developing gradually as I 'watched', until... but where am I now..? Are those voices I can hear? Yes, one of them is Daddy's, but who is the lady who is with him behind the door that stands... that's right ... at the foot of the staircase? I am coming down the stairs, slowly and quietly – I mustn't tread in the middle of the top stair or it will creak and they will hear me. What are they saying? I can hear but I can't understand. Now Daddy is shouting and the door is opening. Quick, hide in the shadows! The lady is coming out of the room. Who is she? She looks kind but Daddy is angry, very angry, with her. Then Mummy is there and she tells Daddy, "calm yourself." And she holds the lady's arm gently and talks to her. So quiet that I can't hear much but now they are speaking words that I know... "tomorrow ...calmer... painful..." And then, "funeral...Tom... estate...father." And Daddy shouts, "NEVER!" and he doesn't sound like my Daddy anymore and I am frightened and run back up the stairs as fast as I can and...

The scene ended, more abruptly than it had begun, and I was back in the snug-room again. I was shaking and cold. And then it came to me! This must be when Grandpa Beresford-Linnel died! I had always known that it was his death that had prompted us to leave our golden French hillside one morning for the grey London drizzle that mingled with the tears that made my cheeks sticky and my nose run and I thought would flow forever... Curiously though – and I wondered why I hadn't been curious before now – no-one ever spoke of it again. Or of the grandfather that I had never known, except as an evil spectre who, from beyond the grave, made us leave the pretty house on the hill, with mint in the grass and ants as big as my little finger on the kitchen floor, and never go back.

And how did 'Mia' fit into this 'once-upon-a-time' collage? Though conscious of the clock ticking where Jamie's social life was concerned and somewhat unnerved by the fact that I hadn't heard anything out of him for an unnaturally long period of time, given that he and I were alone in the house and he hadn't eaten for at least an hour, I could not let it go now that I was this close. Ordering my conscious mind into submission, I let myself drift back into the limitless, velvety-black of my deep-down self...

More shouting. This time it is Mummy and through the wooden floorboards of my bedroom and the soft silky eiderdown that covers my head she sounds a long way away. But I can still hear them. "You don't understand," Daddy shouts back to her, "you've never understood!" "How can I when you won't let me in?" Mummy asks him, quieter now, and I know that they are just below the staircase as I hear the creaky floorboard that is three footsteps out from the bottom stair. Won't let me in where? I wonder, and then a door slams and I guess that Daddy has gone into his study because it's nearest and Mummy says, very quietly now so that I can hardly hear her and I don't think Daddy can at all, "... see you later..." I listen harder and I can hear the rustling of Mummy's waterproof coat as she takes it off the hatstand (the black one that scares me because sometimes in the night it becomes a giant that will eat me if I get too close) and then the bolt on the big front door squeaks and a rush of cold air comes up the stairs and in through the crack in my door. Then the big door bangs shut and Mummy is outside and it's too dark to be outside and I am frightened. I wait. Now, even without the eiderdown on my head, there is no sound at all and that is nearly worse than the shouting. I slide carefully off the bed and put on my slippers. The door creaks when I push it open; the light on the landing flickers, and the shadow of a moth makes a monster on the wall... Why did God make the night-time when the day has sunshine and flowers in it and the night-time just has monsters and the dark?

I keep right to the edge of each stair so I can hold on tightly and I don't make a sound. And because I am quiet there is no sound at all except for the 'bapbap' of the moth when he hits himself against the bulb... The handle on the study door is almost too high for me to reach but I stand up as-tall-as-tall-can-be and turn it with both hands. Now the door is open and I hold my breath and close my eyes so I am invisible. No-one speaks and so I open one eye just a little bit to see if it is just because I am invisible or if it is because Daddy is not there at all but in the dining room instead. The room is nearly dark but the moon is shining through the big window behind Daddy's desk. First of all I can't see him and then there he is, very still in the corner chair. His head is like the sunflowers, too big and heavy for his neck, looking down at the ground. I walk two steps closer and wait for him to tell me "What are you doing out of bed *Abricot*? Go back upstairs this moment!" But he doesn't say a word. He just keeps looking down. So I take a few more steps until I am on the rug and the moon can reach me and so could Daddy if he looked up and stretched out his hand. But he doesn't move. And I know it is not because I am invisible because both my eyes are open wide and so I am scared he might be dead like Maisie's dog that got run over in front of our house and couldn't get up even when I helped him. In four more steps I am right beside the chair and I poke my finger out and touch Daddy's arm. "Daddy," I say. And then he looks up and he is not dead but his eyes are very, very sad. When I am sad a hug is what makes me feel better and so I stretch open my arms wide and all of a sudden Daddy picks me up and holds on to me so tightly that I nearly stop breathing. Something falls off his lap and bangs against the leg of the chair. It is a picture of a little boat. The white sails are shining in the light from the moon...

And then Daddy starts to cry...

Chapter Nine

"Where have you been?" demanded Jamie accusingly, as he burst in through the snug-room door. "I've been calling you for ages! I've lost Toots and I want to take him with me on the picnic to show Max."

How could I begin to explain to him where I had been, or why my eyes were hot with the tears that were queuing up to fall?

Then, "Are you crying?" he enquired more thoughtfully, as he came over to my chair.

I was going to say 'no', when the tears started rolling down my cheeks of their own accord. I squeezed my sleeve to my face to absorb the evidence but Jamie, the Secret Agent, was not to be fooled.

"What's the matter?" he asked.

"I don't know," I answered truthfully. And then, "nothing really," as I didn't want to worry him.

"Oh good," he responded more cheerfully, "then will you help me find him?"

Then, noticing the last rogue tear clinging on to the corner of my eye, he added, "If you are still sad tonight you can have him in your room if you like."

I smiled and gave him a quick hug. "Let's go," I said, the long-ago world already fading into somewhere more distant and intangible. "When did you last see him?"

"Last night," he replied, "before the exhibition, when Nathalie made me put him back in his tank. I think he must have got out of the little hole where the glass broke when I dropped it on the bathroom tiles. Normally I put the soap dish over the top but I forgot yesterday because of the rush."

He looked rather forlorn and I squeezed his hand reassuringly. "We'll find him," I chirped, rather more brightly then I was actually feeling. How strange to feel this lingering sense of sadness without really being sure why. "He can't have gone far."

"But I've looked everywhere already," Jamie protested gloomily. "Last time he was underneath Lizzie's duvet – he doesn't like the cold – but I've looked there."

I shuddered a little. As far as snakes go, Toots was a pretty amiable sort of fellow but I wasn't sure that I fancied finding myself in bed with him at three o'clock in the morning. "Let's check my room first," I suggested.

After a good hour of hunting with still no sight of Toots, we were both starting to feel a bit demoralised. I was also aware that Jamie was due at Max's in about fifteen minutes. Although Max only lived across the square, Jamie was still in his, rather grubby, pyjamas.

"Jamie," I suggested, trying to make it sound like the jolliest of all possible propositions, "how about you go and get dressed and I'll keep looking while you're gone? You could put those pyjamas in the laundry basket on your way past."

Not at all happy with the situation, but, torn between his anxiety about Toots and his having been looking forward to Max's birthday picnic for ages, he made his way back up the stairs to his room.

Moments later there came a squeal of joy.

"Found him!" he shouted happily. "He was in the laundry basket all the time!"

Rather relieved for both Jamie and Toots that it hadn't been Nathalie who'd found him in there, I shouted back, "Hooray! Now hurry up and get ready."

Having safely deposited Jamie and Toots at Max's, where a ventriloquist was practising in the entrance hall and an unicyclist and a stilt-walking juggler vied for space on the front doorstep (whatever happened to good old musical bumps?), I spent the rest of the afternoon in really quite productive solitude.

Nathalie rang at about 3 pm to say that Lizzie had had her leg set in plaster and that the hospital wanted to keep her in overnight for observation. Pod had gone back to the gallery but he would pick up a bag of Lizzie's things from home later on, if I would be an angel and put them together. Although I quite relished the idea of seeing just what Pod's idea was of a girl's 'essentials' for a night away – when Nathalie was rushed to hospital to have Jamie, Pod followed swiftly on behind with a bag containing a pink suspender belt ('I thought it was a pair of knickers'), two pairs of opaque tights (no explanation except, rather feebly, 'you always say you can never have enough pairs'), a copy of 'The Heart of Darkness'

('Admittedly an unusual choice but it was already in the entrance hall as I was using it as a door stop'), and a packet of Jaffa Cakes ('those are for me because I forgot to have lunch') – I folded up her favourite T-shirt ('Save the Whales'), and fetched two pairs of Miffy pants from the linen room, her toothbrush and toothpaste from the bathroom and 'Best Wishes', the peculiar purple and white bear that sat on her bedside table. Though I suspected that she would also be keen to keep an eye on the petri-dishes, I wasn't altogether sure how a hospital would feel about the arrival of a whole host of positively blooming bacteria on their doorstep, and what if, by some terrible chance, they were disinfected to within an inch of their lives along with the rest of the inmates? No, much safer to leave them where they were. Instead I added to the pile the latest edition of 'Science Now' and the packet of Mini-Eggs that I had been saving up for a special occasion, and bundled everything into her rucksack.

Besides this brief interruption I took advantage of the peace and quiet to catch up with a few more of Charles 1st's crowd and managed to tick off a substantial part of my 'revision timetable' in one afternoon. Which was just as well since all that business with Joshua had set me rather off track...

Chapter Ten

Oh, haven't I told you about Joshua? Actually, I rather begrudge him having his own chapter as, frankly, he's hardly worth mentioning. Though, admittedly, if you'd asked me about him three weeks ago you'd have begun to wish you hadn't as you'd have found it hard to shut me up. And then, two weeks and six days ago, you wouldn't have been able to stop me crying which I suspect would have proved equally irritating after a while. In fact this is probably the first safe moment to start enquiring as, up until as recently as yesterday, the whole business was still weighing pretty heavily on my mind. Strange, but somehow the events of the last 24 hours or so have put it all right out of my head – which I suppose means that I am on my way to 'getting over him'. Still, now we've got this far, I may as well fill you in.

It all started at Arabella's Valentine's party. Rather more liberal than most, her parents had agreed not only to allow her to invite a few friends for the evening, but also to vacate the house for the night on condition that a) she keep the music down to a reasonable level, b) she telephone them at 11.30 pm to confirm that everyone had gone home and c) she remember that without her reputation a girl has nothing. Since, where c) was concerned, I suspected they were already a good 3 years too late with their wise counsel, that left only two, relatively straightforward, conditions to which to adhere. Or so we thought. In reality, by 10-45 that evening, it was becoming increasingly clear that a) and b) were going to be more of a challenge than first surmised. For one thing, the number of guests seemed to have multiplied at a truly alarming rate. Rather like Lizzie's bacterium in fact – and by the look of some of them the similarity didn't end there. "I've never seen these people before in my life," Arabella wailed, as a particularly unsavoury specimen, bearing an uncanny resemblance to the textbook 'artist's impression' of Early Man and all but dragging by the hair an equally primitive-looking example of the female of the species, lurched past us into a downstairs bedroom. "Someone is dancing on top of the piano and there's a girl asleep in the bath! The music is so loud that no one can hear me when I ask them to leave and Mrs Fitz-Patrick from next door has already been over twice to complain."

The situation was indeed looking dire. Now didn't seem the time to mention the cigarette burns in the carpet or the fact that someone appeared to have consumed the entire contents of the fridge and brought it back up on the handmade quarry tiles, but clearly something needed to be done. "Can you call Rory?" I bellowed into her ear in a rare moment of inspired genius. Rory was Arabella's older brother who had a flat in the West End, about 15 minutes away (as the car crawls). I could recall a number of occasions in the past when Bella and I had covered for him and his friends when the heat was on and as such we were definitely owed a favour.

"The telephone's not there!" she roared, despairingly. "What if someone is calling Australia?!"

Missing telephones. Ah! There I was on reassuringly familiar ground. "No problemo," I screamed, "I'll sort it." And I dived back into the melee.

Wresting the handset from a girl who, fortunately, (life's all about the way you look at it), was too far gone to know what she was holding let alone to have the self-possession to strike up a conversation with an Aborigine, I searched through the 'address book' listings for Rory's number. After about fifteen rings and just as it was occurring to me that he might not be there, a sleep-laden voice enquired irritably, "What do you want?"

Put so firmly on the spot in terms of my undeniably selfish motivation for calling I was, for a moment or two, rendered entirely speechless. It was a moment too long.

"Go to hell!" the voice growled down the line.

Shocked into speech by my realisation that he was, quite justifiably, about to hang up, I set out to explain the situation as efficiently as possible.

"Hang on a mo!" the voice interrupted, in a far more congenial, even slightly amused tone, just as I was getting into full flow. "It's only fair to tell you before you confess all the family secrets, that I am not Rory. He's out tonight so that I can get a good night's sleep before the Finals exam tomorrow." This last point was made with a hefty degree of irony. "You are in fact the ninth call I've had since I went to bed, although to your credit you did actually speak – eventually – when I picked up."

Somewhat emboldened by my realisation that his original, rather less than warm response, had been meant for the anonymous mute and not for me, I felt not only brave enough to apologise for the disturbance but also to enquire who, in that case, he actually was.

"I'm his flatmate," he revealed, sounding more human – and awake – by the moment, "Josh. It sounds to me like you're in a bit of trouble, not least because your music is making the vase shake on *our* windowsill. I'd hate to think what it's like a bit closer to home. I still bear the scars from a nasty run in with a Mrs Fitz-Patrick, who would have had us all in a police cell in an instant given half a chance."

"*Oh,*" I said, "you're *that* Josh."

"It sounds like it," he quipped back. "So who are you?"

"Apricot," I blushed down the line, all of a sudden, and quite inexplicably, feeling bashful. "Arabella's friend from school."

"Ahh, *that* Apricot," he chuckled, "all red hair and freckles."

It was at that moment that I remembered that of all Rory's friends, Joshua was my least favourite. "Well, if Rory's not there..." I countered stiffly.

"Hey, hey, I'm only teasing – come on, tell me how I can help. Since I am now wide awake, you might as well put me to some good use."

A loud crash from the direction of the 'Chinese Room', Arabella's mother's particular pride and joy, decided me.

Ten minutes later a Vespa scooter was pulling up stylishly at the kerb outside Arabella's, where I was standing shivering and damp in the deceptively light drizzle. If there was a degree of uncertainty in my mind that this was Joshua – it was at least six years since that legendary evening with Mrs Fitz-Patrick and her large, spikey umbrella – the fact that he was sporting a rather natty dressing-gown and monogrammed slippers dispelled it beyond any reasonable doubt. For eccentricity value, however, his wardrobe paled into insignificance alongside the enormous red rose pinned, 'tango-style', between his teeth.

"For the lady," he grinned, on disembarking and coming up the doorsteps towards me. He bowed flamboyantly.

Blushing, for the second time that evening, and more than a little conscious of the fact that my hair, when exposed to even the most inconsequential hint of a shower, becomes possessed of the kind of wild abandon that rock stars can only dream of. By now it would be positively mutinous. My hour-long communion with the straightening irons would be merely a poignant memory...

"Well, my lady," Josh broke into my sentimental reverie, "are you going to accept a gentleman's humble gift in recognition of this auspicious date and show me in, or are we going to stand out here in the rain for the rest of the night?"

At that moment Arabella came bursting out of the front door, all big blue eyes and poker-straight hair . "Oh, Joshua!" she gushed, "I'm so glad you're here. It's all too ghastly for words," and she hurled herself into his arms.

When it comes to dealing with the opposite sex, there's no doubt about it, Arabella has it sussed. 'Shameless', is what Nathalie calls it, but I can only stand by and watch in transfixed awe. On our outings together I had long ago resigned myself to playing Scooby-Doo's Thelma (minus the dodgy socks and glasses) to Arabella's Daphne. The rose, I knew, was now destined for another and I turned to go into the house.

"Wait a sec!" Josh called, extricating himself from Arabella's embrace as I turned back on my heels. He held out the rose. "I can't sort this rabble out whilst minding your rose for the night can I? It rather undermines my credibility as a terrifying force to be reckoned with!"

I don't know who was more surprised, me or Arabella. As I reached out shyly and took the rose, Arabella's eyes narrowed sharply in displeasure and for a moment she looked almost ugly. "Well," she sniffed, as she stomped back up the steps, "are you going to help or aren't you?" And, as she flounced by, I could swear I saw a kink breaking out in her hair...

The first thing Josh did on storming, Terminator-like, (and who's to say whether, of an evening, the Terminator's ensemble of choice isn't his winecoloured dressing-gown with navy piping and co-ordinating monogrammed slippers?), into the drawing room, was to turn off the Hi-Fi. A stroke of genius! Why didn't we think of that? Then, in order to maximise the impact of this devastating initial 'shock tactic', he signalled to me to turn on the lights. Blinking and confused in the dazzling silence, the party animals, deprived of their wall of impenetrable sound to hide behind, looked positively meek. Taking advantage of this moment of bewilderment Joshua addressed the crowd:

"Party's over!" he announced authoritatively, pointing in the direction of the hallway and open front door. "Thank you and good night."

To our amazement, the drunken rabble began, in an orderly fashion, to file out of the room. In a scene worthy of 'The Pied Piper' (only without the rats), they appeared from room after room, smoothing down their hair and straightening their rumpled clothes, to join the departing throng. As the final 'guest' stumbled down the front steps, I felt the house draw a huge sigh of relief and Arabella and I looked open-mouthed at Josh.

"Quick," he ordered, "better shut the door before they start realising what happened!" He grinned. "It's all about the element of surprise; generals have known that for centuries. Of course you can't guarantee there won't be a straggler, passed out underneath the dining room table or asleep in the airing cupboard, but this particular example of the species is not nearly so threatening on its own."

Threatening or no, Arabella turned slightly green at the prospect of her mother alighting on even one such 'straggler', sleeping off the excesses of the night before amongst her lavender-scented linens. Simultaneously she turned her eyes about the room. She gasped in horror.

"It's a disaster!" she cried. "How could they do this to me?" She looked watery-eyed at Joshua, her bottom lip trembling.

I'd seen this performance on a number of occasions, though admittedly none of them were quite in the same league as this when it came to being disastrous. Still, the effect was always the same, with any male within manipulating distance going weak at the knees as they rushed (as swiftly as their knees would allow) to her aid.

Joshua, it seemed, was made of an altogether sturdier metal. "That's not going to get the house sorted, is it now?" he scolded. "Come on, we've got a lot to do if you're not to be looking for a new place to live by tomorrow morning."

Baffled into submission at the failure of her hitherto unerringly successful 'Damsel-in-Distress' routine, Arabella picked up an empty beer can that lay at her feet.

Josh caught my eye and winked. It was then that I realised I was still holding the rose...

Chapter Eleven

Well, as I said, that was how it all began. And for eight wonderful weeks I drifted around on the proverbial 'Cloud Nine' (what is the significance of the other eight, I wonder?). I danced dreamily through each day, grinning like a lunatic at passers by and talking to the flowers (actually, thinking about it, I've always done that) and knew that, for the first time, and forever, I was in love. My heart ached joyously with the longing for him, my head was so full of him that there was no room for anything but his name. 'Joshua!' 'Joshua!' 'Joshua!' The whole world looked different and, when I was with him, I was different too. Somehow his supreme confidence and the ease with which he charmed his way through everything rubbed off on me. Suddenly life opened up before me, full of possibility and excitement. I brushed aside Nathalie's motherly concerns with an airy wave of the hand. "He's far too old for you," she warned, "and you are so new to these things." I could not deny that my brief, uncomfortable encounter with Charlie Brock at last year's 'May Ball' (lots of saliva and the nub-end of the projector in the small of my back) and a moment's clashing of teeth with the German exchange student who was staying with the family next-door two Christmases ago did not add up to a wealth of experience, but, as I explained to her, that was one of the things Josh liked about me.

"He says I'm 'refreshingly different' to other girls," I reassured her – and certainly the other girls within his large social circle were not like me. They were the kind who can toss their hair back, take a long drag on a cigarette, wield a half-full glass of vodka-on-the-rocks, laugh flirtatiously at a passing quip and touch up their mascara all at the same time. To tell you the truth I wasn't altogether sure I liked them that much – they made Arabella seem positively monastic – but none of that mattered when Joshua and I were alone. He made me feel special.

"He's a charmer," Nathalie observed, "there's no doubt about it, but they are often the ones to be most careful of. Before you know it he'll have stolen your heart and galloped of with it, never to be seen again."

But it was too late. Truth be told, I had given him my heart that very first night, in exchange for the rose. For good or for bad, it was his to do with as he would.

Arabella did try to tell me. At least two weeks before I found out for myself she told me about Laura. "Rory says they were together for nearly two years before they broke up," she said. "It was the first time he had really fallen for someone. She felt he was getting too serious and needed some breathing space to work out where she was going with her life."

"Well, it's me he loves now," I replied, disgruntled, convinced that she was just jealous because he had chosen me over her.

And then, one morning, I saw them. I was just coming out of our doctor's surgery that is set back in a pretty mews behind the Gloucester Road. After a horribly wet weekend, the sun was shining and spring was in the air – I almost skipped out onto the main street to catch the Tube back in to school. As I passed the Starbuck's opposite the station, the strong, irresistible aroma of freshly brewed coffee lingered outside. On an impulse (or was it Fate?) I pushed open the door and made my way towards the counter. And there they were. They didn't see me. In fact I don't think they would have noticed if the sky was falling in. Their heads were so close together across the table as to be touching. Her bobbed dark hair, just as Arabella had described, blended almost seamlessly with his and their hands were entwined. Now and again as I watched transfixed – so this, after all, is what true love is – he raised his head and kissed her softly and lingeringly on the lips. I couldn't have confronted them even if I had wanted to. Somehow they were untouchable by the outside world. It was as if their love had formed a kind of protective shield around them that nothing, or no-one, could break through.

I turned back towards the door, my head and heart numb, my legs, as if on autopilot, carrying me out onto the street. I didn't cry then. All the way back on the Tube I stared into the blackness outside the window, through my reflection and into the nothingness beyond. At each stop I barely registered the other passengers embarking and disembarking, going about their daily business when my life was at an end.

I've only seen him twice since then. The first time was two or three days later. He came to the house. I saw him coming from the window-seat in my bedroom that looks out over the square. Nathalie answered the door and told him, just as I had asked, that I wasn't in. But he knew then that I knew.

The other time, quite by chance, I saw him coming out of the little French brasserie a bit further down the King's Road. Laura was with him and he was smiling. With his whole self, not just with his mouth.

And I knew the dream was over.

Chapter Twelve

So that's that. He is, as they say, 'history', or, at least, 'yesterday's news'. read somewhere once that someone, sometime (I've never been terribly good with the 'specifics') said, "If you don't let go of the past, there is no room for the future", which seems like a jolly pithy way of putting something that makes a lot of sense. ('Pithiness' has never really been my forte either. You may have noticed). Maybe it was Winston Churchill – as well as smoking big cigars he, by all accounts, had something of a way with words... *Anyway*, where was I before you started wondering about 'you know who', (I'm determined that his name won't sneak in to a *third* chapter)? Ah yes, getting to know Charles I and just about to collect Jamie from the circus.

Yikes! Is that the time? Hadn't Max's mother said five o'clock? And where were my shoes? Forty-three seconds later, I was leaping down the front doorsteps, (trickier than I remembered it, though I was rapidly suspecting this might, in large part, have been down to my having grabbed Pod's wellies from the under-the-stairs cupboard instead of my own), and out across the square.

"Where have you been?" Jamie called from Max's open front door.

"Lost in traffic?" Max enquired sarcastically. (There's something quite disturbing about a nine-year-old boy who already thinks he's got the whole world sussed).

"I said I thought I could *just about* find my way home myself," Jamie went on in a similarly irritating tone; Max cackled spookily (he is definitely not a good influence on my little brother); "but Mrs Talbot was worried that there would be no-one there to look after me." And then, as an afterthought, and sounding more like himself, "Why are you wearing your wellies?"

"They're not my wellies, they're Pod's," I huffed, "now come on. Have you said 'thank-you' to Max's mother?"

I pretended not to notice Max pulling faces, which were even more hideous than his usual one, and lolloped off back across the square with

Jamie running on ahead. (Important to note that, at least where footwear is concerned, size clearly does matter).

Just as we got to the door, Pod was making his way out, looking particularly natty with Lizzie's "Hello Kitty" rucksack slung over one shoulder. "We're changing the guard," he said. "Nathalie's on her way back from the hospital now – she's going to call in on Giles", ('Ya, Boo, Hiss'), "on the way and apologise properly for today."

'Properly', eh? Oh, yes..? There was a loud rap on next-door's window and Mrs Rainier waved meaningfully at me through the glass. (The soundproofing on these old houses isn't what it might be). Begrudgingly, I got back off my high horse, patted its rump and sent it galloping back off whence it came. This 'benefit of the doubt' thing is quite a challenge...

"She suggested that, if she's not back by seven," (Mrs Rainier shook her head gently at me), "you and Jamie order yourselves a pizza."

"Brilliant!" Jamie exclaimed. "That will be my fourth pizza in one day! Can we have salami?"

"She might be back sooner," I responded tersely, secretly hoping that she was back at any moment, just in time to give her husband a loving hug before he left for the hospital.

Pod ruffled my hair and I tried not to see how tired his eyes were.

"I'll probably stay over at the gallery again tonight," he said. "I'll be at the hospital until late and we've got the shipment for the new exhibition arriving in the morning."

"Oh!" I said suddenly, "what about your post? Nathalie went through most of it when we got back last night, in case there was anything urgent, but she didn't like to open the one from Italy as it is addressed to you by hand." I squeezed past him through the doorway and took the letter from the hall-stand.

I held out the narrow, blue envelope. What happened next could not have been more unexpected.

For a moment my father froze. Then, so slowly as to be barely moving, he reached into his breast pocket. From inside he drew two slim, blue envelopes, their large looped handwriting an exact match to the one in my hand. Without a word he held them out to me and, almost unwittingly, I took them from his outstretched hand. Touching us both briefly on the arm he started off down the steps and out into the square. From behind he cut a comical figure, the fuscia-pink and yellow backpack bouncing cheerfully on his elegant, grey pinstriped shoulder.

Why then did I feel so sad?

Chapter Thirteen

It wasn't until later that evening that I had a chance to look properly at the letters. The pizza (salami, spicy beef and pineapple – not our most successful combination) was well and truly devoured, Jamie was up in his room with a mug of hot chocolate and strict instructions to turn his light out at nine – and Nathalie still wasn't home. Suddenly I longed to curl up with her in a way that I hadn't done since I was small. I wanted to share with her the jumble of thoughts and emotions that the afternoon had inspired, and, yes, to somehow 'hand over' the weighty burden of responsibility that I had been increasingly conscious of since Pod had given me the letters.

What was it that he wanted me to do? To read them? To throw them away? Or merely to hold on to them for him? And why had he kept the other two unopened? I took the envelopes out of my dressing-table drawer where I had 'squirrelled' them before supper. They were, as I had thought, all bearing an Italian stamp. The first, however, seemed, if I was reading the rather blurred postmark correctly, to have been sent last September, and the second just after Christmas.

At that moment I heard a key in the door – Nathalie! But then the sound of voices.

"Thank you," Nathalie was saying, "so much nicer than having taken a cab, and it gave us a bit more time to talk."

She'd brought *him* back with her! Even had he not then spoken, I'd have known she was with a man – her voice took on an entirely different tone, became more 'French', more flirtatious.

"What sort of a gentleman would I be if didn't see a lady home to her door?" Giles replied. (Cringe) And then, more surprisingly, "To tell you the truth, I'd hoped I might have had a chance to see Paul, but it looks like he's still at the hospital."

"He will probably stay at the gallery again tonight," Nathalie said – could there have been a tinge of sadness behind her words? Then, "Is there such thing as an 'Art Widow?'" she continued wryly.

For a moment they were silent. "Perhaps I'll try and catch up with him there tomorrow," Giles said. "Now get some rest."

Silence again and I strained to hear just what might be happening at this crucial moment of their parting. Nothing, until the click of the latch and the sound of Nathalie's footsteps on the stair.

"Apricot," she whispered as she knocked gently on my door. "Are you awake?"

All of a sudden, though I'm not sure why – perhaps it was that sound of his voice where it should have been my father's – I knew I didn't want to tell her about the letters; not yet, anyway. Hurriedly, I pushed them back into the drawer and clambered under my duvet. "Come in," I said, trying to sound sleepy.

"How is she doing?" I asked, as she sat down on the edge of the bed.

"Who?" she replied, with a kind of puzzled distraction.

"Lizzie, of course," I answered, irritated that she was so much caught up in her thoughts *of him* that she was momentarily off guard.

"Oh yes, Lizzie, of course," she fumbled. "I'm sorry, *ma cherie*, I'm so very tired." She put her hand up to her forehead and closed her eyes. How small and fragile she was. For an instant, and perhaps for the first time, I saw her not just as my mother but as another human being, just doing their best to grapple with the whole 'extraordinariness' of being here and now. As she fixed, then, I knew for my benefit, a brighter look on her face and brushed a stray lock of hair from my cheek, I felt a new kind of respect and love for her – a feeling somehow more 'universal' ; perhaps a kind of 'humanity'? "She's doing very well," she continued. "Naturally all the nursing staff have fallen in love with her. She's been so good and patient and not at all difficult about it all considering how much pain she must have been in and the fact that the doctors say it will be at least six months before she can pick up her ballet again. She will miss the summer dance festival altogether and she was so looking forward to playing Peasblossom. Still, she says, she can help out painting scenery."

Lizzie has been reading 'What Katy Did'. If you haven't read it, what Katy did was to have a particularly nasty fall that left her paralysed, possibly for life. Well, she wasn't – quite justifiably in my opinion – taking the fact that she was highly likely to never walk again in terribly good grace. In fact so fed up about it all was she that no-one wanted to sit with her and the like and things were looking altogether pretty gloomy. Then her mother hit on the bright idea of inviting her cousin Helen to stay.

Now, if I didn't know Lizzie I'd have said that besides being nauseatingly 'good', Helen was also entirely unconvincing as a character, but I do, and therefore I have to concede that such people do exist. Anyway, Helen was also stricken with a particularly crippling sort of condition, but, unlike Katy, she was an absolute delight to be with due to her unbearably (sorry) positive approach to the whole thing. Well, everyone lived happily ever after because Helen was able to convince Katy that hers was the happier path (frankly, if she'd never tried it, she couldn't have realised how jolly satisfying a good old wallow in self-pity can actually be). But there it is, Katy was convinced and her room was flooded with sunshine and flowers. The End.

Anyway, the point is that Lizzie was terribly struck by all this business and said that if she were ever in such a position, she would try her best to make her sick room a happy place for people to be. It wasn't, she said, a 'goody-two-shoes' kind of thing but really more of a selfish one because that way they would want to keep her company and she wouldn't have the opportunity to be sad or lonely. She's pretty cool, my sister. But she doesn't half think a lot about things.

Chapter Fourteen

Admittedly though, where thinking was concerned, I'd been giving Lizzie a pretty good run for her money over the past day or two. Even as Nathalie was kissing me goodnight and pulling my bedroom door to behind her, my mind was wandering back to the letters. Waiting for a few minutes until I had heard the water pipes 'clank, clank' with the waste away from Nathalie's wash basin, I climbed back out of bed. The first two letters were rather crumpled, but then if Daddy had been carrying them around in his jacket pocket for six months or more then that wasn't really surprising. Laying them all out in front of me on the dressing-table I wondered what else, if anything, I might be able to tell from the unopened envelopes about the secrets within. Putting myself into Sherlock Holmes' shoes (slippers?), I examined the front of each in turn. There could be no doubt that they were written in the same hand. The script was confident, even flamboyant, difficult to decipher with all its loops and swirls. 'A woman', I decided emphatically – Sherlock Holmes was always absolutely sure about his deductions. Instantly I regretted my conviction. A mysterious Italian woman writing to my father! And he keeps her letters in his breast pocket, close to his heart! Where was Mrs Rainier when I needed her? No, it had to be a man. A poet perhaps, or a painter – someone artistic. But if he was an artist, why was he writing to Pod at home instead of the gallery, and why did Pod not open the letters? This detective business was rather trickier than I had imagined – Sherlock Holmes always makes it look so easy. I tried coming at things from a different angle. How about the paper? Besides the colour, a rather beautiful cornflower blue, it was clear that the envelopes were of a very good quality. Yikes! So, 'she's a mysterious, *rich* (and *bound* to be beautiful) woman who is trying to steal my father away for ever and he's wrestling with his conscience at this very mome...' OK. That was it. No more speculation for me. Clearly, objectivity played a more crucial role in this private investigation business than I had realised. And, after all, Sherlock Holmes has had at least 100 years to perfect his technique...

Just as I was resigning myself to calling it a night, I heard the distinct sound of footsteps outside. Then, a key in the door. Pod! He must have decided to come home after all! I listened. The door shut softly behind him. Instead of coming upstairs, he had, I guessed on the strength of various small, but telling, creaks and clicks (perhaps there's hope for me in the mystery-solving line after all) gone into his downstairs study. It was after eleven and he had already looked so tired when he set off for the hospital. I hoped that, in wishing it, before long I would hear him start up the stairs for bed. By now I was wide awake, my mind skipping and dancing ever further away from sleep. I turned out the light and lay there in the almost-dark. In London the night sky is never truly black. Even after the street lamps go out, a thin, grey light sneaks in through the gaps in the curtains, seeping under door frames, illuminating the quiet gardens with its otherworldly strangeness... How different from the night-time dark of those first few years in France. A darkness that I could almost reach out and touch, so substantial was its presence. It stole my eyes so that the world was perilous and fey. It magnified the sounds a thousand-fold so that the gentle daytime tap-tap of the creeper on my window pane was the chilling rap-rap of a sinister hand on the glass, and the wind in the trees was a coven of witches swooping overhead on giant, 'witchety' broomsticks. Only with the morning light was the world restored. Until then I must hope for sleep to hide me in the land of dreams and pray that any Demons who found me there might be quickly banished on the early dawn...

The clock ticked by on the table beside my bed. There was still no sound on the stairs. Finally, a potent combination of concern and curiosity got the better of me. Careful not to turn on the landing light in case I disturbed Nathalie, (nothing short of a tornado would, I knew, wake Jamie before the breakfast gong next morning), I felt my way in the gloaming to the banister and down the stairs. As I approached the study I paused for a moment, surprised to see that there was no light leaking out from underneath the door. Perhaps I had been altogether wrong and never heard him at all; or had I missed him passing by my room and up to bed? Having come this far I pressed on, still tiptoeing, despite my growing conviction that he was not there. More out of habit than courtesy, I knocked lightly on the door, two quick taps and then a third, our 'signal', devised one sunny afternoon long-ago, when the woodshed was Pod's castle and I was a visiting Elven Queen, tired and far from home. As I had begun to expect, there was no response from inside. I turned to go back upstairs to bed. And then, for no reason that I could give sense to, I changed my mind.

The large brass doorknob was cold in my hand. It squeaked slightly as it twisted, a sound barely discernible in the daytime but by night, even this grey 'half-night', it cut uncomfortably through the silence. I pushed open the door. The room was full of shadows, some familiar – there was the small, neat sofa and, beside it, the large bookcase that I knew to harbour a rainbow of secrets within its myriad, hard-bound volumes on artists and their works. Other shadows were indistinct, taking on more – or less – form as my eyes gradually adjusted to the dark. I smiled to myself as I observed the hideous stuffed-crocodile lamp, that Pod claimed an affinity with and Nathalie had banished assertively to the confines of his study, rising up out of the gloom. I brushed the silky tassels of the shade with the back of my hand, noting that sensations too, like sounds, were somehow heightened when the eyes were obliged to accept their Achilles' heel.

"*Abricot.*"

The voice came from the darkness like a calling from the other-world. My heart leapt in my chest, thumping its surprise through my veins, even after I had realised it was my father. Through the thin light I saw him – how strange to know now that he had been there in the room with me all along – sitting at his decorative Louis XIV bureau, an indulgent gift from Nathalie; unexpectedly feminine perhaps for a man's study, but my father had always loved a thing of beauty above the purely 'stylish' or handsome.

"Daddy," I answered him. It seemed inappropriate to add more. Somehow the room was so full of unvoiced emotion that there was no room for the spoken word. In the grey half-night his sadness reached out and drew me into itself. And at its heart I found my father.

"Should I stay?" Did I speak the words or simply feel them?

He nodded slowly. "Did you bring them?" he asked.

"The letters?" I questioned, but even as I spoke it I knew. "No. They're up in my room – in my secrets drawer."

"Ah, yes." His voice was soft and sad. "Secrets."

"Should I fetch them?" I asked him.

He shook his head slowly. "Not now." Then from a small 'cubby-hole' above the desktop, he drew a folded sheet of paper. Almost tenderly he smoothed it flat, his hands lingering over the creases even after they had been caressed into submission.

"It started with this one." Though his words were directed at me, his eyes had not left the page.

The creamy-white goat skin rug was luxurious against my bare feet as I crossed over to the desk.

Even without the aid of the neat angle-poise lamp, I could see that the letter was written in the same 'looping' hand as the envelopes upstairs.

So, there was a fourth! And this one was opened…

I must have been staring at the sheet for at least a minute before I registered why it was that I was not taking in its contents. "It's in another language!" exclaimed in a whisper. "Is it Italian?"

Strange how the night-time lends its own mystery to all that goes on beneath its cloak. Had the sun been casting its smiling, benevolent beam through the large sash window as we huddled there together at the desk, would I have felt, as I did at that moment, that something remarkable was just beginning?

Remarkable – and perhaps terrible – if the worn, tired look on my father's face was anything to go by.

"What is it, Pod? Do you know?" I asked him.

His response was to change my understanding of our world forever.

There in the darkness he began to read. His voice was strong and calm, the tone and music of the language almost mesmerising in its beauty, though I had no idea what was being said. My father was reading Italian! And reading it as though he had never uttered another language than this. When he came to the end he looked up at me sadly.

"Well, little *Abricot*," he said, "perhaps no-one can keep running for a lifetime…"

"But what is it?" I insisted again, alarmed by the tired resignation in his voice and unsettled by the presence of the unknown.

"It is my past," Pod answered, "tapping me on the shoulder."

"And speaking Italian?"

"Oh little *Abricot*, there is so much that you don't know…"

"Then tell me!" I responded vehemently. Was, after all, my safe secure world built on sand?

"Where would I begin?" he asked hopelessly; as much of himself, I sensed, as of me.

"Begin with the letter," I urged. "Who is it from? What do they want?"

I took the sheet of paper from the desk, my father's hand reaching ineffectually after it as if he were afraid of letting it go but powerless to contest fate, and peered closely at the flamboyant signature at the foot of the letter. "G..iu..li…ana?" I read.

"What is that? Is it a man's name or a woman?"

As though succumbing to the inevitable, Pod sighed and took the page back out of my hand. "It is pronounced like 'Julie', 'Julie…arna', he explained quietly. It is a popular girl's name in Italy."

"It's a girl, then?" I demanded, as an appalling thought, though, I knew, utterly unfounded, flashed into my head. Was she his daughter? Did he have another little girl, just like me or Lizzie, but living in Italy?

My father leaned forward towards the desk and rested his head in his hands. "It is a woman," he replied, his voice muffled. "An elderly woman who knew me a very long time ago."

When did she know him, I wanted to know, and where? Was she in Italy then or did she come to England?

"She was in Italy," he answered. "I was in Italy. When I was a small boy she looked after me for a time" – he hesitated – "and your Uncle Tom."

Uncle Tom! He never spoke of Uncle Tom! All we knew of him was that he and Daddy had fallen out, many years ago when they were young. So violent was their quarrel, we understood, that it could never be resolved and we were never to ask to know more. And 'Never' is a very final word.

They were in Italy together – when they were small! Did they live there or were they just staying? Why had he never told us about it before? Though, thinking about it, he did not really talk about his childhood at all. We heard, all the time, about Nathalie's family – about her sister and her wayward brother, about her eccentric father, our 'Grandpere', and her mother, 'Marie', who still now brought us home-made jam – peach, 'abricot' or sweet, purple-blue 'myrtilles' – that she said tasted like the sunshine and we said tasted 'scrum-licious'. But we knew so little about our father's 'growing-up' world.

I had so many questions. They lined up in my head, one behind the other, in a riotous, disorderly queue, jostling and nudging for 'pole position'. But most of all I wanted to take away his sadness.

"Daddy," I said, "it's alright, you don't have to tell me." I wanted to throw my arms around him and squeeze all the sadness out of him with love. But instead I reached out with my finger and touched his arm.

He looked up and smiled at me, just a slight movement of his lips and a faint crinkling at his eyes. "I'm sorry, little *Abricot*," he said, "the night makes shadows on the wall. You mustn't worry about me."

"Can I help?" I asked.

"You could fetch me the letters," he suggested gently. "Tonight is when I finally stop running."

Chapter Fifteen

Growing up is a strange thing. Mostly it happens without you realising it. One day the bathroom stool is too high for you to climb alone, the next it is an amusing anecdote to remind yourself that once you really were that small. When was it that I stopped identifying with Gretel in The Sound of Music and began dreaming, with Liesel, of love and what it means to be almost a woman? But now and then there is a single moment when I almost feel the 'jolt' as I move a 'giant' step further from being a child towards the mystical realm of 'adulthood'. That night was one such moment. As my father opened one by one those letters, there in the grey half-dark that gradually took on the smoky-yellow and then red-gold of early dawn, I knew that I was changing. I sat quietly, curled up in the corner of the small antique sofa, the soft old eiderdown from the trunk under the stairs wrapped around my shoulders as he read. Then, still silent, I listened as he spoke aloud – to me, to the crazy crocodile and his lamp, and to the coming dawn – of the portentous news harboured within those elegant blue envelopes…

So he had known of Uncle Tom's illness more than a year ago and stayed silent! As each subsequent letter arrived, perhaps with word of his recovery – or even death – my father held it tight against his chest, unopened, as if attempting to cheat fate by his refusal to acknowledge it. Is that hate or is it love? Surely if it was love then he would long ago have left for Italy, and his brother's home, to be by his side. (I thought for a moment of Lizzie, all alone in the hospital through this long grey night, and hoped that she was sleeping deeply, her dreams, peaceful and happy, carrying her through until her homecoming in the morning). But, even as I wondered it, I knew it wasn't hate. Had I any doubt I only had to look at Pod's worn, tired face to know. Then why, when my father's heart was already there, did he not follow it out across the sea?

It was cancer, Giuliana said, and it had spread to Uncle Tom's bones. The doctors said it was 'only a matter of time'. Such a vague, anonymous cliché to write off a life – a short desultory phrase to end a myriad of thoughts, dreams, hopes and ambitions in one solitary, drawn-out wail of inevitability…

Still, time, it seemed, was on Tom's side. Where it might have been death that seeped chillingly out of the final envelope, instead there was life and, therefore, hope. Giuliana's tone was more urgent, even disapproving, but the message was clear; it was not too late.

He must go, I urged my father; and Nathalie too. I could look after things at home until Uncle Tom was well again. But life wasn't so simple, he told me; I wouldn't understand. And, as I clambered back up to bed, through my mind ran a scene from my 'long-ago film'; of my mother, at the foot of the stairs, and her quiet – "How can I when you won't let me in?" And I realised that there was something else. But I didn't know how to ask it and so it lay there hidden, 'between the lines', undisturbed. For now.

The next morning I was woken early by a loud 'Pssst' in my ear. Keeping my eyes firmly closed in the hope that, after my long, wide-awake night, I was actually still fast asleep and that the noise was merely a feature of the (particularly disruptive) soundtrack to my latest dream, I reached out to draw my duvet more snugly around me. Big mistake! "Ughhh"! My eyes shot open, any illusions about dream, sleep and the like vanquished as my groping hand settled on… "Toots!" Leaping out of bed, my heart racing (a friend of the family Toots might be, but, after all, a snake is a snake is a snake), I cast, through the gloom, what I hoped was a withering look at my small brother and turned on the light.

"I only put him down for a moment," he pleaded, spotting the murderous look in my eye. "I had to bring him because he didn't like the shouting." An unfamiliar vulnerability in his voice twanged at my heartstrings.

"What shouting?" I asked him, concerned. "Are you alright?" Then, as I listened I too could hear the raised voices at the top of the house.

"It's Pod and Nathalie," Jamie said. "She says we absolutely must go and he says 'impossible, and that's the end of it!' and that she could never understand. And then they say it all over again."

The muffled sound of a door slamming signalled the end of the 'debate'. Moments later we heard Nathalie on the stairs, passing by my door and down into the kitchen, from where, not long afterwards, rose the rich, comforting aroma of percolating coffee. Toots having been deposited safely (and within full view) in a large upturned hat, Jamie and

I huddled together on the edge of the bed. I wrapped my duvet around us both, and we sat in companionable silence as I recalled the events of the previous night. Clearly Nathalie too was at a loss to understand why Pod was refusing to go out and be with Uncle Tom. Was she, as Jamie reported, suggesting that we all go? And, if so, what about my exams, Jamie's school – and Lizzie's leg?

"Go where?" Jamie suddenly piped up. "Where does Nathalie think we 'absolutely must go'?"

Last night I had resolved to keep Pod's revelations between ourselves, at least until he suggested otherwise, but I supposed that the morning's events had put a different 'spin' on things. Obviously he had told Nathalie about the letters and it didn't seem fair to leave Jamie in the dark when he had already got wind of the surrounding tensions.

"Pod's brother, Uncle Tom, is sick," I informed him. "He might even die. He lives in Italy and he is all by himself so a lady wrote to Pod to ask if he would go and see him."

The room fell quiet again whilst Jamie digested this news. Pod's slow, measured footfall passed by on the stairs. I could feel his sadness in each weighty step.

"It's awful being on your own when you are sick," Jamie mused. "When I had the chicken pox at school, Matron wouldn't let anyone else in to the san for weeks, in case they caught it. Is it catching, what's wrong with Uncle Tom?"

"No," I said, "I don't think so. It's cancer."

"That's what Toby's mum had and she died," Jamie responded, concerned. "They said she was getting better then all of a sudden she died."

"Well, it sounds like Uncle Tom is really very sick indeed," I told him gently, "He might not get better either."

"Then we'd better go straight away, hadn't we?" Jamie retorted emphatically. "I've still got one week left of holidays and Lizzie's coming home today."

His straightforward conviction made me smile. In an ironic change of roles I heard my own voice, now the one of age and experience, echo my father's words to me the previous night. "It isn't that simple," I answered, although even as I said it, I couldn't really see myself why it shouldn't be so.

"I could leave Toots at Max's," Jamie reassured me. "He said he'd look after him when we went on holiday."

Not quite sure where to go from there I relapsed into a submissive silence. And then there was a knock at the door.

Two quick taps – and a third. Daddy!

A fleeting moment of surprise registered on his face at his discovery of me, Jamie and Toots mid powwow at ...only shortly after six o'clock in the morning...(ughhhh, no wonder I was so exhausted), before our father regained his composure and made his announcement.

"Nathalie is just finishing her breakfast before she goes to fetch Lizzie from the hospital. When they get back we are going to have a Family Meeting; 0900 hours." He caught my eye for an instant and nodded gently, then he turned and left the room.

"Wow!" Jamie declaimed melodramatically, though without the slightest hint of irony. "A Family Meeting! Something..." he paused for effect, "...Is About To Happen."

My own response to the news was (fairly racing) along the same lines. The 'Family Meeting' held a kind of mythical status in the Beresford-Linnel household. So much so that there had never actually been one because hitherto nothing had been deemed quite worthy or significant enough for such a rarified appointment. Were we, then, all to go out to Italy? If so, for how long? And when? For the answers, it seemed, I would have to wait until 0900 hours.

Chapter Sixteen

The kitchen, it was decided, would be the most appropriate place for The Meeting. This, I suspected, was largely by virtue of its being the warmest room in the house – there was always a decided chill about the drawing room, regardless of the temperature anywhere else in the world. The other major advantage became apparent on Nathalie's return home with Lizzie. Manoeuvring her red racing wheelchair up the front steps and in through the door proved to be an exercise involving the whole family – though I'm not sure quite how much Jamie, Toots (he wanted to welcome Lizzie home) and I contributed to the procedure besides a lot of encouraging remarks and a good deal of envy over the (exceedingly snazzy) chair. Lizzie's leg, (about which we were decidedly less envious), stuck out at an obstinate 90 degree angle, removing even the remotest possibility for a margin of error when negotiating the furniture in the (surprisingly) narrow entrance hall. Thus, the fact that the drawing room was up a further flight of stairs decided it. The kitchen it was.

Due to the unforeseen circumstances surrounding Lizzie's arrival, it was actually 0923 hours before we were all seated expectantly around the table. At Nathalie's insistence Toots was conspicuous by his absence (despite Jamie's assertion that it was only fair that Toots should be allowed a vote as he was also a member of the family), but otherwise everyone was there. There was a kind of hushed awe about the room in respect of the auspicious occasion as we waited for the Chairman (Pod) to speak.

When did he become so old, I wondered, as I took in his worn, tired features and the grey hairs that (newly?) congregated at his temples. His voice too, as he began to relay the situation to his attentive audience, held no sign of the youthful vigour that had always characterised his approach to everything life threw at him.

The news of Uncle Tom's illness was, of course, new to Lizzie. Just as for Jamie and me, Pod's brother was, for her, a shadowy figure, not so much a living and breathing relative as a character in a book whose name has been mentioned in passing but to whom you have not yet been introduced.

61

Still, like us, on learning that he was so sick she was overwhelmed with compassion. "But Pod!" she exclaimed, "we can't possibly leave him out there all by himself. Can he come and live here with us? There's plenty of room in the big guest room for him to stay; at least until he is better."

"He is too ill now to do the journey," Daddy replied quietly. "Giuliana has another suggestion."

Nathalie took his hand. "She thinks we should all go out to Italy," she explained. "We were wondering how you would feel about that."

For a moment nobody spoke. I looked across at our father. He nodded his complicity. "When?" I asked, "and for how long?" And with these first tentative questions, it seemed, I opened up the floodgates of debate.

"We must go," said Lizzie emphatically. "Though what about my leg? Will they let me on the aeroplane?"

"I've still got one whole week of holidays left!" Jamie responded enthusiastically. "I could make him my special pasta recipe with chillies. Max's Dad said it blew his socks off!"

And then they told us. And what they had to say *really* blew our socks off!

To live in Italy! Not just for a holiday but perhaps for always! My head reeling at their opening proposition, I struggled to keep up with the rest of the information as it came. It appeared that Pod's family had a house in Italy – in fact a whole estate! It was there that Pod and Uncle Tom had grown up, with Grandpa Beresford-Linnel dividing his time between the gallery in London and the Italian home. Grandma Beresford-Linnel – who had always been referred to as Grandma Sophie – was really Sophia Ilaria Katarina Pallavicini and it was through her that Pod and Uncle Tom had inherited the estate. Did that mean that we were part Italian then? And why had we never been told before about this house beyond the sea, with olive trees in the garden, grapevines across the hillside, and sun-warmed figs, to make your fingers sticky and your heart smile, beneath the bedroom window? As he began to speak about his childhood home it was as though our father was a boy again, reliving his walks through the ancient oak woods, balancing treacherously along the rims of the old stone terraces that formed the olive grove, climbing steadily up the narrow, windy path that led to the little church on the hill.

But then, all of a sudden, like a heavy curtain coming down between us and this window on another, faraway world, our father's face clouded over. What was he seeing? I wondered. Where was he now, with us or in a long-ago place where we cannot reach him?

For a few moments there was silence, each of us lost in our own thoughts. Then, finding her voice, Nathalie took over, addressing the here-and-now situation in her characteristically brusque, practical manner. She seemed, to me, more 'herself' than for as long as I could remember. Something about the way she held herself, the spirit behind her words, even the animation in her face revealed that it hadn't just been Pod who had been changed over the past eighteen months or so. Perhaps she, like me, was relieved to have some understanding of what it was that had preoccupied him for so long, stolen him away from his family in body, mind and spirit...

Well, if I still had that uneasy sense that, where Pod was concerned, things were not altogether resolved, there was no doubt that Nathalie was back on form.

"The fact is," she warned crisply, her eyes kind but her tone deadly earnest, "the reality might be very different to the dream. We are being asked to move our lives out to Italy not on a whim, for a holiday or a change of scene, but to help preserve the family heritage. The estate has been suffering for many years – since long before your Uncle Tom became so ill – and re-establishing it is likely to mean a lot of hard work and determination. Your father and I will need all your support and co-operation if we are to relieve Tom of the responsibility and make this work."

We all nodded seriously. Nathalie reached for the small pile of paper and pencils from the middle of the table.

"Now, there is a piece of paper here for everyone," she went on. "I want you all to think very carefully about what it would mean to your lives if we were to decide to go. On one side you should consider what difficulties or problems you can foresee; on the other you might like to write down the things that could be positive or exciting about the idea. After all, there is no doubt that it would be an adventure..."

Jamie, Lizzie and I exchanged glances, each sizing up the other's response to the news. Almost instantly, Jamie began to write, his frantic enthusiasm racing across the page in his large, chaotic hand. Lizzie's mouth was skewed slightly upwards at one corner, in a familiar expression that I knew to mean she was thinking hard. My own reaction, I suspected, was rather more difficult to read, not least because I wasn't altogether sure myself what it was. It was as if my mind was 'frozen' in a kind of 'stalemate' between the positive, excited me that was already halfway through packing her bags and the concerned, pedantic me who was clicking her tongue and muttering things like 'exams' and 'university application' and, more melodramatically, 'yikes!' To leave our home, our friends and everything we knew for another world; a new culture, language and way of life that at this moment were to be prefixed with a giant U for 'Unknown'. My exams, I knew were not really an issue. They would be over in a matter of a few weeks and I presumed that it would take that amount of time to organise ourselves for this gi-normous leap in the dark. In fact where *my* schooling was concerned there could not really have been a better time to leave. Even the matter of university was not really a problem. I couldn't see why my plans needed to change at all – surely, provided my results were good enough (OK – so that was no small proviso!) I could still take up my deferred place at Bristol the following year? So – that just left the 'Yikes!' And what was it that I was afraid of? The big 'U' flashed up in my sight-line once again. But, in actual fact, looking ahead to the world beyond the school gates, wasn't everything a giant 'Unknown'? And wasn't that actually the wonderful thing about life? How dull it would be if the whole road ahead of us was mapped out before we even set out on our journey. I began to write and soon my pencil was whirling over the page almost as fast as Jamie's. I wrote about the excitement of experiencing a new culture; the benefits of mastering a second language; the joy of opening my bedroom window to views that truly justified the words awe-inspiring, that I had hitherto seen only in art or film. I scribbled about sunshine, tomatoes and warm evenings under the stars. And I put down in words my feelings about family and heritage and how important it was that we didn't leave Uncle Tom to cope with his illness alone any longer. As my mind span and danced with these thoughts and images so it wove a kind of 'Tapestry of Certainty', a rich, full picture of my knowledge that, for me, to move out to Italy and take the future that that decision offered was absolutely the right thing to do.

And, when I finally put down the pencil, the other side of my paper remained blank.

Chapter Seventeen

Our first Family Meeting, we all agreed as it drew to a close, was an undoubted success. So much in accordance were we all that it was not even necessary to call Toots in to cast a final vote. We would do it! Once the decision had been made, (and we had all leapt and danced around the kitchen accompanied by the obligatory whoops and cries of "Look out Italy here we come!"; "Is Italy ready for the Beresford-Linnels?" and the like), Nathalie set about making her own list of the very real, practical issues that would need to be addressed in order for us to uproot our lives and embark upon the Big Adventure.

Some of these, inevitably, had made an initial appearance on the flip side of the individual lists. The issue of school for Jamie and Lizzie was bound to be an important one and, although Jamie had graciously offered to leave school on a permanent basis to make life simple, it was clear that it needed to be thought over carefully.

Where Lizzie was concerned, I was of the opinion that, since she already knew more than most people are likely to in a lifetime, she could in fact skip the school and university conveyor-belt altogether, leaping straight to a position of 'professorhood' at a, yet to be decided upon, Internationally Esteemed Institution of Academic Excellence. A long Italian summer, therefore, could be just what she needed, to decide to which such institution she was prepared to offer her services. Strangely, though, our mother did not see it like that. Lizzie had already been 'fast-tracked' through the school system by two years and Nathalie was not sure that the idea of increasing this by another 42 or so was a terribly helpful suggestion. She was not too happy at the idea of Lizzie's education being disrupted at all, let alone at such a critical stage. The fact that she attended a well-renowned day school in West London meant that, unlike in Jamie's case, (he had been very happily boarding at school for the past three years), there was not the option for her to carry on as she was currently doing, once we had made the move. Lizzie herself was, characteristically, much more relaxed about things.

65

"It would be terribly useful to be bilingual," she proposed assuredly, though without a hint of arrogance. "My French and German are coming on and I was hoping to tackle one of the Orientals next, but there's nothing like living in a country for really getting to grips with a language." (I have long suspected that Lizzie is one of those people – I think they are known as 'old souls' – who is actually on her third lifetime of experience, whilst most of us are struggling to get to grips with the first). "I have been wondering whether it might be more beneficial to have a private tutor, someone to bounce ideas off. Perhaps this would be the perfect opportunity to investigate that option. And. of course, the computer is an amazing educational resource that would be available to me just as well in Italy as it is here."

Lizzie is the only person I know that can talk Nathalie into silence. There is something so calmly logical about her tone and argument in any given situation that it leaves any opposing party with absolutely nowhere to go. In fact, not only that, but one is left not even desiring to go anywhere other than in her direction, so reassuring is it to follow her lead.

Nathalie just about managed to murmur something about 'looking into it' and 'putting the final decision on hold for now' and the conversation turned to other matters; the gallery, Nathalie's newly given commitment to Giles (if ever there was a better reason for leaving tomorrow I'm sure I couldn't think of it) and so on... And, as plans were laid and arrangements set in motion, we all knew that from now on, every moment that passed was a moment closer to the beginning of the rest of our lives...

It wasn't until much later that I registered that there had been one person in the room who hadn't danced with such joyous abandon as the rest, nor added their voice to the riotous celebratory chorus – our father.

The rest of the day flew by swiftly. Amidst all the discussions and organisation there was our regular life to attend to. Pod disappeared back to the gallery, the incoming show to consider. Jamie set to his 'holiday project' on Stone Age Man with unusual zeal, fuelled by his anticipation of informing all who would listen of his forthcoming adventure on his return to school. After a brief, furtive ('oops, sorry') phone call, Nathalie announced that she was off to see Giles, leaving Lizzie and me to transform the downstairs 'snug' into a cheerful (remembering Cousin Helen), working bedroom for Lizzie whilst her own was inaccessible. The hospital had passed on some guidelines for ensuring Lizzie's optimum comfort and maximising healing potential but as far as I could gather none of them involved a (shamelessly ornate) 18th century chaise longue, nor, even, a large squashy armchair with no springs, favourite or no. (Our snug room tended to be on the receiving end of any stray pieces that were unable to find a home elsewhere – a kind of 'rescue centre' for furniture). After a brief, enthusiastic attempt to remove the mattress from the bed in the single guest room that resulted in a rather ominous cracking sound from the small of my back but very little else of any significance, I resigned myself to leaving the 'bed' bit of the task to Pod on his return home and set about making the room an otherwise happy place for Lizzie to call home for as long as was required.

And then it hit me. In a matter of weeks none of us would be calling this friendly old house, with its liberal helping of chimneys and lifetime of family memories, home! I sat down all of a sudden in the big armchair, narrowly avoiding missing it altogether, having forgotten in my consternation that I had moved it from its usual position to one further back against the wall. Lizzie grinned.

"I know," she said companionably, "weird isn't it?" (Lizzie does talk like a normal person, as well as like an encyclopaedia, when it is appropriate.) "At least we're not having to sell the house, so it's not like we'll be saying goodbye altogether."

I nodded. "But it will never be the same, will it? Coming back here I mean. I suppose I hadn't registered that all this talk of 'new beginnings' meant that something was going to have to end."

Lizzie wheeled over to my chair. Manoeuvring herself with remarkable dexterity – she'll be doing 'wheelies' by supper time – she reached across and gave me a reassuring hug.

"The way I see it, life is rather like a book, made up of different chapters. Whenever I am a bit scared of something new, like when I started at St Mary's, I imagine a book which is just one long chapter; where nothing ever changes, no new characters are introduced and, when you get to the end you have really learned nothing more than when you started. I imagine how boring it would be and how pointless it would feel having read it at all. And then I think for a moment how dreadful it would be to feel that way about my life and I grit my teeth, give myself a shake and march cheerfully on into my new chapter."

All of a sudden I realised how pleased I was to have Lizzie marching along beside me and how lucky I was that she was my sister. Funny to think that she was actually my 'little' sister. So often her quiet wisdom led me to forget that I was actually the elder by six years. Though I guess that when you are living with an 'old soul' you are always destined to be at least three-hundred years behind...

I gave her an extra big squeeze. "Isn't it strange to think that there is a whole chunk of our family history that, up until a few hours ago, we knew nothing about? I wonder whether our genes will recognise Italy when we get there, making us feel right at home from the start!" We giggled. "Seriously though," I pondered, "don't you think it is odd that Pod has never told us about his family home? And what can be so terrible between two people that causes brothers to practically deny each other's existence for so long? What about Uncle Tom's own family? Do you think he has lived there all alone all his life, with no wife or children? Maybe we have cousins that even Pod doesn't know about – but then surely they would be there with their father, so Giuliana wouldn't have been so desperate for us to visit..."

"For a lot of the answers, I suppose we shall just have to wait until we are out there," Lizzie responded rationally to my sudden barrage of questions. "Pod didn't really seem to want to elaborate on things any more than he had to during the meeting. You know, it was almost as if, at a certain point, he had left the room altogether. He just let Nathalie take over as Chairman for the planning and organising and kind of 'backed away' from it all himself. Somehow it doesn't feel right to press him any further for now. After all, if you were sick and all by yourself as we had had some kind of 'falling out', I know that it would weigh pretty heavily on my mind. Let's hope that us going out there all together will help Pod as well as Uncle Tom – bring about a kind of resolution to their years of separation. It's rather like a novel or a script for a film. You never know, maybe years from now our Big Adventure will provide the inspiration for your first Oscar-winning film!"

We laughed again and I was reminded that one of the things I must do was to contact the University to let them know of my plans. The 'Drama; theatre, film, television' course that I was enrolled on at Bristol was always, I knew, hugely oversubscribed and if I wanted to defer then the sooner I let them know the better. "Well, I'd never find anyone quite like you to play 'Lizzie' would I?" I teased. "You are *definitely* unique! Which reminds me – I can't believe I've left it this long to ask. What *were* you doing on top of the guest room wardrobe...?"

Chapter Eighteen

Well, it seemed that we were *all* about to see the world from a different perspective – even without the advantageous height of a rickety old French armoire. Jamie was to remain a boarder at Philimore's but spend the holidays out in Italy, an arrangement that suited him perfectly as it meant that he did not have to leave his friends behind, (so where Max is concerned I guess I'll have to come up with an alternative plan... 'grrrrrrr'), *and* he still got to be part of the whole adventure. Lizzie, too, was pleased, as Pod and Nathalie were seriously considering the idea of her having a private tutor after the move. Initial investigations implied that the cost would actually work out favourably in comparison with her current fees at St Mary's and she could be entered for the necessary exams in just the same way as through school. Lizzie, they reasoned, was keen to learn (rather understating the fact) and extraordinarily self-disciplined and she could actually benefit from one-to-one tuition.

As for me, my challenge was to be in knuckling down to the final leg of my own education amidst all this excitement. Luckily, my Media Studies project had already been submitted – a short, whacky film pondering the current obsession with youth versus age, entitled 'Hair Today – Gone Tomorrow' and starring Jamie, Mrs Rainier, a number of unwitting 'extras' who were sitting in the waiting-room of Harley Street's top plastic surgeon when I stuck my camera around the door, an extremely irate Harley Street receptionist and, though I say so myself, a pretty cool soundtrack. The rest of my coursework was in and I was as ready as I'd ever be for the English Lit. paper, so that just left History. Ughhhhh! Why, when it should be so fascinating – after all it is really just the study of people and life and we can't get enough of soap operas and reality TV – do I find myself drifting off to sleep from the moment I open my file? Still, my latest technique of picturing the main characters (kings, queens, dodgy politicians and particularly rebellious subjects) as actors in a film or a play and imagining how they behave off screen as well as on (Elizabeth 1st is a real 'Diva'), is definitely bringing them to life. Now all I had to do was remember those pesky dates...

Once again I was alone in the house with my books. Nathalie had taken Lizzie to the hospital for her follow-up 'once over' by the specialist, and Pod was at the gallery, catching his assistants Alice and Charlie up with our news and starting to prepare the ground for his more remote managerial role. Jamie was staying overnight at Max's, as Nathalie felt it would be simpler to get on top of the arrangements without him in the equation (but at what cost..? handing him straight into the arms of the devil?! And she calls herself his mother!). Well, anyway, that just left me, although the house was undoubtedly less lonely by the time I had conjured up a few headless wives, the odd petulant statesman, several thousand revolting peasants and a queen who refused to leave her trailer until the Versace silk babouches and co-ordinating eye mask had arrived.

I was just getting into the swing of the newly-composed 'rap' ditty that I hoped was going to be my secret weapon in the 'dates' war when there was a knock at the door.

"Is Lizzie there?" asked the notably small but cheerful-faced boy on the doorstep. His cheerful face was particularly laudable given the enormous plaster cast that enveloped his right arm and the rather splendid, yellow/green bump on his forehead.

Such good cheer, combined with the almost tangible sense of hope that hung in the air as he awaited my response, dispelled entirely my (rather shameful) irritation at having been interrupted mid 'rap'. I smiled down at him. He waited. I smiled. Then, just as I was resigning myself to having to break the news that Lizzie was not, in fact, in, there was a delighted shout from the opposite side of the square. "Ben!" Within moments Lizzie arrived at the foot of the steps, the wheel-tracks in her wake still aflame, followed, somewhat less enthusiastically, by Nathalie, as their taxi pulled back into the King's Road. Lizzie and Ben beamed at each other. I felt a decidedly 'green and hairy moment' coming on, along with a good deal of sympathy for the poor gooseberry who first gave his name to this, most inelegant, situation. To stay or to go? That was the question.

Fortunately (or not?) it found its timely, and unambiguous, answer in Nathalie. "Don't just stand there," she barked at me, as she arrived at the house, "help me get Lizzie up the steps." Ignoring Ben entirely, she manoeuvred Lizzie's chair to face the doorway and gestured her intention to all who happened to be in the vicinity. Lizzie grinned apologetically at Ben. "We've had a difficult morning," she explained. "The specialist was held up by the tube strike and we had to wait over three hours to see a doctor. Nathalie was supposed to be at the dentists at 11 am and she had to cancel – her tooth is really hurting. But how brilliant that you came!"

"I've thought about you all the time," he whispered back bashfully, glancing across at me awkwardly. All of a sudden I found an especial interest in the jasmine creeper, accompanying my observation with an appropriately nonchalant hum.

"Apricot!" Nathalie was turning purple, resulting, I diagnosed on the spot, from a dangerous combination of overexertion (with the chair) and intense irritation (with me).

"Coming!" I called jovially, in an attempt, for the benefit of our guest, to alleviate some of the tension. To consolidate the carefree mood I gave a flamboyant, balletic twirl – and was promptly ambushed by Ben's rucksack which was lurking enticingly on the second step. Landing conveniently, if a little shaken, at Nathalie's feet, I brushed myself off, made a swift bow, and set to with the chair.

"Your sister is hilarious," Ben grinned at Lizzie, though, by virtue of the fact that she was bent double with hysteria, she was, in that instant, neither able to respond nor to actually see his ear-to-ear smile. She looked up briefly, tears in her eyes, choked and resumed her 'concertina-d' position.

"For goodness sake!" Nathalie admonished impatiently. Unfortunately, as is often the way with these things, her irritation had the ironic effect of providing further fuel to the intensity of Lizzie's shakes. A strangulated wail of laughter came from somewhere between her knees – at which point Ben and I exploded into giggles.

In between snorts, I caught Nathalie's eye apologetically. The corners of her mouth twitched. Then, caught up in that wonderful spirit of "If you can't beat 'em join em', she began to laugh. And, as she and I collapsed companionably onto the steps, breathless with the transforming miracle of laughter, all the tension of the past few weeks rose up and soared out of the square and beyond – never to be seen again...

Chapter Nineteen

The next few days raced by. With the history exam looming, I resolved to converse solely with those cast members born prior to 1750 and, as such, saw very little of my family at all. In between 'takes', however, I thought about them a lot. Particularly Lizzie. Most specifically, Lizzie and Ben.

They had, they informed me when we had all caught our breath that day – though the co-ordinating plaster casts had been a pretty glaring clue – met on the children's ward at the C&W. It had been love at first sight – you know how it is, your eyes meet over the large scary matron – addresses were exchanged, eternal vows made and so forth... Anyway, besides the setting, there was perhaps nothing remarkable about the whole thing. Except that the swooning maiden was my little sister and the handsome prince was, I gathered, despite having known her for only a few days, prepared to die for her. Now, to truly understand my preoccupation with this affair, ('as it were' – or, let's hope at this stage and at their age, 'weren't'), first you really have to be properly acquainted with my sister. Well, let me tell you, if you were, Lizzie Beresford-Linnel would undoubtedly be the most level-headed, sensible, in-control-of-her-emotions person that you knew. Except that, that was the *old* Lizzie Beresford-Linnel, the up-until-a-week-ago Lizzie Beresford-Linnel. This new Lizzie bore no resemblance whatsoever to her former incarnation. (Besides being impossibly pretty, witty and conscientious, but you get my drift...). Ever since Ben's first visit, she had drifted around dreamily, her eyes glazed over, her lips set softly in a permanent half-smile. At table she sat in her own far-off world, pushing her food elegantly around her plate. On two separate occasions, I even discovered the petri-dishes left stranded in the airing cupboard when they were due for a spell on the window-sill.

In the past she and I had talked about love. It was her voice of calm, independent reason that had gone a long way in rescuing me from the depths of my despair over Joshua. I could still hear her quietly-composed assertion that she intended to wait until after university before falling in love, as 'it could really compromise your whole future to let it happen too soon'...Well, when it came to love, Lizzie was clearly the latest in an exceedingly long line of romantics to discover that it's not quite that neat. As for Ben, I feared that, having fallen for my extraordinary, perfect sister, he was hooked for life. And fallen for her, he clearly had. He seemed to have bypassed altogether the 'pinching your bottom and running away', or 'calling out rude words and sniggering' phases of courtship that I (well, OK, for 'I' read 'Arabella') recall being the approach of choice for thirteen year old boys. Instead he had gone straight for all-out romance.

In a matter of days, Lizzie's new bedroom had taken on the guise of an overabundant gift shop, positively straining at the seams with all manner of red and white heart shaped goods. The glorious scent of roses permeated the whole house and our woefully inadequate supply of vases had long since been supplemented by all manner of curious vessels. When the two of them were not actually together, they were sending their 'e-love' out across the ether; imagined their lovelorn e-spirits meeting somewhere above Harrods – just about half-way between us in Chelsea and Ben's home in Mayfair – during the day not a terribly romantic place to convene it is true, but at night, with all those fairytale lights... And with the added poignancy of her imminent departure across the sea...

Anyway, where was I? Well, if I am completely honest, where I actually was was well and truly avoiding the issue. Of course I was happy for Lizzie and, though I was aware that the fact that we were about to leave the country was probably the only reason Nathalie had let the 'situation' develop thus far, I was also sensitive to the fact that when we did actually leave it was going to be very difficult for them both, but I began to suspect that, when it came down to it, the real reason it was playing so much on my mind had rather more to do with me than I'd have liked to admit. Still, the old head-in-the-sand technique was doing the trick nicely... that is, until last night. The two of them were just a silhouette when I caught sight of them through my bedroom window. We had all had a really late supper, over which the rest of us talked excitedly about the move whilst Lizzie and Ben held hands under a faraway table in their own faraway world. Afterwards we played a swift but riotous game of Pictionary before Jamie was sent up to bed, as, I suspect, per Nathalie's plan, happy and exhausted.

I wandered up the stairs slowly. The light through the glass at the top of the door was silvery bright. A full moon! My room, when I pushed open the door, was full of the night that poured in through the open window. Its ethereal light illuminated everything in shades of silver and grey, claiming all for its otherworldly realm. As if compelled by the mysterious force of the moon I crossed the room to the window. I curled up on the window-seat, just as I had done since I was a little girl and looked out over the square. And it was then that I saw them. They were on the bench beneath the willow tree, their giant plaster casts dazzling in the luminous white light. Somehow, between them, they had manoeuvred Lizzie out of her chair. Ben sat upright in the corner of the bench, his back against the arm rest. Lizzie lay back in his arms, looking up at the sky. My eyes held, almost spellbound, the intimate tableau. My awareness of its intimacy, that, I knew, obliged me to avert my gaze, was at the same time the very thing that drew me more irresistibly into the picture beyond my window. So still, so silent. How long was it before I registered the tears that blurred my view and warmed my night-cooled cheeks?

But, even then, I let them come, the tears, though at first I wasn't sure why they were there. Long after I heard my father on the doorstep, the purr of a waiting taxi and Lizzie calling a soft goodbye across the quiet night, they came. Only now they flowed from eye-to-eye, across my nose, as I lay there on my side, my knees tucked up into my chest and my hair damp with the sadness and the being alone. Because that was why they came. To tell me that deep down I feared that I would never know how it felt to be a part of that tableau, not just a watcher from the wings. The ache inside was a space in my heart that cried out to be filled. Would anyone ever look at me the way that Joshua looked at Laura, the way that Ben looked at my little sister who was only twelve and already knew more of love than I? Would I ever gaze at him, my eyes sparkling with a love that reflected back at me from his own? Even Arabella (who truth be told is not even terribly nice) had barely called me over the past few weeks, so wrapped up was she in a new relationship which she said was 'the one'. Would I ever be 'The One'? Why did no one want me? Was it my red hair? My freckles? My unfailing ability to trip over anything that was there for the tripping? Or was it just that I was always destined to be alone? The moonlit night gave no answer. And so I lay there, crying out my innermost fears, to leave them soaking into the soft pillow-down, freeing up my soul for sleep...

Chapter Twenty

All in all, it was just as well that I had my stroppy Tudor cast to take my mind off things. Finally we were beginning to get things together. Elizabeth had been coaxed out of her trailer by the persuasive Lord Darnley, despite the fact that the Versace delivery had yet to arrive, and she was all smiles and lead make-up. The 'overseas set' was almost ready thanks to my last minute recruitment of the revolting peasants to finish painting the backdrop to Versailles. We were pretty much 'ready to roll'. Which was lucky as, before you could say, "Off with her head!", the morning of the exam had arrived.

"Break a leg!" Lizzie called good-humouredly from the hallway as I tripped down the steps (on this occasion, purely in a manner of speaking) and out into the street. I turned back and waved equally cheerily, conscious once again of her generous spirit.

Less than an hour ago, over breakfast, her vain hope that a solution might have been found to her imminent separation from Ben had been well and truly dashed. Her proposal, that I suspected she had been summoning up the courage to present for a good few days, was that she should stay behind in London. Ben's, clearly rather liberal, parents had a self-contained apartment in the attic of their Mayfair home and, remarkably, had agreed to allow Lizzie to stay there on condition that her own parents were happy with the idea. Had Nathalie spat her Special K (with soya milk and sliced banana) six feet across the breakfast table she could not have made her position more clear. Lizzie's eyes were still red and swollen in the aftermath of the battle that had ensued. It was a battle that, inevitably, she had no chance of winning but she was nevertheless determined not to go down without a fight. Fights were something that our mother did particularly well and so the situation had been especially bloody. In fact, Nathalie seemed almost to relish the opportunity to let off steam and I strongly suspected that her dramatic metamorphosis from breakfast-eating mother to fire-breathing dragon was ultimately down to something other than Lizzie's tentative request. Here I had two theories.

One, which I found myself apologising to Mrs Rainier for even before the thought had been fully formed, was that she resented being torn away from Giles in the heat of their passion and that Lizzie's distress over Ben was like a repeated 'poke in the eye with a sharp stick'. This I swiftly disregarded, firstly because Mrs Rainier's disapproval was burning through the wall and into the side of my head in a most uncomfortable way and, ultimately, because my instinct told me that it had more to do with my father.

You would have imagined, and certainly I had, that now that things were all out in the open and such a positive decision had been made, the distant, preoccupied Pod would have been deposed by the rightful holder of the seat. Instead he had remained equally pensive and elusive, dashing off to the gallery whenever he had a chance on some rather flimsy pretext or another. As a consequence Nathalie had been obliged to bear the majority of the practical and emotional weight of the move alone. Added to this, the previous evening had seen an extremely heated debate between the two of them over the travel arrangements.

We had all presumed that we would drive down together through France; Nathalie had hoped that we might even call on her parents on the way. A small removal van had already collected the majority of our things. Giuliana had assured Nathalie that it was unnecessary for us to bring furniture or linens and so it really just came down to clothes, music and various kitchen and household gadgets that we couldn't envisage managing without. Besides a minor difference of opinion between Nathalie and Jamie over just how essential the sandwich toaster was to our daily existence, all in all, the pack-up was pretty straightforward. The few things that we required for these last few days would, we supposed, come with us in the car on the final journey down. At least that is what we had imagined until Pod had arrived home last night.

We had all finished supper by the time he got in. Jamie had gone up to bed more willingly than usual, Nathalie finally having conceded to the sandwich toaster accompanying us on our journey on condition that a) he found room for it in his own suitcase and b) he was no more trouble until we left. I was in my room having a last minute pep-talk with the cast before our critical performance the following day when I heard the click of his key in the door. Spotting an opportunity to be distracted from my over-anxious colleagues I thundered down the stairs to greet him. He smiled wanly – of course, I told myself, it is only natural that he should still be anxious, with his brother so ill – and ruffled my hair as of old. I followed him into the kitchen where Nathalie was removing his rather demoralised-looking supper from the warming oven of the Aga.

"I'm sorry I'm so late," he began, putting down his briefcase by the door and kissing the back of Nathalie's head as she bent over the serving table. "Giles stopped by at the gallery and we opened a bottle of wine together. It's been a long time since we had an opportunity to sit down and really talk."

Both Nathalie and I looked up keenly but if Pod noticed anything unusual about our sudden interest he didn't make any sign. "Is that lasagne?" he asked hungrily. Frustrated, I suspect, in her need to hear more about the meeting and a little too conscious that, having been awaiting his arrival for a good two hours, the lasagne was undoubtedly on the verge of an identity crisis, Nathalie merely deposited the plate on the table and began to rummage noisily in the cutlery drawer. Clearly not altogether sure quite where things had gone off track, Daddy sat down and launched hopefully into a third topic of conversation.

"I also picked up the tickets," he announced. Once again Nathalie and I went into alert mode.

"What tickets?" we asked in unison.

"For the aeroplane," Pod answered calmly, drawing them out of his breast pocket.

Nathalie was anything but calm. "But we are driving down," she asserted categorically.

"I thought *I* would drive down," Pod responded – bravely, I thought – "whilst you and the children follow on by air a day or two later."

"And did you not think that this was something you should have discussed with me first?" Nathalie snapped back at him. "Honestly Paul, is this something that we are going into together, because, quite frankly I am beginning to feel that you have not even begun to consider this move in the context of your family. I have hardly seen you since the decision was made and it has been entirely left to me to make the necessary arrangements."

"That's why I thought I'd sort out the tickets," Pod responded meekly. "I am aware how much you have to manage at the moment."

Uh oh! Wrong answer. Plus, meekness is never a good stance when Nathalie has all guns blazing. From this point things went from bad to worse. In fact I am closing the door behind us so as not to expose you to the rather shameful scene. Suffice to reveal that, whilst I could not say that things were altogether resolved, a shaky stalemate was ultimately reached on the grounds that the tickets had been paid for and were non-refundable. It looked like we had wings...

Chapter Twenty-One

The curtain came down on our historical performance to the roar of the crowds. Everyone remembered their lines and turned up on cue. Treaties were made, battles were won and Elizabeth was every inch a queen. Naturally we would await with bated breath the verdict of the critics but for now we were happy in the knowledge that we had been the best that we could be.

Surprisingly quickly, after the tearful farewells of my classmates and a final goodbye to the familiar old locker-room, now eerie in its silent emptiness, like a long-ago shipwreck brought up from beneath the waves, the world of school, exams and missing gym socks felt like another lifetime. For the first time I was really able to focus on the road ahead; a road lined with cypress trees, stretching out towards our future and perhaps, along the way, challenging all that we had hitherto presumed about who we really were.

Between you and me, just at that moment my family were the last people I would have chosen to embark upon the biggest adventure of my life with, (except Max). The atmosphere in our house was decidedly frosty. Imagine for a moment the Narnia world behind the wardrobe, where the snow-laden land is in a permanent state of winter and then take the temperature down a few notches. Feeling chilly? Me too. Lizzie had barely spoken since all hope was lost and whenever my parents were in the same room an icy wind whipped around your ankles, freezing words mid-sentence and breath mid-air. Even Jamie, who you could usually rely on to lighten a mood, was down in the dumps because Toots was more lethargic than usual and was off his food. Perhaps, I suggested, he was merely coming to his senses, his food of choice generally being of a small amphibious nature that was altogether rather unappetising, but Jamie was not to be consoled. Still, at this stage the plans had a momentum all their own. hurling us through the tundra together towards D-day.

Mrs Rainier had volunteered to keep an eye on the house and, since she had been doing so so diligently for the past 15 years without a need, we felt it was to be left in reliable hands. Giles too was to be entrusted with a key and, truth be told, I was finding it increasingly less of a challenge to give him Mrs Rainier's benefit of the doubt. Though the cynical me could not resist the momentary, insidious suspicion that his recent display of concern for Pod was born purely out of his (well-deserved) feelings of guilt, the 'give-the-world-a-chance' me had to admit that the concern did a very good impression of being genuine. On the two or three occasions during the week that he had popped in to help, Nathalie was equally frosty towards him as she was towards everyone else; the time he accidentally knocked over the nearly-full carton of milk with his briefcase I even felt a wave of sympathy for him.

I had packed my final case, unpacked and re-packed it all over again. Besides my toothbrush (and straightening irons) how could I possibly narrow down a lifetime of 'worldly goods' into one small casefull? We had already sent out three large boxes of books – how I was looking forward to really having an opportunity to read – and all my favourite music was packed and ready to go, so it really came down to clothes and my 'treasure-box'. And therein lay the dilemma. Clothes, for me, (much, I suspect, to Nathalie's eternal dismay) were not really an issue. I had a few items I really loved and, for the purpose of freeing up my case I could always return all the things I had 'borrowed' from everyone else in the family, for their own pack-up. But it was my 'treasure-box' that had me concerned. Actually it was more like a 'treasuretrunk' and, were it empty, my suitcase would have fitted into it twice over. But it wasn't. In fact it was pretty much full to bursting, with all the most precious things I had in the world. Amongst many, these ranged from my very first school project – 'Blood' (by Amelia-Anne agd for) – the watch which taught me how to tell the time, a pink rabbit-shaped button from my favourite cardigan when I was three, my 'Uncle Bulgaria' badge and my signed programme from the Theatre Royal's performance of 'Annie', through to my prized collection of Valentine's cards (most of which were from Max's older brother, Nick, who was nearly as obnoxious as Max and had been pestering me since we were about six – but still, a Valentine was a Valentine...). And then there was my elven cloak, a shimmering sea-green velvet that reminded me that the world was full of magic whenever I put it on. Most precious of all, wrapped safely inside the magic cloak, was Betsy Fingle and the red-gold curl. Mollie's curl.

Mollie was my forever-friend. I promised it when I held her hand at her bedside the night she told me she was dying. She told me she would always look down on me from the sky and I told her I would always look up for her and wave – even if someone was watching. And we laughed. Through our tears. Mollie had cystic fibrosis. We first became friends five years ago when she was six and I was thirteen. For our school 'social awareness' class we were all signed out of lessons for one afternoon a week to perform some kind of voluntary work in the community. We were able to submit a request for a particular field that interested us: the library, hospital or homeless shelter for instance. I had asked to help out at the local community theatre; painting stage sets, repairing costumes and things. But then I heard about Mollie. It was Mrs Rainier who told me. A young couple had just moved in to the house the other side of hers and they had a little girl. Such a happy, smiling little girl but with a sad story to tell.

From the very beginning they had known that she would never be able to run and dance like her brother and sister. But that didn't stop her from trying. And so a lot of the time she and her mother were exhausted. When I asked her parents if it would be a help for me to spend an afternoon a week with Mollie – reading to her, playing quiet games or just to sit, I thought I might be doing them a favour. Instead, it was Mollie who made my life extraordinary. Sometimes we would just be still together. Then she would look out at me from behind the mask that did her breathing for her when her body was tired of trying, her bright green eyes twinkling with all the mischief that her spirit was making whilst the rest of her waited to join it. And I would sit and wonder at her quiet patience. Other days we read, or told each other stories, some out of books, others out of our heads and hearts. And each was greater than the last; more magical, more funny, more preposterous or, we would giggle and tickle and say, "the milly, billy silly-est!"

Then, one rainy November day I thought of The Puppet Theatre. The idea came to me, like all the best ideas surely do, whilst I was on my knees behind the sofa. Mollie lay on her day-bed in the drawing-room and I was entertaining her with my friends, Mr and Mrs Fingle and their eight children. As my fingers sang and danced above the cream silk-covered Chesterfield, it began to take shape in my mind; 'The MA Puppet Theatre – The Most Magnificent of all Puppet Theatres!' the press would announce, and Mollie and I would bow modestly to the gathered crowds and say most graciously, "We would be very proud to leave it to the nation..."

But, of course, first we would have to build it. For the next few weeks, Mollie's playroom was a workshop. We decided on a Victorian model, gilded and ornate, with real fabric curtains at the window through which the Fingles and their friends would make their appearance. Naturally the main 'building' would be red, like our hair, with a liberal smattering of gold. The name of the theatre, M (for Mollie) A (for me), was announced in bold and swirly lettering just below the window. Nathalie even let me borrow her sewing machine, (after a short introductory session), so that Mollie and I could take it in turns to run the busy, whirring needle through the little scraps of velvet that came together to make our 'curtain up!' Pod found two old broom-handles in the garden shed that he sawed to size to make the perfect 'struts' to support the theatre's heavy, cardboard frame and, before we knew it, it was time to call in the cast.

Now that they had such a grand place in which to perform, the Fingles felt they needed a whole new wardrobe. Since, truth be told, their old costumes had relied rather heavily on the 'King's New Clothes' mode of fashion, (plus a few characterful dashes with a felt tip pen), I was inclined to agree with them. Here, Mollie's grandma and her knitting club came to our aid. Before you could say "knit one, pearl one", each of the Fingles was proudly bedecked in the finest, most colourful, knit 'jacket' love could buy. Mr Fingle even had a smart little shirt collar just beneath his new (cheerful but dignified) expression, as befitting the head of such a large and talented family. Mrs Fingle was wearing her favourite hat – the one with the tiny pink carnation on the front, and all the little Fingles had different coloured jumpers, skirts or trousers. My, how proud they were!

So... we were all ready! The Grand Premier was scheduled for Saturday night. The posters had been up for a week, in the kitchens of numbers 45, 46 and 47 Paultons Square, (naturally Mrs Rainier was to be a part of the celebrations), and we had completely sold out of all eleven tickets. Mollie wore her favourite lavender-coloured dress with the apple-green sash and a smile that really did stretch from ear-to-ear. To a packed house, including Toots and Daisybell, Mrs Rainier's cat – we didn't charge for pets – the Fingles gave the performance of a lifetime. After three curtain calls they retired, exhausted but happy, to their dressing rooms, leaving Mollie and me to bask in their reflected glory. And how Mollie's eyes shone as she peeped inside the 'takings box' and counted out the forty-four pounds and fifty-two pence (including donations) – plus a gobstopper which I suspect was Jamie's contribution – which would go towards the Children's Ward re-decoration fund at her hospital. Then; "Can I take the Fingles up to bed with me?" she asked, when the audience had said their farewells and her father came to carry her upstairs. Still now I wonder why I answered as I did, and try to tell myself that perhaps, in a lifetime, everyone has one thing that they will regret for always. "The Fingles are professionals," I smiled back at her, "they're not really toys. They live in the theatre. But when I come again next week we can have as many performances as you like."

And Mollie nodded gently and squeezed my hand. "Thank you," she said simply, "for making the magic..." She waved over her father's shoulder as they disappeared through the doorway. I listened for the footsteps on the stairs before I picked up my bag and went out into the night.

I didn't see Mollie again. The following week's performances had to be cancelled. And then the week's after that. I cried as I folded the Fingles into their little velvet pouch when I left for the funeral that day. And I was still crying when I placed them on the top of the too-small coffin so that she always had someone to play with, and watched them all be lowered into the too-deep-down earth. Except for little Betsy Fingle, who had hair the colour of beech leaves in Autumn and a little lavender dress with an apple green sash.

Because I couldn't imagine life without her...

Chapter Twenty-Two

Pod was even more quiet than usual, the night before he left for home. His home. The place he had lived in for nearly as long as I am old.

The mood at table that evening was subdued, even sombre, all of us sensitive to something that we could not even begin to know. We ate in silence, the periodic clink of cutlery on china painfully affirming the strained atmosphere.

When the meal was over it was Jamie who excused himself first. "Can I go and see Toots before bedtime?" he pleaded hopefully. Nathalie nodded. Jamie's delight at Toot's remarkable recovery, following the worrying period of abstinence, was very much undermined by his realisation that these were to be the last few days they would spend together. Arrangements had been made with Max, (and his somewhat less enthusiastic mother), and Toots was to be delivered to his new home across the square in a couple of days' time. My sympathy for Jamie was great but my sympathy for Toots knew no bounds... Still, Jamie trusted Max, despite the fact that he was clearly the Devil in small boy's clothing, so I guessed that would be enough for Toots.

Lizzie, of course, was equally anxious to spend every possible remaining moment with Ben. That night he was with his grandparents, though, he had assured Lizzie, he had done everything possible to avoid the commitment. Still, with that indomitable generosity of spirit she smiled over at Pod. "Nathalie and I packed you a 'weekend bag'," she told him, "with everything you should need until we arrive on Sunday. We even put in your peanuts, a jar of Marmite and the silver-framed photograph of everyone from the drawing-room so that you have all your favourite things with you until we get there..."

Her bright, positive words skipped out across the table and, delving deep inside, drew Pod out of his distant reverie. He smiled back at her as he stood up. "Then it sounds like I am pretty much ready!" he replied. "Just as well you didn't pack the car, girls, or there may not have been any room for me!" Lizzie and I giggled, relieved that he seemed more relaxed, as we recalled the previous Christmas when the tree that we had chosen had proved so enormous that Pod had had to leave us behind whilst he drove it home. How we had laughed as we watched him pull away, peering haplessly between the thick, piney fronds... "Well," he went on, gesturing at the dirty plates, "let's give your mother the night off." He started to collect the glasses and Nathalie smiled weakly in thanks. She had still not really forgiven him for arranging our journey down separately to his, but at least everyone was trying. "How about some music, Maestro?" Pod suggested to Lizzie. "After all it is our last night all together in this old house for a while – we ought to give it a jolly good send off!"

"My violin is already packed," she reminded him, "but I could see what we've left behind in the CD racks!" Jamie and Toots appeared at the kitchen door 'to see what was going on' and Mrs Rainier popped round, I suspected for much the same reason, bearing a large 'farewell bottle' of champagne. And so it was that, chattering and laughing – and to a riotous combination of Abba, the BeeGees and the jovially unseasonable 'Santa's Christmas Favourites' – we played out our last family evening at number 47...

Pod was leaving early the following morning. He wanted to get ahead of the traffic, he said, and avoid a queue at the 'Chunnel'. We had all said our goodbyes the night before but I couldn't resist creeping downstairs to the kitchen when I heard him pass by the door to my room. "It's going to be alright," I whispered as I made him a large, steaming mug of coffee to set him up for the journey. The smell curled pleasingly up into my nostrils as I set it down on the table and sat down crossed legged on the bench. "It's being all together that makes a house our home." Even as I said it I knew that I was reassuring myself as much as him. He nodded but once again I had the disconcerting sense that he was only partly in the 'here and now'. We sat in companionable silence whilst he munched on a slice of toast and Marmite and sipped at the coffee. When he had finished breakfast I followed him out to the car. As he bent down into the passenger-side door to lay his jacket on the seat I hugged my arms around him from behind. He stood up, surprised, and bumped his head smartly on the frame of the door. I winced. "I'm so sorry, Daddy," I whispered hoarsely, tears in my eyes. And I knew they were tears not just for the bump but for the sadness that clung to my father like a soft, damp shroud. But then he wrapped me up into his big, Daddy arms, just like he had always done when I was small and the Demons were dancing, and squeezed me harder and harder until, just like then, it made me giggle and fight to escape his clutch. And because there wasn't room in our moment for giggles and tears, the tears got squeezed back inside – to wait for a time, perhaps, when we were ready to catch them.

Or perhaps not...

Chapter Twenty-Three

My tasks, Nathalie told me, as she presented the three of us with our lists of 'Things To Do Before We Go', were four. The first saw me meandering down the King's Road to the Post Office to hand in our redirection forms; Giuliana had provided Nathalie with the official postal address. As I wandered, I rolled the words round on my tongue, feeling out the music and 'bite' of the new, foreign syllables that would soon be the tools with which I would build my new life and might, one day, shape and define my very thoughts and dreams... The sounds, even subjected to my 'novice' pronunciation, brought an exotic lyricism to my every-day journey. As I pushed open the heavy glass door to the post office, I fancied myself a mysterious, aloof Countess ... yes... the 'Contessa Albicocca'... (the first thing I had done on learning about our move was to discover the Italian for Apricot!), nodding courteously to my subjects (do Contessas have subjects?) as I glided by. Naturally Contessas are far too polite to queue-jump, despite their status, and so I took my place graciously behind Leonardo da Vinci, three swarthy gondoliers, a large party of Medici, the Mona Lisa and someone who, by virtue of his paint-stained fingers, I took to be Michelangelo on a tea-break. Phew! who'd have thought that this was where it was all happening at 10-30 on a Friday morning?

Twenty minutes later, my task complete, I stepped back out onto the King's Road and took a deep, reassuring breath of its familiar, toxin-laden air. All of a sudden I was very much the English Apricot again – most specifically the London, and the Chelsea, Apricot. The girl in the hairdresser's waved as I passed their window and I grinned back through the glass. Then, with the realisation that this could be the last time for a while that we exchanged smiles, I pressed my nose spontaneously against the pane and watched her giggle as she pointed me out to the client who sat, mid-perm, at her side. Mouthing a final farewell, I darted across the road – in my usual lethal manner, too impatient to wait for the lights – and into The Skylark for part two of my '...Before We Go' mission. I love The King's Road. Which King, I wondered, still claimed ownership of this bustling, eclectic street and would he even begin to recognise it in its current incarnation? Once upon a time 'The Skylark' had been a garage, Mrs Rainier had told me. In another incarnation it was a vast warehouse/market for young fashion designers. Like an actor, I thought, it inhabited each new role entirely. I pictured the long-ago 'grease-monkeys' pacing the lengths, wrench in hand, of what today is a vast and decadent food emporium, straining at its shining glass walls with all manner of delicious things. Huge bowls of herbed and salted olives vie for attention with fresh coral-pink lobster on ice, endless shelves of luxury wines and as-good-as-home-made biscuits and fudge, wrapped in crinkly, transparent film, so that you can't miss seeing how delicious they are... All of these, alongside more mundane food and household essentials for the all-shopped-out Chelsea-ite who just can't face the extra fifteen minute walk down the road to Waitrose. Here you may be paying £8 for your can of tuna instead of 60p but you can be safe in the knowledge that only the most fashionable chunks of fish will pass your (perfectly-lined) lips... And, just in case you are too busy shopping to prepare and cook your own meals or need further temptation to persuade you to indulge in these glorious wares, there is The Skylark Cafe and Brasserie, their 'daily specials' board revealing conspiratorially what might be behind the irresistible aroma that is reminding you that it is much too long since breakfast... Speaking of which... I lingered longingly at the pastries counter like the proverbial Dickensian child with his nose pressed against the toyshop window, lost in self-indulgent reverie...

"There you are!" A triumphant voice crashed through my dream-wall and sent it tumbling to the ground in a scrumptiously gooey convergence of chocolate, jam and cream... "I knew you'd be with the cakes," Jamie announced, "Lizzie guessed fudge and Nathalie..."

"I guessed you would be drifting around somewhere between here and home, lost in your own, who-knows-where, thoughts, and having quite forgotten Lizzie's hospital appointment. Honestly Apricot! I told you time was tight this morning. I've had to cancel my dental appointment again – luckily he can fit me in this afternoon – and arrange to take Lizzie myself."

I looked down at the floor, shamefaced (...was that a squashed olive..?). It was true. I had entirely forgotten that number 3 on my list, after picking up the bread and a pint of milk, was to accompany Lizzie to the hospital for her final check-up before we left for Italy.

"Sorry," I mumbled, looking up, first at Nathalie and then at Lizzie.

"It's not as if this is the first time," Nathalie went on, 'sorry' clearly not being quite enough to put the matter to rest. "If you spent even half as much time in this world as you do in your own, exclusive, faraway place you might remember that it does not entirely revolve around you."

I could feel the tears welling up behind my eyes. I really did feel terrible about Lizzie. How could I have forgotten? She would never have forgotten, were it I who needed her help. I was selfish and thoughtless – an altogether horrible person... The cheerfully ordered displays around me merged into a hot, watery blur as I descended into the equally self-indulgent (and the irony wasn't lost on me here) Mire of Self-Reproach and Regret. To make matters worse, dear, kind, forgiving Lizzie took a sympathetic hold of my hand.

"No problemo," she grinned, blurrily, coaxing me into a smile. Nathalie 'hurrumff-ed'. "I bet you've got so much on your mind about leaving and everything."

I tried to smile back, simultaneously wondering what all the things were that ought to be on my mind about leaving and why they weren't there...

"So," Nathalie broke in, before I could come up with anything particularly illuminating, "at this point I might as well take Lizzie. Do you think you can manage to remember the bread and milk and put together some sandwiches for us all for when we get back?"

I nodded humbly.

"Jamie says he'd rather stay with you."

Jamie grinned at me.

"He can help you sort the laundry into piles – you have remembered that this was also on your list?"

I nodded again and Jamie's grin waned considerably.

"Right," Nathalie announced, "we're off then."

I blinked back my tears, smiled a goodbye to Lizzie and they were off, Lizzie gliding through the narrow aisles like an Olympic ice-dancer on wheels and Nathalie burning her purposeful path into the smooth, shiny tiles for posterity – to observe and marvel...

Chapter Twenty-Four

It was a glorious morning. I couldn't decide whether I thought it ought in fact to have been raining, in mourning for our departure, or whether it was nicer for our dear old house to be seeing us off with a cheery, sun-drenched wave. Still, since there was no doubt that the 'jolly' option had been decided for me, I settled for enjoying the virtues of a true English summer's day for one last time. I lay on my back on the top of the garden wall, looking up at the azure blue sky. Precarious, and not my vantage point of choice, but I promised Lizzie that I would go in her stead, as part of her 'viewing the world from a different perspective' campaign. I felt I owed her. Actually, when I was able to forget for a moment that the wall was clearly a good few centimetres narrower than I was, I could start to see the merits of her investigation. How amazing that simply by turning my perspective on its head I had discovered a whole new world! This one was bluer than blue but, more than that, it had a serenity and peace that took up my soul and carried it higher and higher, far and away from the world I used to know. If it weren't for the tip of the overhanging magnolia branch that peeped into view when I turned my gaze just an inch or so to the left, I might well have left this earth altogether, never to return... Instead, suspended between two worlds, I lay there, my mind drifting, my limbs surrendering themselves to the gentle warmth of the English sun. My eyes caught and lazily tracked a lone aeroplane as it chalked its path across the infinite blue. As the tiny plane dived further into the briny deep, the distinct white line held its ground in its wake. Spotting an irresistible opportunity, my imagination blinked, stretched and shook itself out of our torpor. And sure enough, when I looked again, the simple line was simple no longer but was forming loops and whirls...or, wait! Were they? ... Yes! ... Words! "G-o-o-d-b-y-e..." I read the large smokey letters aloud to myself and to the birds that flitted in amongst the leaves of the old weeping ash at the foot of the wall. "Goodbye A-p-r-i-c-o-t..!" England called fondly from on high, "Goodbye!" The plane did a dashing series of 'loop-the-loops' and I waved my farewell's up at the sky as the letters began to fade...

I might then have drifted back into my sleepy reverie were it not for the decidedly inconsiderate arrival of Marmaduke, Daisybell's fat, ginger adversary who supposedly lived at number 43 but, as far as I could see, spent most of his time in our garden, scaring the birds and digging holes in Nathalie's flower-beds. Jumping up onto the wall, without even a moment's notice, he landed squarely on my middle. My one consolation as I sat up with a start and came perilously close to making a rude and uncomfortable landing amongst Mrs Rainier's lupins, was that Marmaduke was almost as surprised as I. With a strangulated cry he flew off the wall and streaked flat-out across the lawn in the direction of his own, less volatile, terrain. Winded, I took a moment or two to regain my composure (admittedly not something I have a great deal of, even at the best of times), then swung my legs over the edge of the wall.

"Nathalie says you're to stop lounging about and come and help close up the house," Jamie announced gloomily, as he appeared from the kitchen doorway at the top of the scented-stair. That was what Mrs Rainier and I called the little run of stone steps that led from the kitchen into this part of the garden and were lined with pots of gloriously scented herbs on either side. I jumped down and crossed over to the steps, plucking a small sprig of lemon-verbena and rubbing it between my fingers, just as I had done year-on-year for as long as I could remember.

"We'll plant a pot of this at our new house," I said to Jamie, "and then, whenever we feel homesick, we can take a leaf and rub it and the smell will carry us back here for a visit..." I held out the squished green pulp and he took a big sniff.

"I wish there was a plant that smelled like Toots," he mused in response. "Then, whenever I was missing him I could close my eyes and imagine he was next to me."

"Well," I answered, "you know what?" He turned his eyes to mine hopefully. "If you imagine hard enough you don't even need the smell. I imagine all sorts of things and, for as long as I need them to be, they are real. Sometimes they are more real than what is *really* real – but you have to be a bit careful about that."

Jamie's face brightened considerably. Then he closed his eyes, wriggled a bit inside the sleeves of his travel-coat and made a kind of crooning noise. "It works!" he announced triumphantly a few moments later. "It was just like he was there, wriggling around inside my jacket

– and I could nearly smell him! Do you think when I get really good at it I'll be able to smell him?"

Without waiting for an answer he leapt happily up the steps again and in through the door. I shuddered; then smiled and followed him into the house...

Where Lizzie was concerned, I wasn't sure I'd find such an instant fix. She was already ensconced in the front seat of the car when I got there, her tear-stained face testimony to her final, woe-full parting from Ben a few minutes earlier. Though she tried to put on a brave smile as I reached in to give her a sympathetic hug, the effort only brought forth another whole gallon of tears. She appeared to have already cottoned on to the 'reminiscent smell' technique. Every now and again she buried her face in a jumper that I recognised as the one that, up until a short while ago, had had Ben inside it. It didn't seem to be helping. Still, Nathalie was striding purposefully towards the car, so for now there was no time for more than the conciliatory hug. I squeezed her hand and clambered into the back seat with Jamie.

...with Jamie... Yikes! No Jamie!! But he'd volunteered to 'wait in the car' so that he wasn't 'in the way' a good ten minutes ago – I'd even seen him get in... Wait a minute...and I wasn't suspicious??! Clearly I'd had a momentary lapse of sanity. And now he'd probably run away and they'd find him washed up on a deserted shoreline and... Just as my heart had made the decision to stop beating entirely there was a lifesaving screech from Nathalie:

"Jamie! Where have you been? I thought you were waiting in the car!"

Mumbling something about frozen amphibians, which was clearly best left as obscure as possible, Jamie climbed meekly into the back seat beside me. And then, as they say, we were off..!

Chapter Twenty-Five

There was more than a touch of the surreal about our trip. Most unnervingly, Jamie barely uttered a peep during the whole journey. Instead, he sat still and quiet, with a perpetually clown-like, bordering-on-the-psychopathic grin on his face and his arms folded tightly into his chest. Lizzie was similarly mute, although I suspected that her face bore a rather less jocular expression. Every now and again I reached forward and squeezed her shoulder companionably. Even Nathalie seemed lost in her own thoughts, the most clamorous of which, I guessed, would be the fact that Pod had not made his previously arranged call that morning and was subsequently not answering his mobile. Still, the traffic was kind, the sun was shining and we were off on a Big Adventure!

The plan had been to leave the car with some friends of Pod's, Beanie and Robin, who lived near the airport. That way it was close by when our father needed to pop back to London on gallery business and we would have his car in Italy whilst he was gone. Having safely deposited it, with Robin promising to turn the engine over every now and again and Beanie offering us a lift for the final leg, it was only minutes later that we arrived at Departures. The flight to Pisa was to take about two and a half hours and from there we would have another two-and-a-half-or-so's drive to the house. Pod was going to meet us at Pisa airport to take us on to our new home.

Clearly relieved at having arrived safely and in good time, Nathalie smiled gratefully at us all and took Lizzie's hand comfortingly. I grabbed a trolley for the cases and we wheeled into the queue. Jamie remained surprisingly low key, even resisting the temptation to hitch a ride with the luggage. It was, perhaps, at this point my Suspicions should have been aroused. My Suspicions, when it came to Jamie, were usually very much 'on the ball'. In fact, often they were already on the scene before his Mischievous Intentions had even got themselves together. On this occasion, though, they were taken thoroughly by surprise. Actually we all were when Jamie suddenly let out an enormous wail, simultaneously grasping at his body with what I think could only be described as 'reckless abandon'. "Toots!" he moaned anguishedly, looking imploringly up at me as he continued his contortions. In an instant my Suspicions rallied, joining forces with my Reasoning to make what I felt was a pretty accurate on-the-spot conjecture as to the cause of his distress.

"Oh Jamie!" I groaned sympathetically, "have you lost him?"

"Lost him!" Nathalie exclaimed. "But Toots is with Max!"

Jamie shook his head miserably. "Is that where you went just before we left the house," I probed gently. Sherlock Holmes has nothing on me. He nodded.

"I rescued him," he explained miserably. "When I dropped him off Max picked him up by one end and twirled him round and round like he was a piece of rope. And he laughed. He won't love him like I do."

My blood was rapidly reaching boiling point. Well, as far as I was concerned it had definitely been a rescue mission. Imagine spending the rest of your life not only with Max but dependent on him! Ughhhh! Nathalie, however, was still trying to grasp the situation.

"You mean you've had Toots with you all the way in the car? You brought him with us to the airport?"

Jamie nodded again and resumed his moaning. "He's been in my jacket but he must have wriggled out in the last few minutes."

"But you must have realised that you couldn't take him onto the aeroplane," Nathalie continued, not, at this stage, very helpfully. "They have strict regulations about that sort of thing."

"I didn't think they'd mind," Jamie said. "No-one would even know he was there – he's not noisy or anything." Nathalie harumph-ed despairingly.

"It seems to me," I interjected firmly, "that the key thing now is to find Toots before someone else finds him for us."

This was not a scenario to contemplate for more than a moment. As nonchalantly as possible, leaving Lizzie in charge of the luggage, Nathalie, Jamie and I began the search, peering behind chairs, beneath trolleys and in-between the feet of our fellow travellers. Finally, two wallets, one plastic aeroplane and a small green sock later, and just when all hope seemed lost, Jamie gave a yelp of delight. Discreetly extricating Toots from behind the wheels of an abandoned trolly he kissed the top of his head and placed him tenderly in his pocket.

"I'm here now," he crooned, patting the pocket gently, "don't be scared."

I was so moved by this reconciliation scene that it was a minute or so before I realised that a further parting, and one more permanent, was inevitable. If, when he looked up at Nathalie, the pleading expression in Jamie's eyes was anything to go by, this terrible truth was dawning on him too. She led him over to the nearby bank of chairs and sat down beside him. Curiously, at that moment, just as on that night in my room, I found myself seeing beyond 'my mother', to the woman who played her part. She looked so weary and lost, like a small child who found herself a long way from home and was not sure quite how to find her way back. As she took Jamie's hand and began, in uncharacteristically soft and quiet tones, to confirm his darkest fear, I slipped away tactfully to fill Lizzie in on the latest.

The departures hall was positively heaving with crowds of surprisingly aimless looking people. Unwittingly, they wove their strangely choreographed dance around each other, partnered not by tuxedoed beau but instead by precarious piles of cases on wheels. Lizzie was not hard to find. Long before I reached the check-in desk I spotted her, gesticulating wildly, and, I noted as I drew nearer, with a decidedly anxious look on her face.

"They're about to close the check-in!" she exclaimed. "Where's Nathalie? Did you find Toots?" I quickly caught her up with the news, at the same time scouring the hall for a sign of the others. With a huge sigh of relief I identified Jamie haring his way towards us in and out of the milling crowd.

"It's alright!" he called ecstatically as he approached, an enormous smile on his still tear-stained face. "Beanie's coming to pick him up and she says she'll look after him for me and on weekend exeats from school I can go and visit!"

Not far behind him came Nathalie, rather less ecstatic but smiling wanly, nevertheless. Looking increasingly concerned as I ran up and explained the urgency, she rallied us all with due haste, along with the loaded trolley, and approached the desk. We had, it appeared, made it. By the skin of our teeth.

Fifteen minutes later, loitering suspiciously outside the ladies' loo, the furtive hand over was made and we could finally make our way through passport control. Jamie was back to his old – exhausting – self, having taken on the guise of Secret Agent and consequently running a rather less than secret commentary into the radio transmitter hidden in his Secret Agent Watch, on the proceedings and our neighbours in the queue.

By the time we were settling down into our seats the rest of us were altogether fed-up and frazzled – although in the front row with extra legroom thanks to Lizzie's cast – and we had not even left home turf. I looked across at Nathalie. Her lips were set, tight and anxious, and she barely acknowledged my sympathetic squeeze of her hand.

Of course ... there was still no word from Pod.

Chapter Twenty-Six

It was only after we had been waiting for nearly an hour that I began to get concerned. Nathalie, I suspected, had been worried ever since we wheeled through the frosted glass doors of Baggage Reclaim and Pod wasn't there. His mobile was not responding to her repeated attempts to contact him and there was no answer to the two text messages that she had sent earlier in the day.

Initially the novelty of our environment had offered some distraction. Though we were all tired, the substitution of Italian for familiar old English lent a mysterious exoticism to even the most mundane of proceedings. Fortunately, Nathalie had a basic grasp of our new language, though I was realising that my "Asterix Learns Italian" course left one or two distinct gaps in my knowledge when it came down to living in this century. I was becoming increasingly unsure whether, when push came to shove and I was, for example, lost and far from home, being able to inform the authorities that I eat wild boar for breakfast was going to stand me in adequate stead. Still, it is surprising how far you can get with a winning combination of gestures and smiles. Lizzie and I spent a very profitable half hour discovering the latest in Italian fashion in the little airport boutiques whilst Nathalie paced anxiously up and down outside the main exit.

As we wheeled out to join her, small bags in hand – now we'd really arrived! – the early evening sun was warm on our faces. The light breeze still carried the heat of the day, wrapping itself around us in a comforting caress as we wandered over to offer our solidarity to our mother.

"I'm sure it's just the traffic," I reassured her. "It's always hard to judge how long a journey's going to take, especially one that is not very familiar."

She wasn't, I could see, convinced. Nor, if I was honest, was I. Why hadn't he called if there was a problem? He would never willingly leave us stranded, with no word. Nathalie was pale and drawn, a striking contrast to those around us, who sprawled idly on the surrounding grassy banks or chatted unselfconsciously into their mobile phones, tanned and relaxed, in harmony with the golden afternoon.

The next hour ticked by and then a third. At crisis management Nathalie was unmatchable. Sensing our growing concern, she suppressed her own fears and orchestrated a positive symphony of diversions. We had pasta in the restaurant, ice-creams in the car-park and the giggles outside the ladies' loo when a very snooty lady, dressed up to the nines, came out with her dress tucked in her knickers... But finally there was nowhere to run...

Something was wrong.

The time, too, was getting on. Our plane had touched down at 3-10 pm and it was now 7-45 pm. We still had a long journey to make before we reached the house. Where was Pod?! Lizzie began to cry. I, too, was close to tears. Were Jamie not now asleep, his head lolling peacefully against Nathalie's arm, I strongly suspected that, Secret Agent or no, he would by now be scared and upset. How my heart went out to our mother, clearly as confused and anxious as we were, but stoically remaining calm, I knew, for our sakes.

A decision had to be made. Carefully Nathalie handed Jamie across to me and in hushed tones explained her plan. Fifteen minutes later she was returning from the Hertz desk, with hire-car keys in hand, a map of Northern Italy and a firm resolve...

"If we leave now," she asserted, "we should be there by nightfall. I have the address and a good map and we can always ask people on the way. Perhaps there's been a misunderstanding and Pod's expecting to meet us there."

Though we knew that this was extremely unlikely, Lizzie and I smiled gratefully, relieved to have any explanation behind which to hide our fears.

The emergency car, a chirpy-looking Punto, was easy to locate. Whilst I loaded the suitcases into the boot, Nathalie bundled a sleepy Jamie, his flushed face still criss-crossed, not terribly secret-agent-like, with the knit-pattern of Nathalie's sleeve, into the back seat. Then, together, we negotiated the heroically uncomplaining Lizzie into the front. Before long we were haring down the motorway...

Jamie, inspired by all the sudden activity, quickly rallied from 'exhausted' to 'exhausting' once more. There was no doubt that the 'newness' of the fairytale world that was opening up around us as we sped along was thrilling. Somehow, too, the fact that we were taking some kind of action in the face of the unexpected crisis alleviated, to a surprising extent, the mood of rising panic. Jamie's animated commentary on the magical landscape as it rushed by, punctuated by impromptu bursts of earnest, covert instruction into his watch'radio transmitter, lent a welcome touch of normality to the proceedings. Before long, at Lizzie's instigation, the car was positively rocking with enthusiastic, if cacophonous, renditions of Bob Dylan's (Pod's favourite and consequently well-known to us all) 'greatest hits'. You might even have been persuaded that our fears were altogether forgotten.

But you would have been wrong.

Like the covert maggot that leaves his small, clean hole undetected on the surface whilst he eats away at the heart, even as we raised our voices in song, the Fear was busy undermining us all. How glad we were to have the familiar, idealistic choruses to enter into with gusto and help drown out the sound of deep-down rumination...

And when our repertoire was all sung out, we turned, instead, to thoughts and 'imaginings' about our new home – loud and eager so as not to be vulnerable to the silence. Lizzie guessed there would be large iron gates at the head of a long cypress-lined drive. Nathalie guessed an old, beamed kitchen with worn terracotta on the floor and a welcoming kettle on the range. I guessed olive trees as far as the eye could see and Jamie, recalling Pod's memories of lizards and toads and giant winged insects who belonged more to science fiction than to every-day, began to speculate on the creatures and birds who would inhabit the world that between us we were conjuring in our heads.

Made excited by our expectations, we willed the last section of the journey to pass quickly. By now, the day was drawing to its end. In the dusk the landscape took on still more of the mysterious guise of the fairytale. Miniature towns tumbled, higgledy-piggledy, down distant hillsides; tall, elegant trees stood imperiously at the edge of the road, silhouetted black against the sky. And such a sky! Lurid and extravagant. it screamed its glorious farewell to the day – orange, purple, blue and red and gold – ever-changing and wonderful in its brashness. The remaining light was, we knew, essential to this final stage of our journey. The King of the Night – our father had told us tales of his palace in the heavens where the stars were his ethereal attendants and the moon his shining throne – was preparing to take ascendance. Tiny lights already twinkled across the valley and, as we turned off the 'beaten track', the road ahead was almost dark and we no longer had the assurance of other cars to guide us.

I could feel my heart thumping with anticipation as we made our slow and windy way up the hill. "Follow the signs to the *Santa Maria del Bagno*," Giuliana had said in her last letter; to the little church that presides, as of ancient times, over the hillside, so much of which was to be our home. The car headlights picked out the small yellow signs as we climbed; one against a crumbling wall, another on a large and twisted oak tree, a third, almost missed, part buried in a verdant hedgerow. We strained our eyes in the gloaming, eager to glean whatever information we could about our new world before the light faded entirely. There were the olive trees, just as I had imagined, stretching out into the dark, from whence, perhaps, they would go on forever... Now and again a crumbling stone wall or abandoned barn loomed up beside us, only to slip back modestly into the shadows as we passed it by: As if it had heard our thoughts on the balmy wind and considered that it was first and only the finding of our new home that would truly satisfy our search. And then, almost too soon for us to be ready, even after so much anticipation – (could we ever have been prepared?) – there she was: '*Castel di Sopra*'.

'The Castle Above'.

Chapter Twenty-Seven

The name was written into the large wrought iron gates that stood before us straddling the road, so there was no mistake. And Lizzie too had guessed well when she had added her intricate lines of paint to our imagined canvas. But I suspected her vision had told only part of the story...

The gates had clearly once been masterful – and masterly. Even as they were, they rose authoritatively up out of the dark and out of the tall tangle of weeds that wound their vigorous and choking way about the intricate frame. The elegantly-wrought iron stood strong and resolute, as if resisting to the last the verdant green invader that threatened, on a whim, to draw it back deep down into the earth whence it came. Nathalie stopped the car. Clearly we could go no further whilst the gates remained closed. She, Jamie and I clambered out onto the road, which at this point, we could see, was barely more than a track. The headlights illuminated well the challenge ahead. It was clear, on closer inspection, that the gates had not, for some time, admitted vehicles. The silt and mud had long ago built up around the base and large grassy mounds had taken root at either side. They were, in fact, not quite closed. There was, I guessed, just enough room between the two sections for someone, turning sideways, to inch their way through. Beyond the gates the track stretched for as far as the headlights would allow us to see. There was no sign of the house.

"We could leave the car here and walk," I suggested, but even as I did so I could see that my proposal was unhelpful. Without the lights from the car we would be in almost total darkness, feeling our way along a rough and unfamiliar track. It would be impossible to manoeuvre Lizzie's chair through the gap and in any case we had no idea just how far we had to go before reaching the 'castle'. There were no lights, distant or otherwise, to indicate that we were almost there.

"I could squeeze through the gates myself and explore," I said, on second thoughts. "At least I could find out how far we are from the house. You could wait here with Lizzie and the car until I get back."

Nathalie's response was immediate – and adamant. On no account was she going to risk me disappearing off into the night alone, particularly on this unknown road which, I had to admit, was beginning to take on a rather sinister air...

For a while we were all stumped into silence. We stood there in our pool of light, as if it were a small dinghy in a vast dark sea. And then the silence got too loud to bear and so I gave a cough and Nathalie a sigh and Jamie picked up a stick from the undergrowth and began to click-click it along the iron gate.

"What's the plan?" Lizzie called from inside the car.

"Good question!" I answered her. "There's no way we can get the car through the gates. Perhaps there's a way around them?"

It was Jamie who found our answer. At first it seemed impossible. From what we could see, the edge of road fell away sharply at both sides of the gates, forming a grassy bank, studded with tree stumps and criss-crossed with brambles. What we were able to make out of the drive up to the gates was lined by an overgrown 'hedgerow' of sorts, interspersed with densely rooted trees. And then, just as we were ready to despair, Jamie, who had wandered, I noticed then, rather further back down the track than we had agreed to venture by ourselves, gave a shout. Agitating his stick into the hedge he had stumbled upon a large opening leading off the road, screened only partially by soft pine fronds. Excitedly he had discovered what seemed to be deep ruts or tyre tracks packed firmly down into the ground beneath.

Reversing the car back towards the tracks, Nathalie angled the beam of the headlights between the trees. Sure enough a narrow track, little more than the width of a car, was forged through the undergrowth. The tyre-marks were deeply entrenched and it was clear by the lack of new grass or weeds growing in the furrows that this was a well-used path. The angle of the bank was far less steep here and a little further down the route seemed to curve back in the direction of the gates.

And, we hoped, the house...

Nathalie took the makeshift road slowly and cautiously. We bumped our way down from the main drive and, like Good King Wenceslas's page, followed trustingly in the path of those who had been before us.

Just as we had hoped, it wasn't long before the new track swung back up to join our original 'road'; at this point – hooray! – a good 100 metres or so beyond the gates. Though the drive here was peppered with weeds and now and then an overhanging branch brushed creepily at the roof of the car, it was a far less bumpy ride. Still, the ground was unknown and it seemed wise to continue at our slow and steady pace. We felt almost furtive as we crawled along the narrow lane, Jamie, Lizzie and I peering out into the darkness for any sign that we might be nearing the house. Even so, we almost missed the fork in the road altogether.

It was a tiny glimmer of light through the trees, some distance away to the right of our track, that alerted Jamie.

"There it is!" he yelled without warning – and, if there had been a ditch to narrowly miss swerving into, Nathalie would have narrowly missed it. She pulled up to a halt. "Over there!" he exclaimed excitedly, pointing in the direction of the light.

"Well done," Nathalie praised him, though in weary tones, "but might it be possible to notice more quietly?"

Jamie smiled back, peacefully, content in his satisfaction at being the first one to spot 'home'.

The next challenge was just how we were to find our way to the house. It looked very unlikely that the road we were on was heading in the right direction. Nathalie got out of the car to get a greater sense of the lie of the land. She discovered the track almost immediately, though she could see also why we had missed it from the car. It formed a sharp angle with the main drive, almost doubling back on it for the first stretch. Climbing back into the car she reversed back to the narrow opening in the hedgerow and turned in. Once more, now that the end of our journey was in sight, we felt the excitement and anticipation begin to build. 'Castel' di Sopra – did it have turrets like a real castle? Would we each have our own rooms? Would Uncle Tom look just like Pod? And yes, how we hoped it, would our father be there on the doorstep to welcome us to our new home?

It was only as we drew up to the building at the top of the hill that we realised our mistake. The 'Santa Maria del Bagno' was bathed in a welcoming yellow-gold light, courtesy of a large lantern that hung from the branches of the tall beech tree outside. From within, another light flickered and danced, catching intermittently on the colourful, round stained-glass pane that was set high above the mighty wooden door. A small 3-wheeled vehicle, that seemed to me like a cross between a milk float and a golf buggy, was parked beneath the tree.

As we sat there slowly processing our surprise at this unexpected turn of events, one half of the door began to open. At the top of the stone steps appeared an old man, wizened and stooped with age.

He was clearly as surprised to find us there outside the church as we were. Using the handle of the broom he was holding as a kind of staff, he began to make his way cautiously down the steps. Despite his caution, I detected, I was sure, a surprisingly youthful spirit behind the aged facade. Almost as though, in the twinkle of an eye, he would fling off his elderly disguise, twirl that cane like a baton above his head and spring into a cheerful series of cartwheels to the car...

Disappointingly, however, his approach was rather more sedate. His broad toothless grin, as he peered in through Nathalie's window could leave no doubt that he was, indeed, at least one hundred years old.

"*Buonasera,*" he greeted us warmly.

"Tom Beresford-Linnel?" Nathalie supplied, somewhat inadequately.

"Guiseppe," he replied, and stretched his hand in through the window.

"*Mi scusi,*" Nathalie fumbled, rather thrown and taking his hand anyway. "*Dove e* Tom Beresford-Linnel?"

'*Dove e*', I recalled from my Asterix teachings was the thing to say if you were looking for someone – or something – as in '*Dove e il menhir*'.

Guiseppe looked blank.

"*Castel di Sopra?*" Nathalie tried again.

He scratched his head.

"*Una casa grande,*" she persisted, "*di una famiglia inglese.*"

A moment or two passed. Then, as we watched, his face clouded over and the wide perpetual grin pursed into a frown. "*Ah, si,*" he acknowledged darkly. There was a strained silence before he continued:

"*La Casa Senza Occhi. La Casa Cieca.*"

104

Chapter Twenty-Eight

Shortly afterwards, directed back onto our original course, we set off down the hill, leaving the strange old man following after us with his eyes. "What did he say?" Lizzie, Jamie and I demanded insistently of our mother, the moment we were out of earshot. All of us were more than a little unnerved by the sinister turn in the mood of the conversation. "What does he mean, '*La Casa Cieca*'? Does he have the right house?"

I leant forward and poked my head between the two front seats. Nathalie's face was closed and pensive; her front teeth bit down onto her lower lip.

"Sit back down," she instructed, in a distracted rather than a critical tone. "It isn't safe."

More in response to her manner than her request, I sat back in my seat. As our mother fell silent once more we waited, obediently and expectantly. Finally she spoke;

"The Blind House," she said simply. "The house without eyes."

I shivered. For the first time I was aware that the comforting heat of the day had lost its battle with the chill of the night. I shrugged my cardigan further onto my shoulders.

"The Blind House," I echoed, half hoping that I had misheard Nathalie's words. From behind I saw the nod of her head.

"Why would he call it that?" Lizzie asked. "It sounds so sinister. Surely he can't mean Uncle Tom's house?"

"Well, we're about to find out," Nathalie replied, suddenly matter-of-factly, as she swung round a wide bend in the drive. Sure enough, a large house loomed up before us out of the dark. Almost entirely surrounded by trees, it gave itself away only here and there, with a shuttered window; a suggestion of its steeply pitched roof; the ornately railed overhang of an upstairs balcony...

There could be no doubt, however, as to its size. As we drew nearer, more of the house became visible through the trees. From our angle it seemed to form an L-shape, with one part of the 'L' very different in

105

structure to the other. 'Our' side, as we pulled up in front of the house, was by far the grander of the two. Elegant and imposing, it had the very essence of a fairytale built into its old stone walls. Window after window studded its high facade, every one shuttered tight against the outside world. There was not even a chink of light from within.

"*La Casa Cieca*," I mused softly, under my breath.

"The Blind House."

The thin but luminous sliver of moon afforded a surprising amount of light but Nathalie left the headlights on full beam as she climbed out of the car. Caught in their unforgiving glare her face was tight and drawn. A stray tendril of hair had escaped from her usually immaculate French pleat and she brushed it back impatiently from her cheek. But even when it was tucked up safely and neatly behind her ear, I found the thought of it unsettling. As if it represented a loss of control, the relinquishing of my mother's tight and (I realised for the first time) reassuring grip at the helm.

Our lights illuminated magnificently the vast wooden front door, all the better for us to see it flung open wide to reveal our father, arms outstretched to welcome us home. But, despite our willing it, the door stayed firmly shut.

"Where is he?" Lizzie asked pleadingly of the night. I could hear the tremble in her lower lip heralding the close onset of tears. The night gave no answer.

"Perhaps they didn't hear us pull up," I offered in his stead – to compensate for his rudeness. "Let's go and bang on the door."

Actually, I felt more like kicking the door. How dare it, with its solid wooden 'shutness' mock our urgent need for its wide open welcome and reassurance? Cloaking my fears in defiance, I climbed out of the car and, with Jamie close at my heels, approached the door. Like that of the church, this one was in two halves. The wood was dark and weathered and about half way up there was a large iron keyhole. Just above that were two small square holes, as if perhaps, once upon a time, it had borne a handle, in obliging acknowledgement of the outside world.

Reaching the large stone step, I turned back to gain the approval of my mother before I knocked. Defiance is one thing; foolhardiness is quite another! She nodded her consent tiredly and at Lizzie's insistent request crossed to the boot of the car to extract the wheelchair.

My knock was loud and officious in the silence. Instinctively, I realised, I had given the Elven signal – two quick raps and then a third – for our father to hear and to find us. In my heart, I heard its echo as we all stood still and quiet, lest we should miss the slightest sound of a response from within. When it was clear that there was none, I tried again; 'rap rap – rap'. Again the world held its breath. How loud silence was when what you needed was sound.

Finally, Jamie and I turned and looked back hopelessly at Nathalie. Jamie gave an exaggerated shrug of his shoulders.

"What now?" he wondered, voicing aloud the thought that was going through all our minds. What now?

"Surely Uncle Tom should be there anyway?" Lizzie reasoned.

It did seem rather odd. There we all were, his long-lost family, crashing about on his doorstep in the middle of the night, and far from having waited up for us, our Uncle Tom did not so much as twitch at the curtain. Ok, so to be fair, it was quite possible that behind those big wooden shutters he didn't have a curtain to twitch and, in truth, we had no idea just how mobile our uncle was now that his health was in such tragic decline. Still, he might, at least, have left the door on the latch...

I looked back again at our new 'home'. For a moment, I wondered if it was the right one after all. This house was sad. Even from the outside I could feel it. Like something was missing. Its spirit perhaps. As if the old stone walls had long ago given up their hope of being loved. Then, bereft of answers, and just as we were in danger of being overwhelmed altogether by melancholy, there was the unmistakeable sound of an engine.

"Pod!" Lizzie, Jamie and I shouted in unison. Preceded by the bright beams of its headlights a car appeared around the bend. And our soaring spirits came crashing back down to earth. Long before the little car pulled up next to ours, it was clear that it wasn't Pod's large four-wheel-drive. This car, in fact, if you asked me, was more like a shoe on wheels. It had a cute quirkiness about it that I would ordinarily, I suspected, have found humorous and appealing. Instead, in its miniature, ridiculous, 'not-being-Pod-ness', it made me irritable and cross.

The door opened and a distinctly un-Pod-like old lady began easing herself cautiously out of the front seat.

"Nathalie!" she declared rather breathlessly, mid way through the process.

"Giuliana?" Nathalie seemed to crumple visibly with relief as the grey-haired woman grasped her firmly by the shoulders and kissed her warmly on both cheeks.

But then, just as our hopes were preparing to rally: "Where is Paul?" they asked of each other in unison.

If it were possible, our spirits sank even further; down through our shoes, through the stony driveway and deep into the earth beneath. If she couldn't have been Pod then at least Giuliana might have brought word of him, offered some explanation for his disappearance. It seemed that she was as much in the dark as we. Still, there was undoubtedly something reassuring about this small plump figure with the soft, unruly bun in her hair and eyes that twinkled even in the strange half-light. Assessing rapidly the situation, she left, for now, the question hanging in the increasingly chilly night air and ushered Jamie, Nathalie and me towards the house. As though it had been her role since the beginning of time, she took the handles of the wheelchair and, with a quick ruffle of Lizzie's hair, followed on behind us to the door. There was something in her no-nonsense, efficient manner that demanded absolute cooperation and was, I suspected, at this point in our long, unsettling day, a profound relief to us all.

With a large, iron key that she extracted from an apron-like pocket, Giuliana unlocked the door. One side of the door swung open wide. For a moment, we all just stood there on the doorstep, no-one, perhaps, wanting to be the first to step deeper into the unknown.

"Come along," encouraged Giuliana brusquely, with a surprisingly English turn of phrase that belied the rich foreign-ness of her accent. Each of us instantly overwhelmed by an irresistible inclination towards obedience, we then attempted to pile in through the half-open door all at once. Despite the underlying tensions – or perhaps it was because of them – Lizzie and I began to giggle. "One at a time," Giuliana smiled. "Let's get you into the warm and then we can think about finding your father..."

Chapter Twenty-Nine

The entrance hall was even darker than it was outside. It smelt of dust and old floor wax. As my eyes began to adjust, I could make out the foot of an imposing staircase, the sweep of its curved balustrade disappearing back into the shadows. Tall figures, too, loomed up out of the gloom, which, after an initial start. I rationalised must be large statues or sculptures, standing guard over their musty domain.

With an instinctive accuracy, borne, clearly, out of years of familiarity, Giuliana reached her hand around the doorway and turned on the light. After all the hours in the semi-dark, my eyes were assailed by colour. A vast sea of warm, aged terracotta spread out from beneath our feet. The walls were a rich old-gold that, though faded and shabby, reflected back gloriously the light from a large wrought-iron chandelier. Against this lustrous yellow the numerous sculptures that framed the room stood out imposing and black, despite the layers of dust that, on closer inspection, crowned their lordly heads and shoulders.

Giuliana ran her finger over the bald pate of that nearest to her with a resigned shake of her head. For a moment, she seemed lost in thought. Though perhaps it was just my 'imagining', I was sure I heard her murmur something soft and sad to the stern, cold figure beneath her hand. Then, before her long-silent confidant had time to summon up his reply, she was bustling us all efficiently through the hallway, past a number of intriguingly closed doors and beyond the main staircase to a narrow flight of stone steps at the far end of the room.

The staircase was worn smooth with age, the cleanly defined lines of the original stone moulded and shaped by years of clattering feet, just passing through. The passageway was just wide enough to allow Lizzie's wheelchair to make the perilous journey, aided gallantly by the rest of us, down the five steps to the corridor below. From there we made our way, hearts still pumping hard from the exertion, into the kitchen.

If Giuliana had not announced it as she switched on the dim central light of the vast 'underground' room, it might have taken a while for me to recognise this as the '*cucina*'. It could not have been more different from our bright cheerful kitchen at home. (I wondered, fleetingly, how long it would be before this strange, sad house replaced our other in my heart as 'home'?). There were no windows to let the outside in, and instead of the gleaming rows of cabinets, worktops and shining steel it seemed to boast only a huge ancient-looking stove, an untidy pile of pots and pans and an enormous wooden dining table to justify its claim. I caught Nathalie's eye. She was looking rather faint.

Collecting a huge black kettle from the top of the stove, Giuliana crossed to the trough-like sink in the corner of the room and turned on the tap. At first nothing happened and then, with a rush, a stream of water shot out, avoiding the spout of the kettle entirely in the interest of drenching poor Giuliana from head to foot. To accompany this dramatic display, the entire house was brought into play, with an alarming cacophony of screeching and rhythmic bangs that seemed destined to bring the building down around our ears.

"Pipes," Giuliana informed us, entirely unruffled, as, with the stream of water finally finding its equilibrium, she filled the kettle and set it on top of the stove. Although clearly not altogether soothed by the knowledge that the infernal din was 'merely' down to the plumbing, Nathalie smiled weakly and, in a reciprocal gesture of goodwill, began to co-ordinate the rather motley assortment of mugs that stood randomly along a high wooden shelf above the sink, in readiness for tea. Of the six in evidence, only four had handles, one had a large crack down the side and another appeared to have something growing in it that was more than a little reminiscent of Lizzie's bacterial friends. With an air of bold defiance, Nathalie approached the sink with the mug and, standing well back, turned on the tap. Seemingly subdued by the fact that it no longer possessed the element of surprise, the stream of water that flowed out was meek and steady. Bravely poking the revolting green/black gloop with the wooden handled washing-up brush that lay tucked behind the taps and looked scarcely more hygienic than the mug itself, Nathalie rinsed the cup through. Despite her efforts and in the spirit of every-man-for-himself, I made a mental note to avoid the grey mug with the yellow stripe when the hot drinks were being handed out. The violent prod in the ribs from Jamie and the contorted expression on his face as I turned round to prod him back implied that his thoughts were following in a similar vein. OK, so that made the odds slightly tighter but, even if I had also to rule out the option of the cracked mug, I calculated that I still had a good chance of avoiding the gloop if I was quick off the mark.

In the event, however, I was spared from making my rather ignoble bid. The steaming hot mug of tea that Giuliana handed to me as she gestured to us to sit down – a stroke of fortune provided precisely five chairs – was unquestionably white with blue spots. I looked across at Jamie who was nursing, with no small sense of triumph, his bright yellow mug.

Once we were all sat at table, however, there was no avoiding the real issue on everyone's mind. What had become of our father? The fact that Giuliana spoke English was a profound relief to us all. This was not a question about which we could afford to misunderstand the slightest nuance of detail. Nathalie's basic Italian was clearly under strain and Asterix had evidently never had to cope with a missing father – or with the rising sense of dread that I was no longer able to ignore.

"He was here this morning," Giuliana offered, to open the conversation. Nathalie's fist twitched involuntarily on the tabletop and I reached over and took her hand. Then, whilst the night stole silently by and we sought inwardly to make an ally of our strange new world, Giuliana began to tell us all she knew.

She had arrived at the house very early that morning, having understood from Pod that he hoped to make the final leg of his journey through the night. She had not wanted him to arrive, as we had, to a closed and unwelcoming house. 'La Casa Cieca'. I turned the impression over in my mind and then the thought of Uncle Tom slipped in and took its place. She continued. Sure enough, Pod had driven up at about 6 am, tired and dishevelled but very much, she confided in us, the small boy that she remembered so fondly. Impatient for more fundamental news, Nathalie broke in. Where was he now? she wanted to know. But Giuliana, it seemed, had her own story to tell.

Helping him in with his small overnight case – the hint of a smile touched Lizzie's lips and I knew she was recalling packing his favourite things – Giuliana had shown him to a large bedroom on the first floor that she suggested would be the most comfortable for him and Nathalie to make their own. The bed was freshly made and she had opened up the creaky old shutters to let the light, and air, flood in. She had even placed a small vase of wild flowers by the bedside in anticipation of Nathalie's arrival. Her exasperation, then, at Pod's out-and-out rejection of the room, that had once-upon-a-time been that of his parents, was profound. Instead, he had insisted on depositing his things in a small guest room along the corridor, a room that had not seen light or air for more than twenty years and had only a musty old tapestry bedspread to cover the mattress. Still, such was his exhaustion that these things did not seem to matter nearly as much to him as they did to her and he made it quite clear to her that she was to leave him to sleep. Having prepared a breakfast tray for him in the kitchen for when he woke – a plate of salami and cheese with a half-loaf of new bread (Jamie wrinkled up his nose at, I suspected, the idea of this pungent substitute for his favourite 'Frosties') – she resolved to return to the house in three or four hours. After all, she maintained emphatically, she did have a responsibility to 'her other family', the Pittini, whose estate was just across the hillside and for whom she now worked as housekeeper and nanny to two children.

She paused to take a sip of hot, sweet tea. I was finding it hard to remain patient as the story gradually unfolded, so desperate was I to be reassured as to my father's present whereabouts. Nathalie looked as though she might weep with exhaustion and the uncertainty of it all. I just hoped Giuliana had something positive on which to end her tale...

On her return she had heard the angrily raised voices the moment she entered the house. Tom, she knew, would be in his room (it did not occur to me then to find her certainty of this curious), and therefore our father must, on waking, have gone to see him. But before she had time to climb the staircase and intervene there came a loud crash – the slamming of a door, she presumed – followed by the rapid thundering of footsteps. A moment later Pod came bolting down the stairs.

It was as if he hadn't even seen her standing there as he shot past, so close by as to brush her arm fleetingly, and jarringly, with his. (Giuliana could not resist a slight tone of pique creeping into her voice as she recalled the moment). The front door was still ajar after her arrival and he had run straight through the hall and out into the drive. As hurriedly as she could – the problems with her hip meant she was no longer as agile as she used to be – she had followed him outside, where she was just in time to see him start up the car and roar out of the driveway. As children, she said, they had been inseparable – that is until the tragedy – it was only then that this animosity began... How she had hoped that our arrival, especially with Tom now being so sick, would somehow heal the rift between them. Instead, if anything, it seemed that time had merely added fuel to the flames. Perhaps, she mused sadly, they were, as Tom had so repeatedly

The large cream-coloured doorknob squeaked a little as it turned, reminding me of the one to Pod's study in Paultons Square (how far away it seemed just now) and of the night of the letters when our adventure really began...

"I thought these two rooms would work well for the children," Giuliana explained to Nathalie as she pushed open the door. "The large one was once the nursery. This way they are close by each other and perhaps their new home won't feel quite so strange. When you're more settled, we could explore the house together and they could choose the rooms that they would most like to call their own."

I peered in around the door. It was funny to imagine Pod as a small boy, filling this little room with his 'wonderings' about life and his hopes and dreams for the future. Was the life that he had forged for himself today very different from the one he had envisaged when he lay back upon his bed, this bed, with its pointy wooden headboard like a wizard's hat and only just enough room in its length to fit Jamie, or perhaps Lizzie? Would he have felt pleased if he had known then the path that lay ahead? As I glanced around in the moonlight I noticed that, as in the first room, a simple wooden crucifix hung upon the wall above the bed. It was odd to think of religion as being such a feature in Pod's day-to-day world back then, when for as long as I could remember he had been so firm in his atheist conviction that there was no God. It was always Nathalie I went to with my own questionings and uncertainties about faith, so closed was he to considering the possibility of His existence.

Giuliana cut briskly across my train of thought to the little table beside the bed and turned on the lamp. In an instant the silver-blue room was yellow-gold, and the night beyond the window turned near-black. "Well now," Giuliana addressed Jamie, as she hurried over to draw the shutters to a close, "there's water here for you too and remember to tuck the net around the bed when you climb in. Those wily mosquitos are always ready for a feast." Jamie nodded sleepily.

"Now, how about you all start to make yourselves at home whilst your mother and I fetch your overnight cases?" she continued. Jamie had brought his small backpack in with him and, as Nathalie and Giuliana left the room, I eased his arms gently out of the straps and put it on top of the large chest of drawers. It was hard to imagine this being the room of a young, excitable boy like Jamie. Beside the rather ponderous pieces of furniture, the room was sparse and characterless. The walls of Jamie's room at home were positively straining to contain his personality and enthusiasm for life. Still, from the size of the bed I guessed that Pod must have moved to a new room when he was not much older than Jamie. After all he would no longer have needed to be so close to the nursery, and, of course, he would have taken all his things with him.

Looking across at Jamie as I began unpacking his bag I was pretty sure that he would have been happy to sleep anywhere that he could lay his head. Luckily, amongst the rather eclectic selection of 'over-night essentials' – one conker, a small tub of dried 'Toots food' (yuck!), Frank his sock-puppet friend (but no socks), his GameBoy, a pen-that-is-also-a-torch (now, *that's* useful) and a fake moustache (in case a little subterfuge is called for before breakfast) – I found a pair of pyjamas, (hooray!), and, sitting him down on the bed, I started helping him off with his shoes.

Lizzie, in the meantime, had embarked upon a one-legged pilgrimage to find a bathroom. Shortly after her departure, a 'not-very-far-off' whoop announced her mission accomplished. "It's a funny little room," she declared on her return. "It looks like it is embarrassed to be there. A sort of 'don't mind me' bathroom with the smallest bath you have ever seen. It has quirky, sticky-out legs and just enough room to sit up in!"

"I suppose it must have been squeezed in as an afterthought," I mused. "After all, when the house was first built it wouldn't have had bathrooms at all, not like we think of them." I remembered the night stand and its water jug.

Leaving Jamie to pull on his pyjamas, (bathrooms weren't really his thing), I followed Lizzie's leader to see for myself. Sure enough it was really more like a large cupboard than a room. It appeared to have been taken out of another bedroom, now being used as some kind of storeroom, that Lizzie had discovered leading off the far side of the nursery. "Well, it seems to have everything we might need," I observed. I liked the comical little bath and was glad to find a bathroom so close at hand – the idea of creeping around this strange house at night was not terribly appealing.

Just then we heard Nathalie and Giuliana return. "Ah, so you've found the bathroom, then?" Giuliana remarked on seeing us appear, slightly sheepishly, at the new door. And then, spotting the faint flush in our cheeks, "It's your house now, my dears, and one day soon, I hope, it will feel like your home. You must feel free to explore all you want to when the morning comes."

Right on cue, Jamie made his pyjama-d entrance. Despite his exhaustion and still endeavouring to do up the buttons on his jacket as he spoke, he made it loudly and unambiguously known that if there was any exploring to be done then it was not to be done without him. Reassuring him that nothing was likely to happen before daybreak, Giuliana took advantage of his appearance to usher him into the bathroom. Miraculously producing and unwrapping a new toothbrush – "I know small boys," she twinkled at Nathalie – she handed it to Jamie.

"Now," she instructed, "teeth, face, bed – and in the morning I might even show you where we hang the big, iron key to the cellars..."

Moments later, scrubbed and gleaming, Jamie was clambering eagerly into bed.

"Is it a gift?" Nathalie asked Giuliana with a smile. "Or does it come with years of training?"

"Ah!" Giuliana replied impishly, "why, then I would be giving away all my secrets...and without a spot of secrecy the magic dies..." And she began to tuck the mosquito net securely around Jamie's bed.

Nathalie, I felt, seemed happier on her return. I hoped that Giuliana had been able to offer her some reassurance about Pod – perhaps she had an idea about where he might have gone. It had also not escaped me that our mother seemed surprisingly relaxed about relinquishing her maternal responsibilities to the formidable housekeeper. Perhaps it was because she was tired, or perhaps it was down to the reassuringly natural way that Giuliana had slipped into the role? Or perhaps – and here was a thought that had not occurred to me before – continually attempting to keep the three of us safe, well, happy and 'in line' wasn't, in fact, all that much fun? Hmmm..? Well, whatever the reason, on this particular occasion Nathalie seemed content to leave the elderly lady chivvying Lizzie and me about the business of unpacking our cases and readying ourselves for the night whilst she said goodnight to Jamie.

Closing his door softly behind her a few minutes later, she came to join us and sat down on the bed.

"A message from Jamie," she said wryly. "He says he's sorry about the sandwich toaster, Lizzie, but there wasn't any room left in his case."

Lizzie grinned. "I'd wondered why it looked so full", she said. "Well it's a good thing you made him clean it up so beautifully before it came with us, or he'd have been de-crumbing all my things tomorrow! I suppose it will need a new Italian plug though, like my hairdryer, before he can use it?"

"Daddy will sort all of that out when he gets back," Nathalie smiled, positively. And then, seeing our faces cloud over again with worry, she conveyed to us, in essence, her conversation with Giuliana as they had walked to the car. There was, she explained, no way of contacting the house by telephone. The main line had been disconnected years ago and, because of its remote location, our new home had no mobile reception. In fact, the reason why Giuliana had not been there waiting for us when we arrived was that, concerned about our failure to appear, she had driven down to the bar at the bottom of the hill to attempt to call our mobile. Of course, since by that time we were already up here, we were unable to receive her call. Anyway, this may have offered an explanation as to why we had not heard from Pod in the last two or three hours at least. And perhaps he too had been out of range when we had tried to call him. It was a small comfort, but, like Nathalie, we accepted it gratefully.

"Now girls," Giuliana prompted, "hop into bed." Lizzie and I giggled and looked pointedly at Lizzie's one good leg. Everyone grinned as Nathalie and I hoisted Lizzie into her side of the bed, propping up her leg with the ample pillows until she was as comfortable as possible. "Your mother is going to sleep here with you until your father arrives," Giuliana informed us. We looked questioningly at our mother and she nodded. I could quite understand her feeling happier to spend the night here with us than in another part of the house all alone. Of course, like her, I hoped that Pod might appear at any moment, but in the meantime it would be much nicer to be all together. I squeezed her hand. "What fun!" I said. "It will be just like when we were little and we all piled in with you and Daddy on Sunday mornings. Lucky it's such a huge bed now that we are so much bigger!"

And there it was. A few minutes later Giuliana had bid us warmly goodnight, kissing each of us firmly on both cheeks and arranging to call again in the morning with further provisions. At the same time she would be able to advise Nathalie as to the best places to do our regular shop and to give us all more of an idea about the surrounding area.

"Can we have the shutters open?" I asked Nathalie as she passed by the window on her way into bed. Somehow, I felt, it would be reassuring to be able to see out into the night, to look upon the same sky and moon as watched too over number 47 Paultons Square and to know that our old world wasn't so far away after all...

She pushed the old wooden shutters back one by one, securing them fast against the outside wall. Once again the room was filled with an ethereal light. Climbing up into bed, Nathalie kissed me softly on the forehead and drew the silver-white net to a close around us.

Chapter Thirty-One

I lay there still and quiet, allowing my mind to loiter indulgently in the fantastical waiting-room between wakefulness and sleep. The air was thick and exotic with the contented trilling of the crickets; a sound familiar and comforting after the many summers spent with our grandparents in France. When I was small and still afraid of the dark, Grandmere Marie would squeeze onto the bed beside me and stroke my hair. She whispered to me of the 'night-song' – '*la chanson de la nuit*', she said – and told me that if I could hear it then the angels were watching over me and all was well. And so it was. And in the mornings, as I waded through the waist-high grasses of the meadow beyond their house and heard the music at my feet, I would smile to know that I was walking with angels...

The here and now breeze toyed flirtatiously with the net about our bed. Nathalie lay silent and still beside me – too silent and still, I felt, to be truly asleep. Her motionless body seemed strangely animated, as though reluctant to relinquish its place in the conscious world. I wondered whether, like me, she was listening to the angel choir and hoping that they were watching over Daddy, wherever he might be. I felt my mind drifting once more. The soft rise and fall of Lizzie's slumber joined with the night song to lull me further into sleep.

And then – it might have been some hours, or just a moment, later; the Conjuror of Sleep wears an artful smile – all of a sudden I was wide awake. Nathalie, too, now made no pretence at sleep, sitting up attentively against the carved wooden headboard. We both heard it! The sound of a car, crunching slowly and unevenly into the drive! Pod!

My mother touched the top of my head gently in silent greeting and eased herself out of bed carefully so as not to disturb Lizzie. Impatiently, she whisked her dressing-gown from the back of a near-by chair. After a brief flirtation with the fickle breeze, the flimsy silk robe settled dutifully over her shoulders. Then Nathalie picked up her dainty mules – her tiny shoes always make me feel like one of the ugly sisters – and carried them to the door. As she pulled it to behind her Lizzie stirred. My heart was racing.

"It's Pod!" I whispered with excitement, as she opened her eyes sleepily. Attempting to sit up but finding herself thwarted by the giant cast, Lizzie settled instead for a broad grin.

"Fantastic!" she beamed. Then, "Is he alright?"

I couldn't wait to find out.

"Come on!" I urged, still in a stage whisper. I leapt out of bed and rushed round to Lizzie's side.

I sat her up and between us we swung her legs over the edge of the mattress. Tossing Lizzie a jumper to pull on over her nightdress, I scooted over to the folded wheelchair. As if anticipating keenly its role in the action, the chair sprang instantly into form.

"What about Jamie?" Lizzie hissed as we headed for the door.

"Yes, what about me?" Jamie asked, disgruntled, appearing through the side-door. Preceding him was a barely discernible beam of light, which I presumed to be emanating from the pen-torch. "Where are you going?"

I grinned. This was due in part to the enormous sense of relief that was already coursing through me at the thought that our father might finally have arrived and in part at Jamie's particularly anarchic hairstyle. Still, conscious that, in all the commotion, I had not had a chance to check my own 'coiffure', I refrained from comment and instead filled him in on the plan afoot.

"Brilliant!" he proclaimed. "Let's go!"

"It might not be Pod," I cautioned, as much to protect myself from disappointment as to remind the others. But nothing could restrain our burgeoning hope as we stepped out of the old nursery and into the narrow, dark corridor.

Even with the residual moonlight from the open door, the windowless corridor was almost pitch black. As I fumbled ineffectually along the panelled wall in the hope of finding a light switch, Jamie gave a triumphant "Tadd-arrr" and flicked his torch back on. Revelling in its moment of glory, the slender beam marked out, almost instantly, a nearby switch. Did our mother stop to turn on the light, I wondered, as the corridor lit up, or, in her urgency, did she run along the passageway near blind?

We thought it likely that there was a more direct way of reaching the entrance hall than via the kitchen. Given the certainty of added complications with Lizzie's leg if we opted for the (marginally) more familiar route, it was unanimously decided that we try to find the alternative. After a hurried 'eeny, meeny, miney, mo' we plumped for a right-hand turn out of the nursery. There was just enough room for Lizzie's chair as we whizzed along. Jamie ran a few paces ahead. The first two doors off the corridor were locked. The third opened out into what appeared by torch light to be a large drawing room. At the far side of the room was another door and it was through there that we hoped we would find the entrance hall. This close to our goal we could spare no time to turn on the light. Instead, with Jamie and the pen (I couldn't wait to discover the occasion on which the fake moustache saved the day!) leading the way, I managed to negotiate the wheelchair between two rather ornate sofas to the door. Jamie turned the knob. First one way, then the other. It was locked! This was a blow we hadn't anticipated. For a moment we were stumped. Then, just as we were about to turn and retrace our tracks to the corridor, Lizzie gave a yelp.

"The key is in the lock!" She gestured wildly at the door. Jamie and I made a dive for it together. The key turned under my fingers; stiffly – but it turned! The door opened inwards and, sure enough, it led out into the main entrance hall! The front door was open wide, affording enough light to reveal that we were only a few feet from the entrance. I eased Lizzie down the single step between the drawing room and the hall. Now that we were actually there, I felt strangely reluctant to take the final steps to the door. My responsible self nudged my impetuous spirit pointedly. Was it inappropriate for us all to have been racing around this strange house in the middle of the night? And what if it wasn't Pod after all?

I put my finger to my lips in a story-book gesture of hush. We crept softly towards the door, betrayed only by the occasional squeak of a rubber wheel on the tiles. Then, as we held our breath, three pairs of eyes looked out into the night. And there they were. Silhouetted against the sky stood our mother and father, as one. Nathalie's head was buried into Pod's shoulder; his hand was stroking the back of her hair. And we didn't need the angels to tell us that all was well...

It wasn't a scene that required anything, or anyone, else to make it complete. I signalled my thoughts to the others and, with smiles on our faces and relief in our hearts, we headed back to bed. Such was the intimacy of the moment we had just witnessed, it felt imperative to get back before our expedition was rumbled. I bumped Lizzie up the step into the drawing room and we raced back along the now-familiar route. I felt like laughing out loud. With Jamie and me breathless and panting, as much from exhilaration as from the mad dash, we pulled into the nursery. Parking my sister, I flopped down on the bed giggling.

"Hey!" Lizzie retorted laughingly, "no time for lounging around!" She threw her jumper over my face. Springing up in a trice I retaliated with a large pillow.

"I can hear someone coming," Jamie hissed urgently. Yikes! Suspending friendly fire, I helped Lizzie swiftly into bed. I tossed her jumper back into the drawer. Moments later I was tucking Jamie's mosquito net around his bed, just, I hoped, as Giuliana had done.

Right then! Back under the covers! I dived in beside Lizzie and pulled the sheet over myself in a way that I hoped looked artless and natural. My heart was thumping so hard I felt sure they would hear it from the passageway. I couldn't stop grinning.

Just in time! The door creaked open.

"Sprung!" exclaimed Pod and Nathalie together, switching on the light. "Where have you lot been?!"

I tried to look bemused and sleepy but my grin was too wide. I sat up. "How did you know?" I asked. "We were so quiet – you couldn't have heard us!"

"The first rule for any Secret Agent," Pod smiled as Jamie came into the room, "is to cover your tracks..." Jamie, Lizzie and I exchanged glances. What had we missed?

"You left the light on in the corridor!" Nathalie announced. We groaned. Then, with much giggling and ruffling of hair, we all piled onto the huge bed. And, for the next half-hour or so, it was just like those happy Sunday mornings of old. Except we were bigger.

And we were in Italy...

Chapter Thirty-Two

I woke the following morning with what we always called 'one of my Saturday heads', in honour of Nathalie's friend Chloe. I think even Nathalie would find it hard to recognise her without the enormous pair of Chanel sunglasses that were a ubiquitous part of her weekend wardrobe. Her 'skull-splitting' headaches, she informed us, were inevitable for someone who played such a 'high-powered role in PR' throughout the week. We noticed they didn't stop her talking.

Anyway, this was a 'corker' of which Chloe would have been proud. The early morning sun was streaming through the open window and across my pillow. I moaned – but silently so as not to wake Lizzie – and pulled the sheet up over my head. It was not long before I decided that this rather airless alternative was not really a solution. I wriggled impatiently out of the twistytwiney bedclothes and felt for my flip-flops with my feet. Grabbing my sunglasses from the small table (maybe she had something there after all), I wandered pitifully over to the window. It felt good to breath deep of the cool, fresh air. I had always maintained to my 'country-mouse' friends that you could rarely smell the traffic fumes in London. I realised now, as I filled my lungs greedily, that it was more about smelling the absence of them when the air was pure. I looked back at Lizzie. Her eyes were still shut tight.

Well, it wasn't surprising she was tired. It must have been after 3 am before Nathalie and Pod said goodnight and went up to bed. I had slept fitfully. For a long while I had lain awake, my mind playing over the day's events. Though our reunion with our father had been wonderful, I still felt uneasy. The 'something behind his eyes' that had worried me in England was still there beneath his smile. Nathalie's eyelashes, I had noticed, were clumped together with still-wet tears. I wondered too about Uncle Tom. Had he been sleeping when we arrived, or had he stayed quietly in his room to avoid a meeting until the morning? I realised that I had no idea whether he was able to be out of bed at all now that he was so sick. In the interests of sleep I stilled my restless mind. Then, just as

I was finally drifting off, I recalled for the first time that night Giuliana's curious words...

"...as children they were inseparable – that is, until the tragedy..."

Standing there by the window her words came back to me again. A 'tragedy' to my mind was no small drama. To what could she be referring? Certainly, in the context of his rift with Uncle Tom, Pod had never mentioned a significant, or tragic, event. But then, thinking about it, he had never really mentioned anything at all. My head was beginning to throb with speculating.

Suddenly the lush green of the grass beyond the window combined with the beneficent breeze to seem irresistibly inviting. The window, I assessed spontaneously, was wide and low. If I perched on one or two of the large hard-covered books from the shelf I was sure I could climb out without too much trouble. Selecting a large tome on Florentine art – definitely something to dip into when my head was feeling less like a cabbage – and another that appeared to be about Romanesque churches, I positioned them carefully in front of the window. With one foot squarely on Pisa cathedral, I swung the other over the window-frame.

Before you could say 'Michelangelo' I was standing in a large meadow. The long grass streamed out before me in the wind, the early dew still shining silver on its wide blades. I wriggled my surprised toes, introducing them formally to the cool, wet green. At this hour, though which hour that might be I had only the vaguest idea, the ground nearest the house was still in deep shade. The grass was laced with wild flowers, grown long and leggy in their competition with the neglected lawn for light. There was a wild, unkempt beauty about it all. My mind flashed up an impression of the neatly manicured garden in Paultons Square where only the most reactionary of daisies dared to challenge the social order.

It was the more distant view, however, that made me draw my breath in awe. It left no room for even the most tenuous of comparisons with our old world across the sea. The olive trees spread out before me like an immense benevolent army; rigourous in their regimental discipline, incalculable in number. This army, though, was no novice platoon, on shaven-headed first release from military school. This army had many stories to tell. Tousle-haired and battle-weary it had long abandoned hope of loving care. Tall weeds and grasses grew up around the base of every tree, and bedraggled shoots shot out chaotically from each gnarled and twisted foot. Yet still they had a strange ethereal beauty. Catching the

127

morning light, their leaves shone silver-green above the dark trunks. Their long, slender boughs were caught up on the wind, joining the grass beneath in its fluid, perpetual run for freedom. How glad I was to have this moment of quiet contemplation. Taking a deep inward breath, as though filling myself to brimming with the magical scene, I resolved always to remember my first real view of 'home'.

I kicked off my shoes. Wet and slippery with dew they would be uncomfortable to walk in and, I felt, would serve better, along with the little stack of books, as a 'Hansel and Gretal' kind of signal to Lizzie, should she wake and wonder where I'd gone. I balanced them rather precariously on the narrow window ledge. There was still no sign of life from my brother or sister. Having appropriated a little too much of the early morning shiver that still permeated the ground nearest the house, my feet were now decidedly cold. Despite my thumping head, the warm sunlight was appearing increasingly inviting. Valiantly I donned my sunglasses and strode out into the light. The strength of the sun on my bare arms and legs took me quite by surprise. The grass here was already warm and soft, with no hint of the damp chill of the shadows. Resolving to stay at this 'sunny distance' from the house, I embarked upon a further exploration of our new environment. My new perspective enabled me to take a look back at the building itself. Beside those of our open window, the rest of the shutters on this side, and there must have been at least a dozen, were firmly closed. After the previous night I could only think of them as eyes, shut to the world – 'blind'. I recalled my childhood drawings of safe, happy houses with wobbly picket fences, disproportionately large flowers and, it was true, windows that were really four wide eyes on the world. Was this house trying to shut something out? Or perhaps – my thoughts grew darker and despite the sun's warmth I shivered a little – to keep something in?

"... that is, until the tragedy..." What had she meant by that? And why had Pod never told us about his childhood home? Giuliana had clearly loved him very much and so much of his early life must resonate within these walls.

I followed along the line of the house, stopping now and then to select the prettiest flowers from the lawn. I planned to gather a large bunch for Nathalie. In my mind I pictured handing them to her – a bouquet, of pinks, yellows, blues and white, interspersed with my love, remorse, respect and new-found trust. Spotting a particularly striking cluster of pink blooms beside what looked to be a big, outdoor rubbish bin I crossed back into the shade. As I bent down and thrust my hand into the abundant foliage I gave an involuntary yelp of pain. A long splinter was embedded in the soft pad of my middle finger. For a minute or two I squeezed ineffectually at the offending article. Finally I resigned myself to its being a job for a needle and my mother's steady hand. Clutching the hard-won flowers in my other hand I was about to stand up when, my eyes having adjusted further to the dark, I spotted what it was that had caused the injury. Had I not seen it somewhere before, I might have mistaken it for any old piece of wood. The two long sides were smooth and refined and it had clearly been broken off at both ends. It was one of these splintered ends that my fingers had inadvertently grasped hold of. But it was the distinctive 'wave-like' markings carved into the gilded surface that could leave no room for doubt in my albeit confused mind.

Just then I heard a rustle from behind. I stood up quickly, the piece of wood still in my hand. Then, almost afraid to have my instinct confirmed, though I wasn't sure why, I turned slowly to face the figure standing before me. How had I had known it would be my father? He looked down at my hand and I held the piece of picture-frame out to him, an unspoken question in my eyes. Without a word, he walked over to the large bin and extracted something from inside. The canvas was torn and crumpled. Parts of the frame still clung to the edge.

"Was Mia your boat?" I asked him softly.

In the silence that filled the space where my words had been I began to wonder whether perhaps he had not heard my question.

Finally he spoke. "No," he answered simply. And then, as though I might have guessed it all along;

"Mia was my sister."

Chapter Thirty-Three

At first I thought I had forgotten how to breathe. Then the thumping in my chest felt as loud as if I was shouting my bewilderment to the world. Even if I could have found the words, it did not feel appropriate for me to say anything. So I waited. Thumped and waited. Finally, after all the years of silence, my father began to talk...

Mia had died, he told me, when she was fifteen. He paused, his head bowed. My thoughts raced with my heart. When they told me that Mollie had died, at first I wasn't angry. I wasn't even sad. I was surprised. Her death was a huge, terrible surprise; a monstrous jack-in-a-box that shocked me out of my comfortable world where everything made sense. Even though I thought I'd known that she was dying. So I had needed someone to blame. Because if I found out who it was then I could ask them why it happened. Why a girl who loved to live so much would never have a chance to be. But I never found the culprit, so an answer never came. Was that how it was for Pod?

So Mia, like Mollie, would always be young... I ached for the once-upon-atime girl who danced now through my head. She would never again wriggle her toes in the dew-laden grass or feel the warm prickle of the first light of summer on her skin. She would never know the man her brother had become, find true love or carry a child of her own. How desperate the living seem to be to outwit the hand of time. How ironic that the only foolproof way to do so is to die before your life has ever really begun. Were Mia's hopes and dreams buried with her, I wondered. Or were they instead a forever-vital part of all that I could see around me? My father, I felt, was not the one to ask. And now was not the time.

He looked up then and caught my eyes, though I had the strangest sensation that he wasn't really seeing me. It happened shortly after he had left for France, he said. He was nineteen, and had been eager to strike out and find his place in the world. I pictured for a moment the impoverished young artist, straw in his hair, the soles of his shoes flapping. I nodded. We knew that part of the story well. Or so we thought. They had, his mother said later, tried hard to find him. But haystacks don't have telephones and one old barn is too much like another. So it was many weeks before they told him and Mia had long lain cold in the ground. The sadness in his voice I would have expected but I was disturbed by an undertone of something darker; bitterness, or even anger. The youthful, dancing vision in my head turned sinister and fey.

Before I lost us both entirely into his pain, I took my father's arm and led him out of the shadows into the bright sunshine. Standing here, of course, the story was no less mournful but somehow I felt the light would help us to retain a foothold in the 'here and now'. Still, it seemed my mind, like his, was in too deep. How was it that she had died? I longed to inquire. Was it morbid of me to wonder? But I didn't like to ask and he did not offer it. So I remained wondering.

"Did Nathalie know?" I asked instead. He hadn't told her yet, he confessed. They had resolved to have a proper talk today. She had known there was something. And after last night...

This reference to the drama of the previous night seemed to call him back firmly, and reassuringly, to his role as my father. Now when he caught my gaze he held it earnestly. "I'm so sorry, little Abricot," he said then. "You know that you all mean more to me than anything, don't you?" His tone was urgent and insistent. "I will never forgive myself for letting you down."

I felt the petulant child in me rising up in response to his contrite 'parent'. Where had he been? I wanted to know. We had waited and waited.

He looked down at the broken pieces of the 'Mia' painting. "Lost in the past," he answered cryptically. "But it is not an excuse, only an explanation."

I recalled our anxiety and Nathalie's strained, pale features as she tried vainly to reassure us that all would be well. Even in the light of this morning's revelation this was not my idea of an adequate explanation.

"We thought you were dead!" I threw out at him melodramatically, in my need to draw out of him a sufficient justification for our distress.

"I'm sorry," he said again, hopelessly. "Everything started to go wrong as soon as I got here. Your Uncle Tom wasn't expecting us and..."

"Hang on a sec!" I interjected. "What do you mean, he 'wasn't expecting us'? What about all Giuliana's letters?"

"Exactly," he said. "Giuliana's letters."

131

Pod went on to explain that the whole thing had apparently been all Giuliana's idea. Clearly she had had some idealistic notion of him 'coming home' to care for his ailing brother. What better way to bring about their 'long-overdue' reconciliation before it was too late? Which was all very well, but she might have let both parties in on her plan before setting it into action. As it was, relations between him and Tom were, if it were possible, now worse than ever. Convinced that Pod had only come out to Italy in order to secure his inheritance now that he was on his deathbed, Tom had declared himself unwilling to even acknowledge their presence in the house, let alone welcome the family into their new home. As a violent confirmation of this resolve, he had broken Pod's reconciliatory gift, the 'Mia' painting, into a dozen pieces before his eyes, and hurled them across the room. The next few hours were a blur. My father remembered storming down the stairs, though he was surprised when I told him Giuliana had been there at their foot. It seemed to him that no time at all had passed before he found himself parked high up on a mountain ridge, with no recollection of his journey or idea as to his exact location. Checking his watch he was horrified, and not a little afraid, to discover that more than eight hours had elapsed unaccounted for. And, seemingly miles from anywhere, he had less than an hour before our plane was due to land. Still traumatised and shaken, he had set out upon the road.

How terrible, I thought, feeling rather shamefaced at my petulance.

To make matters worse, having left in such a turmoil Pod did not have his mobile telephone with him. He had stopped at a couple of bars to try to call us but had no luck – he suspected we were out of range. In the end he had decided to head for the airport as swiftly as possible in the hope of finding us there.

He must, I realised, have been as concerned as we were. How horrid to have been alone with his anxieties – and to carry too the feelings of responsibility and guilt. I couldn't imagine how I had ever felt angry. I flung my arms around my sad, remorseful father. We were all safe and well, I reassured him. Mia's ghost danced hauntingly across my mind. I clung on to him even tighter. And I was sure, I joked, that once Uncle Tom got to know us all, he couldn't fail to love us! I tried to coax a smile out of him. He kissed the top of my head.

"I am sure you are right, little Abricot," he agreed softly and I was convinced his eyes looked a little happier. Still, he seemed pensive for a moment. Then he shook his head sadly to himself. "But I should have been there..."

I took my father's hand and we wandered into the house for breakfast in companionable silence. His last words lingered poignantly in our wake, somehow reluctant to let us leave. But it was only as we passed, one after the other, through the small side door and into the cool dark of the house that I realised why. He hadn't, just then, been talking about the airport...

Chapter Thirty-Four

It was strange sitting down to breakfast knowing that I brought Mia with me. Nathalie still looked tired and drawn, though the smile on her face as we entered was reflected in her eyes. I registered happily the warm, tender look that she exchanged with my father as he sat down beside her. Lizzie had noticed too. She nudged me as they took hands discreetly under the table. How would Nathalie take the revelation? I wondered. It was such a big secret to have gone unspoken between them for so long. I looked over at Giuliana who was bustling to and from the table, taking obvious delight in surprising us with all manner of delicious things for our first meal together in our new home. From her comment the previous night, it was clear that she thought we had all known about Mia. And surely that was the natural assumption. So why had Pod never felt able to share his sadness with us? For a terrible minute, I allowed my imagination to explore how I might feel were Lizzie or Jamie to die suddenly. But the place I had entered was so dark that I couldn't see anything at all. So it didn't illuminate things any further. Giuliana caught my eye and gestured encouragingly towards the food before me.

With a sense of relief I closed the door to my inner world and surveyed the one around me. In comparison to the dim, underground kitchen, this room, the 'sala da pranzo' Giuliana told us, was light and cheerful. Its windows were large and the shutters were flung open wide to welcome the now late-morning breeze. This apparently was the 'informal' dining room. There was another, much grander, Pod said, that had been reserved in the past for the notoriously glamorous dinner parties held by his parents. Its great swagged curtains were tied with silken tassels and a sparkling chandelier hung in the centre of the room. The rugs on the floor came from Persia and the guests from all corners of the world...

I couldn't help feeling rather glad that Giuliana had chosen, instead, this simple, airy room for our breakfast feast. And feast it undoubtedly was! An immaculate white cloth was spread on the table. Down its length were set two large platters, each laden with all kinds of cold meats, salamis and sausage. A third plate was for the cheeses. One of these, Giuliana insisted, we must all try. It was from her 'family' the other side of the hill, she announced proudly. The 'Pittini', I remembered. They kept goats, and this cheese, like the milk that filled a large earthenware jug at the other end of the table, came directly from their estate. The bread was baked that morning – irresistibly soft and white inside, with a thick, hard crust – and there were even ripe strawberries from the farm in the valley. And, of course, presiding over all were two elegant glass bottles of olive oil, gleaming green-gold as though lit from inside as well as out.

"Today you eat like 'principi'!" Giuliana declared with a flourish – and we didn't need Asterix to tell us she meant princes!

It seemed that our 'after breakfast plans' had already been hatched whilst Pod and I were in the garden. When finally we pushed our chairs back a little from the miraculously still-laden table in reluctant defeat, Giuliana clapped her hands briskly.

"Come along, then, you three! Let's leave your mother and father in peace."

She arranged to meet us in precisely three minutes at her car. Our invitation from the Pittini extended through the rest of the morning and over lunch. We were welcome to take our afternoon siesta with them if we felt happy to do so. If I was honest, I wasn't feeling terribly much like going at all. My head still throbbed unpleasantly and my heart was weighty with my newly-aquired understanding of Pod's past. Still, I was glad to give him and Nathalie some time alone together. How I hoped that sharing 'the secret' would bring them still closer, rather than cause further sadness.

Though I had got away with my oversized night/T-shirt at breakfast, I wasn't sure that it was altogether the most appropriate attire for my first meeting with our new neighbours. I was suddenly conscious of the fact that I hadn't even had a chance to wash. Therefore, with an apparently un-containable enthusiasm for the expedition, I raced out of the breakfast-room and, after two false starts, (finding myself in a boot-room – inexplicably chock-full of boots – and a small sitting-room, respectively), I found my way back to the 'nursery'. Diving into the 'bagno', (the incongruous image of Asterix wallowing in a lavender-scented bubble bath flashed into my head), I was dismayed to discover that my hair had entirely abandoned its sense of reason. Conscious that my three minutes was well-and-truly straining at its confines, there was nothing for it but to compromise. And

135

after all I was hardly going to meet the man of my dreams...

I pulled my hair swiftly back into an elastic, splashed some water onto my face and flew back into the bedroom. Hoping that the aeroplane creases would have miraculously dropped out of my favourite old sundress by the time we arrived, (perhaps all that palaver with the tissue paper that Nathalie swears by might be worth a try next time after all), I pulled it on over my head. Grabbing my large, floppy sunhat from my overnight case – all this 'glorious sunshine' had my skin on freckle alert – I screeched out of the door.

Jamie and Lizzie were, of course, already waiting at the car when I arrived.

"Well, you didn't clean your teeth!" I retorted, when Jamie was rather too eager to make a point of this. Naturally omitting to mention that I hadn't either, I instead climbed disdainfully into the car. Two minutes later I climbed, equally disdainfully, back out again. I had forgotten to help Lizzie into the front seat. I had just got Lizzie installed when Giuliana appeared out of the house.

"Well, don't you all look lovely?" she beamed. "How proud I shall be to introduce you."

Jamie and I scowled amicably at each other across the car and set about squeezing into the shoebox-on-wheels. Even before I had manoeuvred Lizzie into the front, this task would have been against the odds. At this point, the old chestnut about how many elephants you can fit into a mini – or not? (what was the punch line of that joke anyway?) – felt acutely pertinent to the occasion. Or it might have done, if only I could remember what exactly transpired in that famously cramped scenario. Anyway, suffice to say that by the time we were ready to pull out of the drive we all felt as though we were a part of a minor miracle.

Or were those elephants in a phone box..? Hmmm?

Chapter Thirty-Five

Lizzie knew that something was up. "What is it, Ab?" she had asked me when I was helping her out of the car. I liked it when she called me 'Ab'. It reminded me of Pod and, I think, of France. It made me feel safe. She pointed out that I had not said a word on our bumpy, ten minute journey.

"There was no room for words in that car," I joked. Anything longer than three letters and it would have exploded!" But I wished, instead, I could tell her.

Inspired by Giuliana's warning that we must look out for snakes, a delighted Jamie had launched into the unabridged version of 'My Adventures With Toots'. "Is it Uncle Tom?" Lizzie asked me discreetly, keeping one eye on the others.

Giuliana, it seemed, had the ears of a bat. "You mustn't be worrying about your Uncle Tom," she said, interrupting Jamie in full flow. "He's not used to sharing his house, or his life, that's all. I took him up his breakfast this morning and the nurse is visiting today. She won't stand any nonsense. You'll see, by the end of the week he'll be sitting up in his favourite chair reading you some of his fairy-tales. His head is full of magic, you know. Or it was, once-upon-a-time..."

She looked sad then and I was conscious again of how much she loved her 'children'. "Does he write fairy-tales?" I asked more chirpily than I actually felt. I was eager to dispel Giuliana's moment of melancholy, but genuinely interested too that Tom was a writer. Her face brightened again. She spoke proudly. "The first two volumes published were fairy-tales and the others were the 'Little Lady Clementine' stories." Then she looked puzzled. "But surely you have read them?"

It was our turn to look puzzled. Lizzie, Jamie and I shook our heads. "We didn't even know he was a writer, " Lizzie said. Then, a little embarrassed, "Pod doesn't really talk about him much."

"But I have sent a copy of each book to your father as it was published." Giuliana was clearly dismayed by this revelation. "And I know for certain that he received the first because I delivered it by hand. You were up in bed, Amelia-Anne – she seemed determined always to call me by my 'formal name' – you must have been about three years old. It was the night your grandfather died."

Something stirred vaguely in my own mind but I was conscious that now was not really the time to explore this issue further. "We'd love to read them," I smiled at Giuliana, squeezing her hand. "How exciting to know we have a famous author for our Uncle!"

"Well," Giuliana said, almost bashfully, "they were a tremendous success, both in England and America. And, with him writing under your Grandmother's maiden name, at one time there was even talk of translating them into Italian..."

So, the books were written under the name Pallavicini. That would explain why our attention had not been caught by the name on the cover when we were in a bookshop or at the library. How strange though that Pod had never even mentioned his brother's writing to us. As a family we had always read avidly. When we were small, 'story-time' was the most eagerly anticipated moment of our day...

My thoughts were interrupted by a warm, musical voice, singing out across the neat gravel drive in which we were parked.

"Buongiorno!"

We all turned to see a tall, graceful woman approaching the car. Her dark hair hung long and straight down her back, swinging out a little to one side with the rhythm of her step. Her long, flowing gown was the colour of sea-spray – bluegreen-grey and, somehow, at the same time no colour at all. We watched her approach. There was something strangely captivating about her ethereal beauty.

"I'm Eleanor," she smiled, holding out her hand. I took it, feeling suddenly clumsy and self-conscious, as though I had wandered into an elven gathering, of which I was too mortal be a part. She closed her other hand around mine and, with a touch so light as to be no more than the brushing of a butterfly's wings, kissed me on both cheeks. Then, "What beautiful hair!" she said as she stepped back again to look at me. And I knew I would love her for ever.

Greeting Jamie and Lizzie with a similar blend of courtesy and warmth, Eleanor beckoned us all towards the house. I had at first imagined her to be Italian, though her pale, luminous skin was undoubtedly remarkable in this land of sunshine and outdoor living. When she spoke, however,

I was sure that her soft, lilting tones were Irish. Dancing to her strange, unearthly music, we followed irresistibly after her, like the mythical children behind the Pied Piper.

For the first time I was really curious about the rest of the family. There were two children, Giuliana had informed us in the car; a boy and a girl. There was also a grown-up son of twenty-four, of whom we must not speak. He had greatly disgraced the family in the Autumn by disappearing with the newly-married wife of a local aristocrat. Sad, because he was a lovely boy, bright and witty and passionate about life. Still, there is a way of behaving that is simply not acceptable and, though she would have hoped she had taught him better, in part she considered herself to blame.

What a responsibility it is, bringing up children, I mused. I wondered if Nathalie would feel herself culpable if Jamie ran off with someone else's wife. Then, finding I couldn't really imagine either Nathalie's guilt or Jamie's lust, I concentrated instead on the more seemly world outside my mind.

Like ours, the Pittini villa was entered through a large, double front-door. How different it felt, though, from the moment we stepped inside. From the entrance hall we could see right through to the back of the house. As we ventured further inside it was dark and cool, but the uninterrupted view to the large French windows, flung wide to admit the day, lent a cheerful, sunny aspect to the whole interior. The spirit within these walls was animated and alive, dancing uninhibited between the large, elegant rooms and the olive groves without. This was a happy house, full of the love and hope that 'La Casa Cieca' had long since lost.

A large paved terrace opened up beyond the back doors. As we stepped out, we each caught our breath. The views across the valley were spectacular.

"Wow! It's like standing on top of the world!" Jamie pronounced vehemently.

Eleanor smiled. "When he was a boy, my husband's great, great grandfather felt just as you do," she said. "He vowed that one day he would build a house here. Many years later he made his fortune selling beautiful cloth – the finest hand-woven silks, in so many glorious colours that only God had dreamed of more. And so the first stone of our 'Pelagio' was laid. It, and each stone that followed, came from this very hillside."

Still looking out over the vast plain, Jamie seemed lost in thought. I suspected he was making his own vow; to one day find a hilltop just like this one on which to build his dream. Or perhaps that was just me...

Just then the sound of footsteps inside turned our attention from the view to the doors behind us. "Alessandro! Aisling!" Eleanor called into the dark interior, "Venite qui, voi due! Come here, you two!" A few moments later, a tall dark-haired boy stepped out onto the terrace. I have, as you know, always been struck – you might even say staggered and could almost certainly add cheesedoff – by how unlike my own mother I look. Well, I was, if anything, still more astonished by the extraordinary resemblance between Eleanor and her second son. Like hers, his skin was pale and luminous. His eyes were similarly green and piercing. When he moved it was with the same liquid grace that gave his mother her bewitching, other-worldly quality. The unmistakably Italian accent behind his English as he spoke, then, took me quite by surprise.

"I can't find her anywhere," he declared to Eleanor. "I've looked in all the usual places."

He flashed his eyes at Lizzie, Jamie and me. "Hullo," he said distractedly, and turned back almost immediately to his mother. I was suddenly conscious of how intently I had been staring. To my horror I felt the unmistakable prickle of the mother-of-all-blushes, rising up from my chest. Not now! Please, not now! I begged silently. I took a small, nonchalant turn on the terrace, suddenly gripped by an irresistibly urge to survey once again the remarkable view.

"Amelia-Anne!" Oh no! "It is Amelia-Anne isn't it?" Eleanor pressed, drawing me (callously) onto centre stage. I smiled wanly – if it is possible to be wan when your whole face has taken on the guise of an overexerted beetroot – as I turned back to face the group. "Most people call me Apricot," I replied, trying not to sound like I was wishing the ground would open up and swallow me. Hoping fervently that Jamie wouldn't come up with the fact that at that moment 'Strawberry' might have seemed more appropriate, I tried to remember that one day I would be ninety-three and all this would be just a distant memory...

"Ah! Because of your beautiful hair?" Eleanor, dearest Eleanor, presumed.

But before I had time to smile graciously and move things swiftly on, Jamie leapt in. "No!" he responded gleefully. I cast him the most meaningful of meaningful looks, verbally translated as 'I'll give you fifty euros if you stop now'. To no avail. Like a train thundering down its track there was no stopping him. "It's because she ate a whole jar of apricot jam and was sick on Grandma's shoes!"

I was rapidly becoming a threat to global warming. Just as I was about to internally combust, I raised my eyes a fraction in farewell to the world. Alessandro looked back at me, his eyes twinkling with amusement. "I'm told I did a similar thing with a jar of bottled figs," he grinned. "Unfortunately a valuable antique rug was in the wrong place at the wrong time!"

I grinned back. And I didn't feel embarrassed any more. Instead I felt a kind of squeeze inside my chest; as if something was going to happen that I wasn't quite prepared for. But it was going to be a lot more fun than a chemistry test.

Chapter Thirty-Six

The sun was warm on our backs as Alessandro and I set off across the 'campo'. Here in the meadow, in contrast to the neatly clipped lawn, the grass had been allowed to grow long and lush. The wild flowers bobbed and danced in the wind and I was reminded of the conversation with my father that morning. Still, so as not to be distracted from our mission, I tried to dispel the feelings of melancholy that threatened to creep in amongst the flowers.

I was, in fact, more than a little pleased that, on his mother's suggestion that he take someone with him in a further hunt for his independent little sister, Alessandro had chosen me. It felt entirely natural to call out "ciao!" to the others as we left them to sup home-made lemonade on the terrace and wandered off together. The relaxed, happy sense I had of having known him for years as opposed to minutes, sat alongside feelings that were altogether new to me. There was not quite enough room in my ribcage to breath and I could feel my heartbeat quicken in a way that was not adequately accounted for by our leisurely stride, whenever he looked my way.

"She's a little minx, really," he smiled across at me. "But it's impossible not to love her. Sometimes I think she is half-wild; that she doesn't belong to us at all, but instead, to the wind and the trees and to the clouds that are already moving on, even as they first appear... Only music seems to hold her spellbound for a while; perhaps whilst her spirit is roaming her body allows itself a moment's stillness. When I play for her she will sit quietly for hours, her legs crossed underneath her on the floor at my feet. Though even then," he mused, "I am never altogether sure that she is there in the room with me."

I liked listening to him speak. His accent was slight but distinctly Italian. I thought for a moment of my mother, who, despite having been in England for almost fifteen years now, had not lost the attractive French lilt to her voice. Was that deliberate, I wondered for the first time? Or had it grown as much a part of her as her eyes and fingerprints? More than

Alessandro's accent though, it was the lyricism of his words that made me want to hear more. How differently he spoke to the other boys I knew. As though he lived as much inside his thoughts as in the world around him.

I recalled, then, something Giuliana had been saying in the car. It was about Alessandro's older brother and his disappearance. My thoughts had been so much with Mia that I was not really paying attention, but it had something to do with Alessandro and his being unable now to take up his place at a greatly renowned music school in Siena next year. I wondered what instrument he played, but, conscious more of what I couldn't remember of Giuliana's conversation than what I actually knew, I felt it would be too intrusive to enquire. So instead I wondered aloud about his little sister.

"Ash-ling..." I spoke her name just as Eleanor had done. It was an Irish name, he told me, in answer to my unspoken question. It was written 'A-i-sling' and was the Irish word for 'dream'. It was beautiful, I told him. And it felt appropriate for the free-spirited little girl who roamed this vast hillside all alone, from morning until dusk.

"Ah! But not quite alone," Alessandro smiled, as the pretty tinkle of a bell sounded out on the wind. "The bell was our mother's idea – find Star and you can be sure that Aisling is close at hand..."

I was intrigued, but Alessandro would only smile secretively, determined to keep me guessing for as long as possible. He had visibly relaxed on hearing the bell, knowing that his sister was just across the way. The hillside, though, he warned me, was enchanted. It was a master ventriloquist. It could throw a sound that you would swear was at your feet, from right across the valley. The compact ring of hills was like a giant natural amphitheatre, having delighted for centuries in confounding the human senses.

The bell sounded again. At the same time we spotted a flash of white in the long grasses of the field next to ours. Now with an additional sense to rely upon, we set off towards the sound of the bell, breaking into a run as the slope of the hill carried our legs faster and faster beneath us. Using the momentum of the downhill run to take us, panting and exhilarated, part way up the next slope, we gradually came to a halt.

I watched, curious, as Alessandro tilted his face up towards the sky, his hands cupped to his mouth. He had pushed back the sleeves of his loose white linen shirt to the elbows. The skin on his forearms and hands, I noticed, was tanned pale gold. His fingers were long and slender, the nails clipped back short and blunt at the tips. I wondered again what instrument it was that he played so beautifully as to hold Aisling spellbound. Then, from the hollow between his fingers rose the haunting strains of an owl hoot – three 'hoo-hoo's' and he paused to listen. To my surprise there came an answering call, more high pitched and wavering but unmistakably in response to his own. "There she is!" he announced triumphantly. A tiny figure was running down the hillside towards us. Unexpectedly, Alessandro hooted again, though the little girl had surely seen him? She changed her direction slightly at the sound and I noticed that behind her skipped a small white kid, the bell around his neck tinkling as he came. As Aisling approached, Alessandro made a low crooning sound and she threw herself into his arms. He swung her up onto his shoulders. "There!" he exclaimed. "Now I have you!" She giggled. Now and again, as Alessandro set off down the hill, Star jumped about him, keen not to stray too far from his little mistress.

"Did you say 'hello' to our new friend?" he asked her as she bounced up and down atop his shoulders.

"Hello," I said. She turned her face towards me, looking down from above. The delicate features were framed by a tangle of shining dark curls.

"Hello," she whispered back shyly. Her bright green eyes were so like her brother's ... and yet ...

We meandered lazily through the long grass. Instead of following the most direct path back to the house we were heading for the olive trees across the hill. The sun was strong now and the world about us shimmered with the midday heat.

The realisation came upon me slowly, as though my mind worked in harmony with our relaxed pace. I reached up and took the tiny hand that wavered in the air above my head; but it was to her older brother that I looked for confirmation. "E vero," he nodded, 'it is true'. His own eyes betrayed fleetingly the sadness behind his words. "Lei e cieca." 'She is blind.'

How I had hoped that, after all, I had been mistaken. It hurt to think of all that she was missing. I felt the hot prickle of imminent tears. Then I remembered again about Mollie and how I had wanted to know 'why?' Until finally I had stopped looking for answers and started thinking about Mollie instead. And I found it made me smile. I had remembered her excitement as she unveiled the Fingle's hand knitted costumes, one after the other with an increasingly tuneless trumpet voluntary. I had thought of our mischievous laughter when the cat next-door fell suddenly out of the tree and landed squarely on Mollie's mother's new sunhat. And I had remembered my promise. And each day whenever I think that she is watching, I look up at the sky and wave. And it doesn't 'make sense', but it does make me happy.

I took Aisling's hand still further into my own. Her fingers curled tightly around mine in a simple expression of trust. It didn't 'make sense', I thought, that Aisling couldn't see. A virus stole her eyes forever, Alessandro told me, when she was just a few months old. And it really 'wasn't fair'. But instead of looking for answers Aisling was busy being alive. Her delight reached out and tickled my own, so that I felt my heart expand with it. Her footsteps, as she ran down the hill towards us, had been confident and sure. Far from being cut off from the world around her, she was, as Alessandro had observed, an inextricable part. My thoughts were interrupted by a high-pitched bleat as Star launched himself into the air with happy abandon. "Whoa!" Alessandro laughed, staggering to one side in an exaggerated gesture of surprise. Aisling giggled. I giggled. And I didn't need to look far for the smile that lay beyond the fact that it 'didn't make sense'. I could feel it inside me. the fact that it 'didn't make sense'. I could feel it inside me.

Chapter Thirty-Seven

The Pittini olive groves, unlike ours, had clearly benefited from years of care and attention. The ground beneath the zillion trees was neatly tended. Around each trunk a small ring of earth had been exposed to aerate the roots, Alessandro explained, and to prevent encroaching weeds from stealing valuable nutrition from the soil. Where the land fell away, there were mossy stone walls built into the hillside, creating narrow grassy platforms – like a meandering green staircase for giants. On each of these 'terraces', there was room for one or maybe two rows of neatly clipped trees. Here and there were interspersed newly-planted saplings, spindly and frail-looking but already sporting vigorous leaves.

We spread our picnic out on the blanket underneath a group of ancient trees. How glad we were that Eleanor had thought of sending us off with our lunch, all packed neatly into small tinfoil parcels. What fun it was opening up just one end of each and guessing what was inside by the delicious smell that escaped from the shiny folds.

"Salami!" Aisling shouted with glee as we held the first up to her little turned-up nose. Then "Pomodori con basilico!" she cried discovering the redder-thanred tomatoes, packed together with the intoxicatingly fragrant leaves of basil. "Pane!" came next, as we unwrapped the pillowy 'focaccia' bread, rich and golden with olive oil and earthy-scented with the rosemary that had been baked into the unctuous dough. "Formaggio!" Cheese!

"Pesce!" I interjected, before she had a chance, keen to show off some of my newly acquired language skills and instead succeeding in sending the others off into peals of laughter at my mistaking the glorious ripe 'pesche', peaches, for pungent 'pesce', fish. We took it in turns to drink from the large bottle of home-made lemonade and it was as though we had been friends forever.

When we had finished eating, we lay down in the kindly shade of an old, wizened tree. The feathery grass was cool and tickly on the back of my neck. I was conscious of Alessandro's arm almost touching mine.

"This is my favourite part of the whole estate," he murmured lazily. "I persuaded them to leave the grass long here and let the flowers grow up. In April everywhere was a sea of colour. But they had to cut most of it back, to give the trees the best chance to fruit."

Whilst we whispered, Aisling slept, curled around the warm body of the little goat.

"That's how we found her on the night he was born," Alessandro said. "Star's brother was born first. We hadn't realised his mother was carrying twins. don't think she had either. The estate-hands didn't expect the second kid to last the night. He was so small. When everyone had gone, Aisling and I crept out again to say goodbye. We stayed with him a while. Aisling held her hands against his body, feeling the breath fluttering inside him. In the morning when she didn't come to eat I knew where we would find her. I'm pretty sure she saved his life, keeping him warm through the night. Anyway, since then they've been inseparable."

I closed my eyes. The breeze that ruffled through the grove was warm on my skin. How strange it was lying there to think that only the day before I had been stretched out along the garden wall in Paultons Square. So much had happened since then.

"How's Tom?" Alessandro broke in suddenly, still in a whisper. His question jolted me out of my sleepy reverie. Somehow our new home, Tom – and the ghost of Mia – felt like they were just my secret. It was odd to think that these two worlds might overlap, more than just in my happening to be there. I was conscious too that I didn't have an easy answer to the question. Perhaps because I didn't respond immediately, Alessandro tried again. "We were sad when he got sick. Aisling loves his stories. We've read them over and over. Lady Clemmie is her favourite. I think it is the combination of mischief and goodheartedness that she likes!" Again I was stuck for a response. I was embarrassed to admit that I hadn't read them, hadn't, in fact, even known that Uncle Tom was a writer until that very morning. And I was piqued too that he had shared his books and, it seemed, his life with strangers and yet had been so cold and unwelcoming to his own family. Irritated by my irritation, I sat up awkwardly and brushed impatiently at the egg-yolk yellow pollen that dusted my arms.

"What's up?" Alessandro asked, forgetting to whisper in his concern. He turned on his side and propped his head up on his hand. "Did I say something wrong?"

And then an extraordinary thing happened. I told him. I told him everything. Right from the start when the letter arrived and Pod didn't open it. First, though, I made him promise that he wouldn't tell anyone – ever. And I trusted him when he said he wouldn't. It is strange when I think of it now – that even then I knew he would never let me down. I didn't stop until I got to where we had left Pod and Nathalie alone so he could tell her about Mia. I'd never really talked to anyone like this before; telling not just what had happened but also how it made me feel inside. Except perhaps Pod. The only bit of me I kept back was the part that was afraid that I still didn't know the whole story. That there was something more to come. But I didn't know why I felt it, or what the thing that still lay hidden might be. So I held on to it for now. Alessandro didn't speak until I had finished. And the only thing that could have surprised me more than my having told him, was what he told me.

"I know," he said gently. This time it was he who seemed embarrassed. "About Mia." He paused again. "It was before I was born but there are lots of people who loved her and still remember. Mum had only just arrived in Italy. She was studying at the Accademia d'arte in Florence – that's how she met your grandfather."

He told me that Grandpa ('Nonno') Beresford-Linnel had been one of her lecturers at the art school. She had been only a few years older than Mia and so they had become friends. It had been Grandpa and our Nonna Sofia who had introduced Eleanor to his father, Marco. Alessandro thought that, by then, Pod had already left – for France, I told him, filling in the only gap that I was able. Tom, he said, had kept himself to himself whenever Eleanor was at the house but Mia's obvious love for her brother had left Eleanor with affection for the man whom she, in fact, hardly knew. When Alessandro was little, he remembered, Tom had come to the house now and again. Once he had even read to him from one of his books. But that was a long time ago. For the past ten years or so, according to local gossip – here again Alessandro looked a little embarrassed – Uncle Tom had hardly left the house. The family had all been surprised when one day a few months ago Tom had sent some books with Giuliana especially for Aisling. Giuliana had taken Aisling with her to the house that morning when she went to look in on him. He had seen her playing in the garden from his bedroom window.

"Giuliana had tears in her eyes when she gave Mum the books," he went on. "She's so proud of your Uncle's writing. It makes her sad, how he's there all on his own, with the house all closed up like that. Part of her, she told me once, can't bear to let go of how it once was. She talks about Mia as though she is still alive sometimes..."

My emotions scrambled over one another for pole position. The most bolshie was one to which I could not give a name, but I was sure it had to do with all these 'strangers' knowing so much more about my family than I did. On a few moment's reflection I realised that it was, in fact, a number of emotions, masquerading as one. Shock, Pique and Sadness had got together, in order to bully the others into submission. I tried to get the unruly rabble under control. Finding Sadness particularly difficult to appease, I resolved to come back to it later and had a quick scan of the rest. Further down the line I was surprised to spot Curiosity.

"Do they really call the house 'La Casa Cieca'?" it asked of Alessandro.

He pulled a 'I'm-sorry-to-have-to-tell-you-this-but-I'm-afraid-so' face and nodded. "I don't know when it started. Ever since I can remember it has had its 'eyes' shuttered to the outside world. Like it's always been in mourning, local people say. But to tell you the truth, when Tom got sick Mum told me that it was always a sad house, even before Mia died. Despite your grandfather having been, she said, one of those 'impossibly charming' people who could persuade you to anything..."

I thought about the secret staircase behind the dresser-that-wasn't-really-there. I tried in vain to form a picture of my grandfather with the two small pieces of the puzzle that I had acquired since we'd arrived. The problem was, they didn't seem to fit at all with the few bits that had I picked up from Pod before. And without putting together the background setting – composing the rest of his family around him, perhaps – I would never be able to see exactly how his portrait fitted in. I thought about how, with a jigsaw, it is sometimes just one piece – usually the one that has disappeared under the sofa – that solves the whole puzzle. With a rush, all the bits that up till then seemed to have come from another box entirely make perfect sense. With it in place the entire picture becomes clear. So, when it came to my Grandpa Beresford-Linnel, maybe all I needed was the bit that was hidden under the sofa and the past would come together before my eyes...

Still, I had discovered enough for one day. Perhaps even for a lifetime. Suddenly I was keen to get back to my family – the living part rather than the ghosts.

Right on cue, Aisling stirred. Star wriggled over and onto his feet. He nudged her softly in the back.

I was surprised to learn from Alessandro that it was almost 5 o'clock. The air was still warm but, when I squiggled my toes beyond the cool shade of the tree, there was a new, evening softness to the sun's smile. We gathered up our picnic things, unable to resist nibbling at the one or two delicious morsels that remained as we did so. Aisling and I sat cross-legged to share the last succulent peach, giggling mischievously together as the sweet, fragrant juice ran down our chins, through our fingers and onto our feet.

"Dad said he'd run you home tonight if he was back in time," Alessandro told me, as we set off up the hill. "Which is lucky because after all you've eaten over lunch the chance of you squeezing back into Giuliana's car is, at best, minimal!"

With a grin, I swung the rolled-up blanket at his unsuspecting back. Then, in fear of retaliation, I took off speedily up the hillside. Sensing our fun, Aisling broke into a run, and, with Star bounding madly alongside, followed on at our heels. We arrived back at the house breathless and laughing. Lizzie and Jamie were on the terrace, just as we had left them.

"Where have you been?" Jamie called out as we crossed the lawn towards him. "You missed the best lunch ever. This afternoon Eleanor showed us where they make the wine. They have their very own bottles and all the grapes come from this hill. She said that when they are pressing this year's grapes in the Autumn we can come and see. And I might even be able to help!"

I smiled at his enthusiastic account. I was pleased that they too had had a happy afternoon. Lizzie, I thought, looked a bit tired – it occurred to me that her cast must be especially uncomfortable in the heat. How good she was never to complain. All of a sudden I was overcome with warmth towards her. I skirted round the table and gave her a huge hug. "What's that for?" she chuckled bashfully. But I could tell she was pleased. Then, when she was sure the attention of the others was suitably distracted, she whispered into my ear. "You'd better tell me everything tonight!" She flashed her eyes suggestively and I made a pretend swat at her arm as though she was being ridiculous. But I only just managed to keep the blushing under control.

Fortunately everyone's focus shifted to little Aisling, as, at the sound of footsteps inside, she gave a happy cry. "Babbo!" Daddy! She ran in through the open terrace doors.

"She knows everyone by sound," Alessandro explained. "And sometimes by their smell. She's never wrong about footsteps."

In the few moments before he appeared, I found myself forming a mental picture of their father. Of course, I thought, he would be slim and dark. He too would have that sense of belonging to another world about him. Perhaps an aloofness, not cold but rather distant all-the-same. He would be sensitive and wise, firm but fair. As would be right and fitting for the head of a small elven clan.

By the time anyone actually appeared through the doorway, I had so convinced myself of this imaginary portrait that, were it not for the fact that Aisling was clinging steadfastly to the fellow's right leg, I would have presumed that Signor Pittini followed on behind. Freeing up his leg, Aisling's un-imaginary father swung her up into his arms with a broad smile.

"Buonasera!" he greeted us heartily. Aisling reached up and ran her fingers softly over his broad, tanned face, planting a kiss loudly on one cheek. He chuckled and, balancing her skilfully under one arm, he crossed the terrace to introduce himself warmly to each of us in turn. His wide smile seemed to come from deep inside and was instantly infectious. In moments we were all beaming. Conscious of how utterly different this father was to the one I had conjured, I consoled myself with the fact that his appearance was indisputably extraordinary. Set against his dark tan, his wiry blond hair and eyebrows had a curious effect. It was a bit like viewing a face in photographic 'negative'. Far from being tall and slender he was not much taller than me and his frame was muscular and stocky. Everything about their 'babbo', I surmised, was a celebration of outdoor living. Not only did he exude health and vitality but he seemed to dispense it to all those around him. No, he could not have been more different to the cool, aloof figure that I had created in my mind. And I could not have been more glad.

"I hear you three do actually have a home to go to!" he joked. "I thought at first that Eleanor had picked up a few strays from across the hill and we were going to have to find room in one of the barns." It was funny to hear such relaxed English banter combined with his strong Italian accent. I wondered briefly whether Asterix and I would ever be able to slip so naturally from one language to the other. It seemed unlikely. Signor Pittini winked at his wife who had appeared on the terrace just at that moment.

151

As she approached he caught her around the waist with his free arm and drew her close. What an unusual couple they were, I thought, seeing them side by side. But how happy they seemed. And I was in no doubt that, just like my 'imaginary father', this one was indeed 'sensitive and wise, firm yet fair'. So at least I got something right. And, after all, that was the most important bit.

Chapter Thirty-Eight

Sig. Pittini swung Lizzie with ease into the front of his jeep. The canvas roof was rolled back, much to Jamie's delight. "Can I stand up all the way home?" he asked excitedly. Unfortunately for him, and with an extraordinary prescience, Giuliana appeared, as if by magic, on the scene. In an instant my small brother's enthusiasm was knocked kindly but firmly down into a seated position.

"You've caught the sun," Alessandro observed, as I was about to climb up into the car myself. Could he have been trying to delay me leaving for another moment or two? Hardly daring to hope it, I squirrelled the 'wondering' away – to dig up and savour later on, perhaps, when I was on my own. In any case, for now, I had more urgent things to attend to. Those dashed freckles! I brought my hand up instinctively to conceal my nose, though I was aware that where my rampant freckles were concerned this was likely to be only the tip of the iceberg. How could I have forgotten to take my hat on our picnic? Alessandro grinned back at me. "They're pretty," he said. "I like them." And you know what? For the first time ever, so did I.

I was still smiling when we pulled up into our own drive. And there was a surprise too! Someone – I guessed it must have been Pod – had freed up the old gate from the mounds of earth and weeds that had prevented it from flinging itself wide. How proud and happy it was to welcome us through! It was almost a disappointment, then, to approach the house and find it still bearing its tired and melancholy air. Nothing, I felt, could altogether dampen my spirits that evening. Nonetheless, our new home, particularly in contrast to the bright and cheerful one that we had just left, looked shabby and forlorn. All but one set of shutters were still firmly shut and, arriving this time in the daylight rather than late at night, I was even more aware of the sense of foreboding that lingered about its greying, dilapidated facade.

Still, there were our smiling parents waiting for us at the door and, in terms of cheer, they made up for any number of closed shutters!

The moment Sig. Pittini pulled up to a halt, Jamie stood up. He waved a 'look-at-me-standing-up-in-the-car' wave. Pod and Nathalie waved back. A 'yes-we've-seen-you' kind of a wave. "Giuliana said to tell you that, if it's alright, she will call by later to look in on Uncle Tom. She's made an enormous lasagne for our supper!" He gestured to the large ceramic dish on my lap and Nathalie came thoughtfully over to the car to relieve me of it.

Sig. Pittini jumped down from the front seat to greet her warmly as she approached. Holding her face between his hands he planted a kiss firmly on each cheek. Slightly taken aback by his enthusiasm, but in a pleased sort of a way, Nathalie fumbled for the appropriate Italian response. "Buonasera," she settled for after a few moments. She smiled graciously at him. Luckily for my mother, all she has to do is smile graciously at someone and she has won a friend for life. Sig. Pittini seemed delighted. Refusing to let her take on the burden of the lasagne, he insisted, with a flourish, on doing so himself. With a neat bow to Nathalie and a wink at Jamie and me, he zipped across the drive and handed it straight to Pod! Like a lasagne version of the 'hot potato'. We all laughed.

He and Pod smiled warmly at each other. "Ciao, amico mio", Sig. Pittini said, a more dignified composure and sincerity coming into his voice. Of course! I thought. Pod and Alessandro's father must have known each other as boys! Despite my conversation with Alessandro, it was still hard for me to envisage the recent revelations about Pod's past in a real context, particularly where other, 'ordinary' people were concerned. "Come stai?" he asked, enquiring after Pod's well-being.

Where would Pod start in answer to that question? I wondered ironically. It seemed to me his whole world had been turned upside-down in the past few weeks. Wisely, Pod stuck to reassuring his old friend that all was well. Alessandro's father beamed – surely unable to conceive of any other answer? And then, as they began to chat, I recalled Giuliana's reference to his eldest son and the sadness and shame bound up with his disappearance and was reminded again that things were not always as they seemed. What an extraordinary capacity for hiding their secrets people had, I thought. The conversation continued in English. How glad Sig. P. was that Pod was back where he belonged! How much he was looking forward to catching up with him. Had he seen Bertie? he wondered. Our ears pricked up. Who was Bertie?

"Bertie!" Pod exclaimed. "Surely he is not still here?"

"Larger – and noisier – than life!" Sig. P. chuckled. "In fact I have it from Giuliana that he's about the only one that brother of yours will speak to nowadays." I was sure I saw a shadow cross Pod's face at this reference to Uncle Tom and his strangely reclusive behaviour. Sig. P. had, it seemed, picked up on Pod's discomfort too. I knew he was sensitive and wise. "How is he?" he asked more soberly.

Sensing things becoming awkward, Nathalie crossed over to Pod and threaded her arm through his.

"The nurse says he's doing surprisingly well," she said brightly. "He's still defying the rather gloomy predictions of the doctors. I think she's hoping that having family around him will boost his spirits though. Help to bring him out of himself a bit after being shut up and alone for so long."

Sig. P. nodded sympathetically. "There's no doubt that being surrounded by the people you love helps put a more positive spin on things." He looked thoughtful for a moment. "Well," he announced after a respectful pause, "I'd better be getting back to my own family before their spirits begin to flag! We really are so happy to have you near-by. You must call if there's anything you need. Giuliana, of course, will be back and forth but if we can help with Tom and the hospital visits at all, do let us know. Eleanor thought you might like a trip into Cortona with her sometime, Nathalie. To help you get your bearings around here."

Accepting the suggestion gratefully and arranging to call and make plans in the next day or so, Nathalie bid him "Buonanotte" and, excusing herself and the lasagne, she disappeared off to the kitchen.

Sig. P. and Pod wandered over to the jeep. "Is this one of yours?" Sig. P. quipped, looking in through the open window at a fast-asleep Lizzie.

Pod scratched his head, Laurel and Hardy-style. "Hmmm. I think I've seen her somewhere before," he teased.

Lizzie opened one eye sleepily. "Well, I'm not at all sure I recognise you!" she grinned. Still, giving him the benefit of the doubt, she let Pod scoop her up into his arms and carry her towards the house. We stood all together at the door to wave Alessandro's father off. Just as he began to rev. the engine, Jamie gave a shout.

"Hey! Who's Bertie?"

Sig. Pittini held his hand up to his ear, pretending that he couldn't hear above the noise. Then, making a tight turn in the drive not far from where we were standing, he leaned out of the window.

"You'd better ask your father!" he chuckled. And he was off.

Chapter Thirty-Nine

Pod would give away nothing about the mysterious Bertie, except to say that he wasn't someone we'd forget in a hurry. On further pressing, he did suggest that we always had plenty of cheese about our person just in case he arrived unannounced. Needless to say, these enigmatic titbits of information served only to inflame our curiosity.

I might have been more dogged with my interrogation – though Jamie was more than compensating for any lack of persistence on my part – were it not for the fact that I was rather more concerned to have news of Pod's discussions with Nathalie whilst we had been away. "Did you tell her?" I whispered urgently at the first opportunity. Nathalie had sent me out to the garden to pick some of the mint that grew wild and rampant just beyond the house, for a fresh batch of iced-tea. Leaving Jamie and Lizzie setting the large oak table for supper, I dived gratefully out through the door. Pod was standing by the old stone wall that, once upon a time, he said, had formed a part of an enclosed kitchen garden. He was wrestling with what looked to be an equally ancient barbecue, in the (blindly optimistic) hope of restoring the rusted bits of old iron into a working proposition. "It seems that everyone around here knows!" I hissed. "It would be awful if she found out from someone else."

I was glad to learn that they had talked together about Mia. They had discussed, too, Pod's failed attempt to reconcile things with Tom and how they might approach him again in the light of this. Pod did not elaborate further, but, for the moment, I was happy enough in the conviction that, if anything, the revelations had strengthened my parents' relationship rather than undermined it further.

The rest of the evening was uneventful. Giuliana's delicious lasagne was worth a mention, as was the fact that Lizzie fell asleep whilst actually still at table, which was a first for any of us! Besides that, Pod seemed reassured by Giuliana's report that his brother had managed supper and though he had not actually had anything positive to say on the subject of his uninvited guests, he had calmed down greatly since the previous day.

All in all it was an evening that called for an early night. And for once even Jamie didn't answer back.

It it hadn't been for the fact that Lizzie was also wide awake, with a rather alarmed look on her face, I might have thought I had dreamt it. But no, there it came again. It was an extraordinary sound, a high, plaintive cry, that seemed to linger in the air even after it was over. "What is it?" Lizzie whispered as it filled the heavens a third time with its melancholy wail. Dawn was breaking and beyond the open window the sky was tinged with pink and gold.

"It must be an animal of some kind," I answered her, not very helpfully. I was as much at a loss as she was to conceive of the unearthly sound as something belonging to this world. By now we were both well and truly awake, with all our senses on alert. I reached over to the table by the bed and grabbed my watch. I groaned. "It's only 4-35 am," I informed Lizzie. "Whatever it is, it has no respect for propriety!" We grinned, then, and felt rather less spooked out by the unknown, but decidedly inconsiderate, perpetrator of the strange noise.

I sat up. Now that it had succeeded in waking us so irrevocably, the peculiar sound had stopped. "Well, I don't know about you," I said to Lizzie, "but I'm far too awake to simply snuggle back down and sleep." All of a sudden, the idea of a hot, fragrant bath was extremely appealing. In all the rush before we left for the Pittini house I had barely had a chance to wash and I had been too sleepy that evening to bath. Lizzie thought she might try and read for a bit in the hope that it might help carry her closer to sleep. Frankly I suspected I would only have to scan the cover of 'A Closer Look at Bacterium' to be asleep within moments – but then, that's me. Looking forward to my soothing soak, I slipped purposefully out of bed. Liberating a large bar of chocolate from my bedside drawer I broke off a few squares and handed them to my egghead sister. "See you in a bit," I whispered and I tiptoed into the bathroom.

The ancient brass taps squeaked reluctantly as I turned them on. With still greater reluctance, they began, at a trickle, to relinquish their water. Then, inspired by the momentousness of it all, the antiquated pipes struck up their infernal chorus. I giggled. So far this was not the sublime, soothing experience that I had anticipated. To cap it all, accompanying this astonishing din was the unmistakable pong of bad-eggs. Stink bombs, if you will. Though this element of the proceedings was not entirely unexpected – Giuliana had warned us all that there was a very high

158

sulphur level in the water supply from our well – it did not contribute favourably to the overall sublimity of the occasion. Recognising that additional resources were called for, I darted for the bedroom and my washbag, in which, I recalled, languished a lavender-scented 'bath-bomb' positively yearning to come to my aid. The next thing I knew, I was lying in a tangled heap on the floor.

Though it was initially a challenge to discern anything amidst all the stars, I gradually came to identify the secondary component to the tangle as being Jamie.

"What are you doing charging about in the middle of the night?" I demanded crossly, conscious that there was clearly no longer a need to whisper.

"What are you doing having a noisy bath in the middle of the night?" he batted back. "Is that chocolate?"

"It might be," I answered enigmatically, following his gaze to the top of the small bathroom chest. Equally motivated by this latter exchange to find the where-with-all to stand up, we got shakily to our feet. Fortunately, being marginally closer to the chest at the outset, I managed to alight first on our mutual target. I waved it tantalisingly under his nose. "Six pieces and you go back to bed," I bargained.

"Ten!" he shot back. Respecting the conventions of the proverbial 'haggle' we settled on eight.

I broke off the squares and wrapped them conveniently, if not terribly hygienically, in a strip of loo-roll. "Thanks!" Jamie said graciously as I handed him his ill-gotten gains. Keeping to his part of the bargain, he set off for bed. Then, with a second thought, he paused for a moment in the bathroom doorway.

"Oh!" he tossed casually over his shoulder. "Did you hear the peacock?" And he disappeared out of the room.

Chapter Forty

So, it was a peacock, I mused, as I eased myself into the now sweetly fragrant water. Of course! Though how different this had sounded, rising mystically out of the night, to the cacophonous gaggle behind the high wire fences of Battersea Park. Ours was clearly an altogether nobler branch of the family. My thoughts drifted as I relaxed into my liquid cocoon. There was something rather fairy-tale-like about having a peacock at the bottom of the garden. liked to think its being here was not simply by chance. That it had chosen us. Would it stay, I wondered, or was it just passing through? From the dusty archives of my mind, I called up a file marked 'Peacocks: information on'. It was not, admittedly, a weighty tome, but it was a promising start. The single flimsy sheet informed me cheerily that the peacock was a harbinger of good fortune. As such, they were in many countries greatly revered.

I thought of Mia and of Uncle Tom and his illness. There was no doubt that our house could do with a bit of good fortune. It was so strange to think of Uncle Tom ensconced somewhere in the house with us, but refusing even to acknowledge our arrival. It seemed particularly ironic, given that he was the very reason we were there. I felt a shameful moment of pique that we had all given up our lives across the sea – Pod and Nathalie their friends and jobs, Lizzie, Ben and Jamie, Toots – to keep him company and he preferred to be alone. But more than that, I just felt sad.

How I hoped that through being there we might find a way to reach Pod's brother and draw him out of his loneliness and isolation. For ten years, Alessandro had said, Tom had barely left the house. And for nearly twenty before that he had remained cut off from the only family that he had in the world. I imagined for a moment that it was Jamie, watching his life tick by from the melancholy confines of his room. I drafted myself into the scene. Sure enough, I was hurling myself at his closed door, diving over to his bed and throwing my arms around him. I saw myself vowing never to leave him alone again and forgiving him for everything that had ever come between us. (Even the time he used my toothbrush to clean out Toot's tank and forgot to tell me until I was using it that evening: 'Eeewww!'). Simple. ('Eeewww!').

Why then was Pod so unable to make amends? What was it that happened all those years ago that was worth sacrificing the rest of their lives over? Was it, in fact, the reason Pod left home? Mia, he said, had died whilst he was in France so, terrible as that must have been, it couldn't have been the tragedy that tore them apart. My brain ached with trying to form a sound construction on shifting sands. In the past few weeks, even the foundations of my own world had revealed themselves to have been built largely upon the shaky ground of presumption and myth. Each successive replacement of these with the small fragments of truth that had come to light about the past, had seen the hitherto established picture of my childhood shift, re-form and shift again. Like the quixotic image in a kaleidoscope, it seemed destined never to come to rest.

I shivered a little. The water was becoming decidedly chilly. The night temperature too was surprisingly cool after the heat of the day. I rubbed at my knees – conveniently close my chin, due to the miniscule proportions of our inherited bath – in order to inspire a bit of warmth. Finally accepting defeat, I stepped up and out. My 'soothing, relaxing' bath had not entirely lived up to its mission statement. Still, I felt glad to have had a chance to reflect.

I slipped gratefully back into bed. Lizzie was fast asleep, her hands and book still resting on her tummy. I lifted off the book carefully and pulled the covers up and over her exposed arms. Snuggling in close, I relaxed indulgently into her residual warmth...

Zzzzzzzz.

I wasn't sure how long I had been asleep when I was conscious of another extraordinary noise. This one, however, had rather less of the sublime about it. Not to mention an impressively implausible measure of the ridiculous. It was best described as a loud, nasal honking – and it appeared to be emanating from something just beyond our window. After a brief intermission, the performance began again. This time the 'honk' had more of a forlorn air about it. Its delivery was rather more tentative. It was, I would say, a kind of 'pardon-me-if-I-am-disturbing-you-but...' honk. (Though, admittedly, my experience with 'honks' and their more subtle intonations was somewhat limited). Still, I determined, such politeness should not go unobserved.

As I was clambering out of bed for the second time that night – although

I supposed that to the early-bird, this one might legitimately be considered morning – Jamie appeared through the door. I put my finger to my lips and gestured towards Sleeping Beauty. Jamie nodded his understanding. He and I crept over to the window.

From the moment we looked out, it was as if we were caught up in an enchantment. Breathless and wondering, we were swept up out of the real world and assimilated into the land of fairytale. The peacock was standing in the shadows, only a few metres away. If I stretched out my arm I could almost touch the rich glossy feathers that, even without the light of the sun, emanated a strange unearthly gleam. Jamie and I touched hands briefly, not daring to leave the sight with our eyes for a moment lest we should return to find it just a dream. Neither of us spoke.

Hypnotised by the awesome spectacle we were both slow to survey the surrounding scene.

We saw it in the same instant. Jamie grabbed my arm. Alarm caught me tight by the throat. A fox! His belly lay close to the ground, his legs almost quivering with intent. Beady, amber eyes fixed unwaveringly on their exotic prey. Everything about him exuded sly malevolence. The peacock took an anxious on-the-spot turn, as though bewildered into a futile display of narcissism by the imminent danger. Run! Why didn't he run? I urged, silently. Or fly? Could he fly? The fox closed in further.

I could bear it no longer. My body was seized by something deep-down and primordial. Its action was instinctive and decided. Finding Pisa Cathedral still where I had left it under the window, I sprang up and out into the garden.

The dozy bird did not bat an eyelid, let alone a tail-feather, as I hurtled by. Eye to eye with Mr Fox I lay down the gauntlet. Entirely un-perturbed, he made no attempt to amend his schedule. Clearly, to him, the mad, crazy loon charging across the lawn, far from representing a serious threat, was merely an unwelcome distraction. He grinned. (I'm telling you, he actually grinned). This fellow was really getting my primordial goat. Waving my arms wildly, I charged straight for him. His conviction wavered.

"Go away!" I shouted, at the top of my voice – my primordial spirit is not yet confident in its grasp of the Italian laguage. Still, some forms of communication are universal, I noted with satisfaction, as Mr Fox made one final assessment, took to his heels and ran. I gave one last burst of "Wollawollawolla!" that saw him off into the distance and turned to go back to the house.

My bare feet and legs, I noticed now, were wet with dew from the long grass. My heart was thumping with the thrill of the chase and, most especially, of victory. I tipped my head up to the sky and took a deep, long breath. And then I saw him. Up at the window directly above our room stood a man, looking out over the lawn. Set inside the dark of the interior, the figure was almost entirely concealed from view. But I saw him. Then, eliminating any doubt at all, came the slow clapping of hands. I smiled and gave a small, embarrassed bow.

"Brava!" called my Uncle Tom from his window. I looked over to our room. Jamie was crouching down in the grass beyond the window. He was busy feeding the peacock something that he had been carrying in his pyjama pocket. From where I was standing it looked decidedly like cheese. Hello Bertie! I smiled to myself. I raised my hand tentatively up at the window. Hello Uncle Tom.

Chapter Forty-One

I was eager to recount my exchange with our elusive uncle to Pod and Nathalie over breakfast. Lizzie, who had woken just in time to see me dive out of the window, had been filled in entirely at the first possible opportunity. For the first time since her accident, she expressed frustration at being so immobilised by her leg. She was sad to have missed the whole drama.

"Jamie did give me a very entertaining running commentary, though," she grinned, with her usual grace. We both felt so sorry for her that Jamie rushed off to his room to fetch his three remaining squares of chocolate – an enormous testimony to his love for her and his sympathy for her situation. I presented her proudly with the exquisite tail-feather that Bertie had left behind as a parting 'thank you' after the rescue mission. We all marvelled together at its beauty and intricacy of design and colour. Divorced from its owner, it was somehow even more difficult to conceive of its being 'of this world'.

We arrived down in the 'breakfast room' in an excited flurry. I was sure that my parents would be thrilled by our 'news'. After all, everything was going to be alright now. Uncle Tom was going to come downstairs, Bertie was safe and Pod didn't need to be unhappy any more!

Jamie screeched in through the door with Lizzie, who brandished the feather to the fore. "We met Bertie, Pod!" he called out, as though Pod was actually back in Paultons Square rather than sitting a metre or so away from him at table. "The fox was going to get him, so Apricot went crazy and scared him off. And she saw Uncle Tom and he saw everything, so it's all going to be alright now!"

It wasn't exactly how I would have told it. I had been looking forward to savouring each dramatic moment of the story in its telling. But, I conceded, all the essentials were there. We all beamed at our mother and father expectantly. Nathalie, in turn, reached across to Pod.

"That's wonderful, isn't it?" she said. Which should have been just what we were hoping to hear. But somehow, instead of sharing with him her elation, it felt like she was pleading with him to feel it.

Coming down a little from my own emotional 'high', I took a moment to actually look at them. Pod's smile was strained and tired. I was conscious, too, of the enormous effort he was going to to convince us of his delight at this dramatic turn of events. Nathalie tried hard to introduce a light and cheerful tone into her voice as she bustled us all into our seats and urged us for a more detailed account. But I could see that she was anxious. That same worn, distracted look was back, after the brief, joyful twenty-four hours on Pod's safe return. How I had hoped that finally sharing all that was on his mind would succeed in erasing it once and for all.

And suddenly I knew it. For sure. She hadn't shared all that was on his mind. She, like me, sensed that there was something more.

I ate my breakfast in subdued silence, in marked contrast to my expectations of triumphant celebration. But I had much to ponder – and silence goes particularly well with both pondering and eating, so silence it was. In the event, all that silence went largely unnoticed. Jamie delighted in being the bearer of our dramatic news all over again. My parents were thoroughly occupied with trying to convince him that they were not somewhere else entirely. Only Lizzie, on a rather pointed request to pass the milk, caught my eye with a questioning look. Sending it, rather ungraciously, straight back to her along with the milk, I buried myself again into my thoughts and my plate.

It had to be something to do with Mia. I felt the now familiar wave of sadness wash through me at the thought of Pod, his little sister and all the years of secrecy and pain. How strange it was to feel so unable to approach my father and simply ask him. Since I was two years old, and afraid of the shadows on the wall, I had been able to confide my fears and share my thoughts. Why was I so reluctant now? Perhaps, in part, I was afraid of what I might learn if he did open up his heart in response to mine. I had not even asked how it was that Mia had died. In part that was down to Pod's reluctance to tell me. But in truth I did not trust my reasons for wondering. Was it merely salacious curiosity? Or might it hold a key to the past that still had such an oppressive hold over my father?

I toyed with the last piece of cheese on my plate. And then there was Uncle Tom. Was it really going to be alright now? Might what happened that morning have acted like a kind of magic spell, lifting the veil from his eyes and freeing him from his lonely enchantment? Or might, instead, nothing have changed? I was beginning to wonder whether I had imagined the whole thing in any case, and that even Jamie's role in the proceedings was merely a part of my delusion, when there was a tentative knock at the outside door.

Pod stood up from the table.

"Buongiorno!" Alessandro smiled. "I hope you don't mind us coming round the back. Giuliana thought it would be OK."

For an extraordinary moment I had been convinced that it was Uncle Tom: That somehow I had conjured him to the door by my fevered imagination; spirited him downstairs in my burning need to find resolutions.

Still, if it wasn't to be answers knocking at the door, then I was jolly pleased that it was Alessandro. Real as real. And in a further bid to rescue me from Delusion City, he had, it seemed, brought along resources. Clinging shyly to the back of his legs was little Aisling. Tangled up in hers was Star.

"Aisling has something for Jamie," Alessandro said, urging her gently out from behind.

Squashing his last piece of bread into his mouth all at once and missing Nathalie's frown of disapproval altogether in his excitement, Jamie got up from the table. "Hey – thanks!" he mumbled – at least, I'm guessing that's what came out, along with the considerable shower of crumbs (gross!) and the broad smile.

"Jamie!" Nathalie admonished with dismay. "Sit down and finish your breakfast properly." And then, with a warm glance at Alessandro and his sister, "I'm sure our guests will be happy to wait for another moment or two."

"Of course," Alessandro answered politely. I found myself feeling inexplicably proud of him. We grinned at each other across the table.

But someone, it seemed, was feeling rather less patient. With a leap and a bound a small white goat, bearing a large blue bow, burst in to the room, nearly knocking Pod off his feet with surprise! "Bacchus!" Alessandro cried with horror as the excitable kid proceeded to charge madly about the room. 'Crash!' as Pod's chair came down. 'Smash!' That was the large – but luckily empty – milk jug, brought tumbling to the ground with the tablecloth from the small side table. Every bit as excitable as the goat, Jamie made a wild lunge for the lithe little body as it disappeared under the breakfast table. Moments later, the two of them reappeared as one long wriggle, Jamie clinging steadfastly on to the hind quarters of his new friend.

Aisling giggled. As the little goat came to rest under Jamie's hands, Alessandro took hold of its makeshift 'reins'. "I thought you were holding on to these," he said sternly to his mischievous sister. With the innate sense of the world around her that had so astounded me the previous day, she crouched down beside Jamie and Bacchus.

"Sorry," she said quietly, stroking her hand gently along the goat's back. Jamie was making the low crooning sound that seemed to so entrance the creatures that came under his spell. The animal was now perfectly calm, nuzzling now and then into Jamie's hand.

"I love him!" Jamie declared passionately looking up at Alessandro. Then, of Aisling, he asked, "Can he stay? Is he really mine?" She nodded and reached out her hand. Recognising her intention, Jamie leant forward so that she could brush her fingers across his face. It was all rather moving actually. (But don't tell Jamie).

"She heard you telling Mum about Toots last night and how much you missed him." Alessandro explained. "She asked whether we could give you Bacchus so that you weren't sad any more. He's Star's big brother. Mum thought you might like to get a female one too." He turned to Nathalie. "We could show you how to milk her when the time came – and even how to make cheese."

The thought of our chi-chi mother milking goats and making cheese was beyond hilarious! Jamie, Lizzie and I exploded. Pod chuckled. Nathalie looked bemused. And then amused. The whole room dissolved into laughter.

When we had finally managed to catch our breath, Alessandro looked nervously at Pod and Nathalie. "Is it OK?" he asked. "Mum said we must check with you before we left him?" Pod nodded, still smiling broadly.

"If only because it leaves open the possibility of my seeing my wife on a milking stool!" he teased, catching Nathalie's eye with a wink. Jamie leapt up and threw his arms tightly round first one parent, then the other.

An outdoor shelter would be required, Alessandro explained. He could help put something together in the 'campo' beyond the house. Recalling an old barn that might be 'just the ticket', Pod suggested that they go out and take a look.

The morning sped by. The barn needed patching up a bit here and there, but it was basically dry. Any straw that remained inside the mellow stone structure was mouldering and black, but Alessandro was sure that they could bring over a crop of fresh hay from 'Pelagio' to make a luxurious bed for our new friend. Various old, rusted pieces of iron, long-ago having lost sight of the original purpose to which they had been so keenly set, were carefully collected from the barn's earth floor. With great excitement, Jamie found some rather beautiful pieces of broken tile, part buried in the ground inside. When all the large obstructions were cleared, Alessandro set about raking the remaining muck and debris, depositing it in a handy wheelbarrow that I found underneath the olives not far off. I liked to imagine the rickety old barrow having been left for just a while under the trees by a once-upon-a-time gardener – perhaps whilst he tucked into his lunchtime bread and cheese – but for a reason now buried with him, never actually picked up again until this very moment.

The barn was near enough to the house for Bacchus to feel part of the family and far enough away from Nathalie's proposed kitchen and herb garden to keep her happy too. He would, Alessandro warned, eat anything. He was a wonderful dustbin for scraps but not someone to have around the dinner table. His name, he told us, was well and truly earned by his penchant for a glass of craftily appropriated wine, revealed one lunchtime when Eleanor had had her back to the outside table for the crucial instant. And more than one of her sunhats had provided a hearty midmorning snack for the mischievous goat. At least until he and Jamie were well and truly acquainted it was probably most sensible to keep him on a long tether.

We had just finished clearing the barn when the first spots of rain began to fall. They had, Alessandro said, forecasted rain. He and Aisling had hoped to make it back across the hill before it did. But of course, no one would hear of them setting out for home now – especially with it being so close to lunchtime!

Nathalie agreed wholeheartedly, when we arrived back at the house. She had, in fact, already planned on inviting our friends to stay for lunch. A large, steaming pan of water was already on the kitchen stove for the pasta when I went down to investigate. There was, however, our mother announced, one vital condition upon which everything hung. She paused. We all held our breath. A thorough wash was to be had by all – and that included Pod!

It was just as we were called to table that Alessandro took me to one side. We were alone in a small, fusty 'salottino' just off the main entrance hall. He handed me a mysterious package, discreetly wrapped in brown paper. "I thought you might like some of your Uncle's books," he explained in a hushed voice. "They really are wonderful and perhaps, in a sort of way, they might help you to get to know him a little." A rush of warmth and affection for him in this thoughtful, hopeful gesture rose up inside me with a rather reckless abandon. Before I knew what was happening I had leant forward and kissed him quickly on the cheek! Then, without giving him a chance to respond – and before he had a chance to see the hot blush rise up into my face – I disappeared; for the welcome sanctuary of my room.

Depositing the precious parcel beneath my pillow, I sat down on the bed. I took a long, slow breath. The rapid thumping of my heart, I knew, was not merely the result of my rapid escape. I willed the heat out of my burning cheeks. The blush, of course, was all too familiar, but no-one had ever made me feel like this before. I was thrilled and terrified all at once. At times, the squeeze in my chest when I was with him made it almost impossible to draw breath. Did he feel it too? I wondered. Could it really only have been yesterday that we had met, for our lives to feel so inextricably bound? The intensity of the past few days had undoubtedly been extraordinary. Was I mistaking this for something else, something of which, after all, I had no real experience? But then, perhaps I was thinking about it all too hard. Perhaps it was simple. For Ben and Lizzie it had seemed simple. She liked him and he liked her. But that was before our lives changed forever and nothing was really as simple as it had seemed.

Two minutes before lunch was, I realised, not the ideal time to attempt to unravel this tangled ribbon of emotions. Attempting to coil it up just neatly enough to avoid tripping over it on my way into the dining room would have to do.

I tried hard not to catch Lizzie's eye as I sat down at table. I was not ready to field another of her quizzical looks, although a part of me was longing to find a moment to confide something of the past two days to my wise little sister. I was equally anxious to avoid confronting Alessandro across the table. At this rate I would have to spend the entire mealtime looking at Jamie! I almost smiled at the absurdity of it all when, with a chill, it struck me. What if Alessandro was horrified by my kiss?! What if he too was doing his utmost to avoid catching my eye, in case I interpreted his glance as encouragement? My attempt to tidy away my emotions had clearly been woefully inadequate. The latter thought was too much to bear unsubstantiated. As the lesser of two evils, I raised my eyes in the direction of Alessandro. His clear, open gaze met my cloudily, fuddled one head on.

"We're glad you decided to grace us with your presence, Apricot," Nathalie admonished disapprovingly. For an instant I had forgotten that she was in the room at all, or that I was actually there for the rather prosaic purpose of consuming a meal.

"Eleanor is going to take us into Cortona this afternoon," Lizzie cut in breezily, spotting the awkward ball in my court and coming neatly to my rescue. She handed the large earthenware bowl of pasta down the table to me and continued her bright, distracting discourse. I could have kissed her! Oh help! I'm doing far too much of that just at the moment!

Though, with all the turmoil inside, I was sure there couldn't be room for food, I helped myself to a generous plate of fragrant, 'tomato-y' tagliatelli. At least, I surmised, if I was tucking into lunch then the world was temporarily safe from my wanton kissing frenzy.

The plan, it seemed, was for Eleanor to meet us here at the house. She was looking forward to introducing herself properly to Nathalie and Pod. We would then take one car into town. Regretfully, Alessandro said, he and Aisling would not be accompanying us. He had promised his father that he would help out on the estate that afternoon. Now that his elder brother had made alternative plans for the future – we all sat down hard on Giuliana's revelations of the previous morning – the running of the estate would eventually be his responsibility. The next four months or so until the grape harvest were critical in the 'year-of-the-vine' and he was eager to learn as much as he could about the whole process.

Emboldened by the knowledge that I would have a whole afternoon in which to get know my unfamiliar emotions a little better, without Alessandro close at hand to stir them all into an unidentifiable melee, I exchanged a glance with him across the table. Our eyes met somewhere in the middle, with a broad smile. Resisting the urge to break into song – or at the very least do an animated jig in amongst the plates and glasses – I looked bashfully back down at my rapidly congealing pasta. And therein lay the next challenge. How to convey the long, sauce-laden strands to my mouth with natural – and irresistibly appealing – aplomb, when the best I had managed to date was to avoid splattering more than three other members of the dinner-party with tomato and parmesan along the way?

God's Angels, the Fates, Father Christmas and all were on my side. The remainder of lunch passed without incident. My emotions, and tagliatelli, were irreproachable models of orderliness. Happy and replete, we pushed back our chairs from the table and Alessandro and Aisling excused themselves to leave. They graciously declined Pod's offer of a lift home. The rain had proven to be a short, sharp shower and already the sun was breaking through the gradually dispersing cloud. They were looking forward to setting off into the hills and, 4WD or no, they weren't altogether sure how Star would have taken to 'buckling up' into Pod's leather-upholstered back seat! Everyone chuckled and it was the perfect note on which to say goodbye.

At least, it would have been, if it weren't for the brief, but strong, squeeze of the hand that Alessandro gave me just as the others turned back towards the house. Now that was perfect. house. Now that was perfect.

Chapter Forty-Two

Nathalie and Eleanor got on like a house on fire. Nathalie even bypassed the bit where she hides behind her 'frenchness' and a too-high-pitched laugh, lest she actually make the mistake of getting to know someone better. It was four o'clock when Eleanor arrived and they would probably still be sitting there in the shade of the 'loggia' now, if it wasn't for our persistence in cajoling them to the car.

The ten minute journey into Cortona was really just a simple matter of sailing down one hill and up the next. Still, it was a journey to remember. Round each bend in the winding road I left a part of my soul, to gaze for eternity in awe and wonder at the beauty and magic of our newly discovered world. An age-old castellated land, where reality is just a breath away from fairytale.

It was nearly five-thirty by the time we arrived at the little car park at the foot of the hilltop town. We drew ourselves in just far enough to squeeze between two large camper vans that had staked out their plot with monumental purpose. Ignoring their bullyboy frowns, Nathalie gave a defiant crunch on the handbrake and we leaned over to open the doors. Jamie and I inched our way out of the back of the car, with Eleanor making a sedate exit from the passenger side. We had left Lizzie back at the house with a large tome on Etruscan history that Eleanor had lent her the previous day. She was keen to discover more about Tuscany's past and the legacy of the people who seemed still, more than two thousand years later, to exert such an influence on the region's life and culture. "I'm hoping to be inspired upon a new project," she had announced. And, after all, she had gone a whole three days without one.

Pod too had stayed behind. I wondered if he would try once more to approach Uncle Tom. How much I hoped he would – especially after the tentative exchange that morning. I thought of the intriguing parcel of books under my pillow, my one regret at having decided to accompany the others into town.

After the rain, the air was cool and clear. The climb, Eleanor told

have missed it altogether, in fact, were it not for my elbow knocking a small, unusual pipe and sending it to the ground. Observing, with immense relief, on picking it up, that it did not appear to be damaged, I placed it carefully back on the dresser. As I did so, a flash of pink caught my eye. I moved the monstrous wireless gingerly over to one side. It was a puppet theatre! 19th Century, it said on the label. It was, perhaps, a little over a metre wide and about half as high. The structure seemed to be composed of a kind of stiff board, painted in minutest detail. A aged-pink silk curtain hung ready to drop at the first sound of applause. Exquisitely crafted stage sets, with their fairytale architecture and idealised landscapes, told umpteen stories of romance and battle, idyll and dream. Even the actors, tiny and perfectly formed, still waited patiently in the wings for their cue – which, for so long now, never came. Though there was an air of faded grandeur about it, this, I thought excitedly, was a theatre longing to be filled, once more, with life. I could almost hear the orchestra tuning up in the pit, smell the greasepaint and feel the heat of the lights... This theatre needed me. I would bring it out of the shadows and restore it to its former glory. And it would be called, 'Mollie's'...

"Apricot!" Nathalie broke into my reverie. Drawing Jamie away from a monumental juke box – disappointingly, he informed me, playing only Italian songs – I led him back through Gulliver's legs to the main body of the shop. Our mother surveyed us briskly. The business with the fabric, it seemed, was all wrapped up.

"Eleanor and I have one or two things to do in town. Mr Gimble has kindly said that he will keep an eye on you here for half an hour or so, if you'd rather stay."

Mr Gimble twinkled his consent. (How could anyone not realise he was a sorcerer?).

"Thanks!" Jamie enthused keenly, and, as they say, in the twinkling of an eye, he disappeared back into the melee.

As for me, despite appearances, I had never actually left the theatre. Still now, I was basking in the crowd's thunderous applause. Waving goodbye to Nathalie and Eleanor in between bows, I realised how very much I longed to own this wonderful part of imaginative history. I fingered the dusky-pink curtain tenderly. Then, hardly daring to look, I turned over the small yellowing label that had initially announced the theatre's date. 450 Euros! Imaginative history clearly did not come cheap!

"Ah, so you've found it," the wizard said, clambering over an untidy pile of leather suitcases to join me in my yearning. "Magical, isn't it? I rather suspect that it's been hiding here all these years waiting for someone just like you to come along and bring it to life once more."

I nodded.

"It belongs to a very elderly lady who lives up in the hills near Perugia. It had been her mother's when she was a little girl, and her grandmother's before that. Once-upon-a-time the family were very wealthy and their home was the setting for some of the region's most feted parties. Now, the house is almost all shut up, the beautiful gardens are tangled and overgrown and money is scarce. But a more gracious and elegant woman you are not likely to meet," he added thoughtfully, and I wondered...

But before my wonderings revealed themselves even to me there was a 'ting' at the door.

"Lucius old fellow!" called Mr Gimble, beginning to negotiate his way back to the centre of the shop. "Come and meet my new friends!"

Even without the battered panama hat and the brightly coloured umbrella that he set down, opened wide, just inside the door, this man would have been extraordinary. For one thing he must have been close to seven feet tall. His long gangly frame was clad entirely in crumpled white linen and his feet, I noticed with surprise, as I came out from behind a pair of grimacing merry-goround horses without their 'round' (or, for that matter, their 'merry'), were entirely bare. His voice, when he spoke, was like those you only ever hear on old-fashioned newsreels, only three octaves higher:

"Half a cheese!" he called out blithely.

Feeling rather out of my depth, I turned to Mr Gimble for reassurance, but he was already disappearing into the back of the shop. "Righty ho!" he called over his shoulder.

He emerged a few minutes later with a large bundle of wood that looked to be comprised of an assortment of broken chair-legs, picture frames and the like. Together with the astonishing man, he began to load the wood into the umbrella. On completion of the task, Lucius reached inside his breast pocket and drew out a large piece of cheese. Handing it to Mr Gimble, he gave a strong salute, picked up his umbrella and disappeared back out into the street.

Just when I was beginning to fear that it was I who had completely lost my marbles, or that, as Nathalie had always warned might happen, I had stepped over into my imagination once too often and now there was

178

no going back, Jamie appeared.

"Who was that?!" he gasped in wonderment.

I smiled at him gratefully. "I can't imagine what he does with all those pieces of wood!" I called out to Mr Gimble, who had dissolved into the back room once more.

"Neither can I!" he replied cheerily. "Mad as a hatter, I expect."

There was a loud crash and the sound of something rolling around on the floor.

"Ah! Skittles!" Mr Gimble declared. "I wondered what had happened to those."

"He seems to have left his stick," Jamie observed, peering into the dim little room after Mr Gimble.

"Yes. He always comes back for his cane. In about thirty seconds..."

Sure enough, the doorbell 'tinged' again.

"Forgot my stick!" proclaimed Lucius, as, as if by magic, Mr Gimble reappeared in the shop. Then, spotting Jamie and me loitering amongst a veritable solar system of globes, he took a low bow. "Lucius Pomeroy, at your service."

"Meet Apricot and James!" Mr Gimble replied, equally flamboyantly.

Jamie and I bowed politely. And then, just as though it had been dislodged from underneath the sofa, another piece of the jigsaw made an unexpected appearance.

"They are the Beresford-Linnel grandchildren," Mr Gimble went on. And then, to us: "Many years ago, Mr Pomeroy was employed by your grandfather as tutor to his children. He even lived at the house for a while," he explained.

"There's Lizzie too," Jamie interjected helpfully.

Lucius Pomeroy's response will remain with me always. His already grey face turned deathly pale. He staggered backwards a little towards the door. The words came in a ghastly, hoarse whisper, an instant before he rushed back out into the street:

"Poor Amelia-Anne. Poverina!"

And he'd left his stick in the stand by the door.

Chapter Forty-Four

How had he known my name? I wondered, still reeling after witnessing such apparent distress. Why did he feel so sorry for me? And why was he so terribly disturbed by the mention of our family?

Theophilos shook his head sadly.

"He took the loss of dear Amelia-Anne very badly," he mused, patting me sympathetically on the arm. "I think in part he blamed himself. Perhaps if he had still been around he might have been able to prevent what happened. Still, we all felt something of that at the time. And after all, it was nearly three years after he left that little Mia died."

My thoughts tripped over themselves, trying to keep up with all that he was saying. Mia, Amelia-Anne, Mia, Amelia-Anne, Mia, Amelia-Anne – the names ran round and round in my head until they became the same. So she was Amelia-Anne too. My father's dead sister. The first Amelia-Anne. And he had never told me. So every time he said my name, my 'real' name, he must have thought of her. And he had never told me. Was that why I had always been Apricot, so that it wouldn't hurt each time he called my name? How much, though, he must have loved her, to have called his first child after her memory...

My amplifying thoughts were so big that there was almost no room for Jamie's increasingly insistent question:

"Who was Mia?" he pleaded, tugging on my arm in a bid to draw me back into the room.

Of course! He didn't know. Pod had not yet had a chance to talk to Jamie – or Lizzie – and I had not felt that it was my place to tell them. Well, there was nothing for it – I would have to tell him now.

I sat Jamie down beside me on a convenient pair of stools. Mr Gimble had sensitively taken his leave. Our faces appropriately sombre, I told my little brother all that I knew about our family's tragic secret.

It wasn't much, I realised, as I told it. It really posed more questions than it answered. But it was somewhere to start.

Melting back into the room as we fell silent, Mr Gimble looked at us both with kindly eyes. "I'm sorry," he said, putting a gentle hand on each of our heads. "I hadn't realised it was all so new to you."

And there we were, the three of us in quiet reflection, when the doorbell 'tinged' and Nathalie and Eleanor came in.

"Well, Mr Gimble, I don't know what magic you have cast, but I haven't known the two of them that quiet this side of dreamland," Nathalie teased heartily. We all smiled broad, counterfeit smiles so that she didn't feel bad about crowding out our contemplative mood.

"I've liked having them about the place," Mr Gimble replied courteously – although I think he really had, you know.

"Can we come back?" Jamie asked eagerly, of Nathalie and Mr Gimble simultaneously.

"Well, I'd been meaning to ask your mother whether she might spare you, and perhaps your sisters too if they would like, every now and then, to help me with a project here in the shop." Mr Gimble replied, chuckling at Jamie's enthusiasm.

He went on to explain how he was hoping that his nephew might one day take over the business, but before things could be arranged, he needed to catalogue the store's innumerable contents. Could we be persuaded to give him a hand? We could, of course, negotiate our terms. He looked smilingly at me. There was, he recalled, a certain puppet theatre in need of a new owner...

Need he say more? A provisional deal was struck. Nathalie made it clear to all that if Jamie were to choose something from the shop as 'wages' she would prefer it not to be the grizzly bear. We all laughed, and set off for home.

But my thoughts were still with the other Amelia-Anne. And what actually happened thirty years ago...

It wasn't until after supper that I had a chance to talk with Pod alone. In fact, it was he who sought me out. I had finished my kitchen chores for Nathalie and was just escaping off to our room to finally delve into Uncle Tom's books, when he called out after me. Catching me up in the corridor, he wondered whether we could speak for a minute. If it might, even for a moment, have rid him of that strained, anxious look, I would have agreed to anything. How I hoped that this, at least, might be a start...

We chose the small 'salottino' that had been the scene of my assignation with Alessandro and the parcel of books, to sit down together. Whilst we had been in Cortona, Giuliana had clearly been working her magic on the pretty little room. Although it was after nine o'clock, the rich light of evening still poured in like molten honey through the open shutters. The cool, fresh breeze that had replaced the weighty air of disuse and neglect toyed with the silken key-tassel that hung from the window frame. As much, I suspected, in the interests of privacy as of night-time prudence, Pod strode over to pull the windows to a close. He stood silent for a moment, surveying the field beyond, as if to reassure himself that we were entirely alone. Was it the living he was scouting for, or was it the ghosts?

There wasn't a sound. Only a solitary rosebud peeped in through the shining glass. Pod came over to the pretty little sofa beside my chair and sat down. "It is not easy for you, little Abricot, I know." He spoke softly and the combination of his words and the solemnity of his tone took me back to that night in the study when I had first learned about the letters.

I waited silently, to find out where he was going. Then, despite my patience, I sensed his sudden – and uncharacteristic – resolve to come straight to the point.

"Uncle Tom has asked to see you."

I felt a thrill of excitement and...was it fear?

"Did you talk to him today?" I asked him eagerly.

"No," he replied, almost shamefully. "He won't see me. Giuliana spoke with him whilst the nurse was here."

So, he wanted to see me! I couldn't help a faint sense of pride at having been singled out. "It's because of this morning," I explained, "with Bertie." We both knew I was trying to make him feel better about the request. I could not have been more taken aback, then, at the next turn in the conversation.

"I have said that it is out of the question." He could not look at me when he spoke. His voice had taken on an unfamiliar, brittle edge. "I hope you will understand and respect my decision."

The emphasis was on finality. This conversation, his tone said, had nowhere else to go.

I, on the other hand, was only just beginning. Understand?! How could I possibly understand? I had no idea what was happening to our once happy, uncomplicated family life. Most disturbingly I was beginning to fear that my naive impression of it always having been so was, after all, just an illusion.

"How can I understand when you don't even try to explain?" I demanded. "Isn't this our chance to make everything alright?"

"I do NOT want you involved!" he responded explosively. If there had been a table close at hand I felt sure he would have banged it.

"Involved in what?" I pleaded desperately. I could feel the tears beginning to form, born in part out of frustration but primarily, I suspected, in my childish need for Pod's approval. "Is it about Mia?"

Pod's anger drained away as fast as it had arrived. I saw it leave. His face, for a moment flushed and animated, relaxed into its sad, too-familiar facade. The rage had left me shaking, but it was almost more unbearable to observe the tired and drawn expression take back its seat. He reached out and took my hand.

"I'm sorry," he said quietly.

Emboldened a little, I tried again. "Was she sick?" I probed tentatively. "There was a man in the antique shop who said..."

The anger was back. "How dare people make idle talk about our family?!" Pod bridled. "They know nothing about how it was. Nothing about my sister. I forbid you to listen to such gossip. Mia was sick for a long time – for three years – and she died. That is all you need to know."

But he was wrong. It did not even begin to answer the concerns and unease that shivered inside me. For one thing, I was sure that had Mia been so very sick, for so very long, then Pod would never have left, purely on a whim, for France. And it did not begin to explain why still now, more than thirty years later, my father and his brother were unable to face each other and their past.

Nevertheless, it was clear that the conversation was at an end. Pod stood up from the small sofa that was too delicate and frivolous to bear such weighty emotion. As if to let out a little of that weight, my father sighed. He reached over, touched my head softly and went out of the room. And it was then that I made up my mind...

Chapter Forty-Five

I hugged the plan tightly to myself as I pulled my night shirt on over my head and slipped into bed beside Lizzie. A part of me longed to share it with her – to spread out on the eiderdown before her all of the thoughts and uncertainties that had led to my making the momentous decision to defy our father's wishes. But the consequences, I knew, could be far-reaching and it did not seem fair to involve her in such a conspiracy. Besides, if I was honest, I was afraid she might try and dissuade me from going ahead. She was wise and prudent and had teased me repeatedly for the impetuous streak that had, all too often, seen me landing flat on my face. But this time I was not just acting on impulse. Instinct was different. Something, I felt sure, was wrong. Something that had been left for too long unspoken, to undermine and to fester... and to gnaw its way into the heart of our family.

What I could share with Lizzie, however, were Uncle Tom's books. For a while, at least, I would channel my trepidation over 'the plan' into my genuine excitement about the brown-paper-wrapped parcel of enchantments beneath my pillow. We unveiled the contents eagerly, though with no small amount of reverence. The three hard-backed volumes were bound in soft green leather and I recalled Alessandro telling me that they were from a limited run of 'presentation' copies. I ran my finger gently over the gilt-brushed, indented lettering on the front of each. The first, my finger read, told of 'The Mountain of Here and There – and other stories'. The second was slimmer and entitled simply 'The Town that Looked Down'. As I swirled my finger over the final title, 'Little Lady Clementine Makes a Difference', I gave a smile. Aisling's favourite.

Lizzie and I looked at each other with glee. Which to choose first?! The fattest of the books appeared to be a collection of short stories. Opposite the title page was a wonderful line-drawing. A majestic mountain rose up in the centre of the picture, swathed mystically in a swirling, ethereal mist.

"Oh! I must try this one!" Lizzie exclaimed in delight. "Do you mind?

184

If you like we could take it in turns to read one story at a time."

But I had already decided. Well, really it was Aisling who had decided for me. I placed the third book reluctantly on the bedside table – what a shame one can only ever read one book at a time – and snuggled down beneath the covers with Little Lady Clementine.

At first when I woke I thought I was back in Paultons Square. My mind lingered nostalgically in my dreams. Then, even before I had opened my eyes, the singing of a solitary cricket had carried me back across the sea to our Italian hillside. Somewhere far-off a dog was howling. It was a surprise to find the bed still bathed in a pool of yellow light. Lizzie lay awkwardly, as though she had struggled to find a comfortable position in which to slumber. Her book, I noticed, lay neatly on the table beside her; mine was resting at my side where I must have let it fall as I was finally overcome by sleep. What time was it? I wondered. I fumbled for my watch. Two o'clock. I 'scrunched' the top pillow back into shape and curled up, slightly irritably, on my side.

'The plan' came back to me first as a constriction in my chest. Something was about to happen. Then I remembered. My idea had been to wait until about 6 am. That was, I thought, late enough for Uncle Tom to be awake – the sick, I understood, slept fitfully and woke with the dawn – but early enough that no-one else would be around to hear me creeping up the wide stone staircase. Of course, this all relied upon being awake myself. My mobile alarm was set for 5-50 am – on 'vibrate' so as not to wake Lizzie. The phone was tucked securely under my bottom pillow. I reached out and turned off the light. Perhaps there was a chance I might sleep again now until 'zero hour'.

I lay there for a while thinking. Lady Clementine's impish adventures danced about my head. I thought of Tom's kindness to little Aisling and then of his brutal response to Pod's attempt to make amends. Like my inscrutable grandfather, it seemed, Uncle Tom was a man of contradictions. How then would he respond to my arriving unannounced at his door? He had, of course, requested to see me, but on what terms? Pod had made it clear that he was not prepared to discuss the issue further with me. So I really had no choice but to take matters into my own hands. Having convinced myself, if a little shakily, of that, I snuggled up more peacefully. Lizzie stirred a little. Her hand came to rest in the small of my back. The bed was warm and soft. Even the companionable cricket had settled down to sleep...

Strangely, in that extraordinary quirk of circumstance that it is impossible to explain, I woke again at precisely 5-48 am: two minutes before my phone was due to 'buzz' its 'Good Morning'. Congratulating my internal 'clock', I turned off the alarm and slid stealthily out of bed. Given my need to wake early, I had wondered whether it had been a mistake to close the shutters the previous night. The light that now fingered its way through the cracks in between was surprisingly bright. At least in this semi-dark, Lizzie might not wake until my mission was safely over. The night-chill had infiltrated its way into the small pile of clothes that I had set out the night before in readiness for 'Operation ...' what? My sleep-warmed skin shrank back a little from the cool fabric as my dress slithered on down my back. As if responding to a formal invitation – which, after all, in a sense I was – I had selected the most presentable of my summer outfits for my first-ever meeting with my uncle. Slipping my arms into the sleeves of my cardigan, I felt my way into my mules with my feet. Then, on second thoughts, I kicked them off again. Though bare feet undeniably undermined the formality of an occasion, they certainly made for a more discreet passage. I hoped that, in the circumstances, Uncle Tom wouldn't mind.

Then I was turning the smooth, round door handle and creeping out into the long dark corridor towards the staircase. I didn't dare turn on the light. Instead I felt my way along the now familiar panelled walls to the appropriate door. Still, I would have been glad of Jamie's pen-torch. Where were all the secret agents when you needed them? The thought made me smile and I was glad to be distracted from my growing sense of nervousness about the plan. Was it Uncle Tom's reaction I was afraid of? Or Pod's response when he discovered what I had done? Or was it instead that deep-down inside I was afraid of what I might learn? There was, I recalled, a saying about letting sleeping dogs lie which had undoubtedly been coined for a pretty astute reason. But the thing was, this dog wasn't sleeping. He was gradually gnawing his way through his chains. And perhaps what I was really concerned about was knowing the right way to handle him if we finally came face to face.

Well, I thought, as I tentatively approached the door to the room directly above the nursery, at least I couldn't hear him growling. In fact, I couldn't hear anything at all. Was Uncle Tom still asleep? There was no light coming from underneath the door.

I was standing in a wide corridor, just off the main landing. Just the other side of the staircase was the handsome master bedroom that I knew to be Pod and Nathalie's. This part of the house was much grander altogether than the lower floor that I was used to. The staircase swept up to an elegant marble-tiled floor, cold and hard beneath my bare feet. I remembered Giuliana saying that there was a rather beautiful 'salotto' up here in which Nona Sofia would entertain her closest – strictly female – friends. I surveyed the unaccounted for doors in the dim light. They looked back at me darkly, with blank, unyielding stares. A part of me wished I was still safely tucked up in our congenial nursery bedroom. No, I determined, now was not the time for further exploration. I drew my focus back to the matter in hand.

Should I knock? I wondered. I didn't imagine he would be pleased to be woken and there was always a risk that knocking too loudly might alert Pod or Nathalie too. But this must be the right place. It was unquestionably at the window of this room that I had seen Uncle Tom the previous morning. I had even slipped out of the nursery window to make certain before getting into bed. Once more I made a mental picture of the layout of the house. Finally, unable to bear the thought of sloping back to my room in defeat before I had even attempted my mission, I gave a hesitant knock at the door.

Silence. I tried again. I could hear the blood pounding in my ears. But it was the only response to my boldness. So I should have stopped there. I should have done the 'right thing' and gone back to bed. But I was being led by something stronger than reason or etiquette. That is not an excuse; just an explanation. You see, before I had really registered what I was doing, I was turning the handle on the door! By rights it ought to have squealed loudly at my unauthorised intrusion. Instead it opened smoothly, as though it was a door well used to the comings and goings of the 'no-nonsense nurse' that I knew attended to Uncle Tom each day. As I stepped into the room I was dimly conscious of stepping over the proverbial 'point of no return'.

If I closed my eyes would I be invisible? Just like when I was a little girl? I wished I still lived in that place where the imagination reigned high over all. My eyes were all-too-open. Thin shafts of light, like in the nursery, pierced the impenetrable dark of the solid wood shutters. I could see almost instantly that I was alone in the sparse, characterless room. The air smelt of sickness and despair. A stifling combination of age and antiseptic. It made me think of Great Aunt Emily and the exclusive nursing home to which she had been moved after her stroke. Even wealth, it seemed, couldn't eradicate the smell of decline.

But Uncle Tom wasn't old! He was three years younger than Pod. That made him forty-six. I felt a surge of anger and determination. This wasn't how it ought to be! I strode over to the shutters and flung them open wide. My eyes were smarting with tears. The new day sped in through the window, banishing the demons in one almighty gust. But for how long? Just at that moment I knew that I would not settle for anything less than forever.

The sunlight was kindly on my face. After its initial rush inside, it seemed now to hover hypnotically about me, tiny particles of jewel-like dust drifting lazily in the radiant beam. I felt my anger soothed and calmed.

A half-filled glass of water stood on a small table beside the neatly made bed, together with numerous bottles and packets of pills. Loitering awkwardly alongside was a tall, spindly drip-stand. A small vase of fresh flowers on the nearby chest of drawers attempted to soften the impact of its portentous companions. Good old Giuliana.

So, everything, it seemed, was here to point to this being Uncle Tom's room. Except for Uncle Tom. Hmm! I sat down on the edge of the bed to think. The wind had been altogether ousted from my sails. Where was he? I felt like crying again. The bedroom ceiling gave a sonorous, sympathetic kind of creak. Or rather, I supposed, the floor of the room above it did. It creaked again. Hang on a mo! Floorboards don't creak like that unless something – or someone – is creaking them. Well, it was either a very heavy mouse or somebody was creaking around upstairs! My heart jumped back to attention.

I knew that there was a third floor to this part of the house. But why would anyone be up there? Giuliana had told us that the attic rooms had long ago been left to while away the years alone. How much of a mystery it all was still – even our own home was one of locked doors and secrets. The floorboards creaked again. And I was decided. I left the windows flung open wide, unable to bring myself to condemn the room once more to its unhappy fate as the province of decline. The compliant door clicked softly shut behind me. I wasn't even sure how to get up to the top floor from the main landing. Conscious of the eager morning skipping on towards the day, I knew that not only would I have to be stealthy, I would have to be swift. A further corridor stretched out from the top of the staircase. Taking extra care as I passed by Pod and Nathalie's room (no discernible sound from within), I tiptoed (killing both the 'cold feet' bird and the 'noisy feet' bird with one stone) along its considerable length. Where our Paultons Square house was all 'up', this one was all 'along', I thought distractedly.

I was aware that the stairwell I sought might well be hidden or, at least, discreet. Sure enough, the door could not have been more unassuming. Rather than a handle, there was a small, round hole bored into the dark wood. Unless it was a stack of brooms and dustpans, a narrow wooden stairway was just what you would expect to find behind such a door. I stuck my finger into the hole and drew it open. And there it was! Surprisingly, a welcome shaft of natural light illuminated the narrow stairwell from above. Now for a bit of 'up'! There were ten steps in all. I found myself counting them instinctively as I climbed. 'One – creak', 'two – cree-eak', 'three – crak', all the way to the top. Whoever was up here would undoubtedly hear me coming...

The chamber that opened out from the stairwell made me gasp. It was a world away from the main body of the house. A vast pitched roof, supported by giant timbers, lent an air of majesty to the otherwise simple space. Light poured in through two round windows set just below the eaves. The floor was constructed of short wooden boards. Myriad magic-dust hung in the radiant light. (Still more, I observed in the large footprints that betrayed my every move, was settled, rather less transcendentally, at my feet). But it was the cobwebs that made this world truly miraculous. I craned my neck up to follow the delicate traceries from beam to beam. Here and there they plunged into shadow, to emerge again resplendent into the light, at once sinister and sublime. When the family retreated downstairs, the spiders had made this their realm...

Still, they had not been undisturbed. Besides my enormous prints – I wish someone would write a story about a beautiful princess with gi-normous feet – there was a good deal of disturbance in the dust around the stairs. Tellingly, from there the tracks led out in one direction only. It was harder to get my bearings on this floor, but all I really had to do was follow in the path already made. Was I, with each step, coming closer to the answers?

The confused footprints finally made their befuddled exit under a door. The most beautiful door I had ever seen! I gazed in awe. Where the other doors in the house were simple, if imposing, this door was a

189

work of art. The peacocks were carved into two columns, one at each side of the central panel. The tiniest details were picked out in the rich wood. I couldn't resist running my finger down an elegant neck, tracing downwards towards the glorious, half-fanned tail. Instead of answers I had found more questions. There were those that began with 'who' and 'when' but, when it came down to it, they really all meant 'why' Inexplicable beauty, hidden away here with the dust and the spiders. It made no sense. My hand fell reluctantly away from the wondrous image. Truly a house of mysteries...

"I hoped you would come."

The voice was so low, I thought I might have imagined it.

"It is open."

So this was it. After so much anticipation I found I was not ready at all. Still, taking a deep, inward breath like before a too-high dive, I pushed the door open slowly and stepped inside.

Chapter Forty-Six

"Giuliana said you were like her," he said simply. "She was tall too." There was a pause. "Do you dance?"

The words were even more disconcerting in that I could not see where they were coming from. I shifted awkwardly from one foot to the other, uncomfortable under the 'one-way' scrutiny. Without waiting for an answer, he went on.

"They told her she was too tall to dance. I think that was what killed her in the end. Knowing that she wouldn't be able to dance her way out of it all."

At first it didn't occur to me to look for a physical explanation for the eerie green light that pervaded the room. The strangeness of the conversation was enough. When exactly I noticed the high round window, almost entirely obscured by new-green creeper, I don't know for sure, but I remember it being a comfort.

"My sister, Lizzie, is a dancer," I offered, as though this were a polite chat over tea and cakes. I was relieved to be able to make out a tall, slightly hunched figure standing in the far corner, to put the words to. But his thoughts were already moving on without me.

"Always, she danced and danced, her red hair whirling about her, her eyes flashing. As though, if she whirled fast enough, the 'knowing' would not be able to keep up and the pain was left behind."

None of my 'imaginings' about the meeting had prepared me for the reality. Uncle Tom moved slowly across to a chair and eased himself down. The initially imposing figure was somehow diminished, shrinking gratefully into the support of the small tub chair. My heart reached out to the man who was at once a stranger and an inextricable part of me. But, for now, the rest of me stayed put.

"We wanted to thank you, Mia and I," he said. "For saving Bertie. He is old now and his instincts are not what they were. When he arrived, she said he was an angel, here to set us all free. Still he comes each day to stand beneath her window and entice her spirit down. Yet she remains forever shut away in this lonely room, afraid to come out into the light even though the demons are long gone..."

I shivered in the sinister green. Were they gone? I wondered. I fancied I could sense them, now indolent wraiths, sneering in the shadows. I fingered the pretty friendship bracelet around my wrist. It had been a parting gift from Arabella – not the greatest of friends but somehow thinking of her opened a window back into the 'real' world where the sun shone and the trite and the frivolous had somewhere to play.

"I was glad to help," I said brightly, determined to draw the conversation out into the light. "He left us a tail feather to say 'thank you'. Is it him on the door outside?"

"And on the bedposts," Uncle Tom replied. I took a few steps nearer to the large four-poster bed that stood between us in the centre of the room. Reaching up I ran my hand down one of the corner posts, marvelling again at the intricacy and beauty of the design. Each post looked like it bore a slightly different image – here the magnificent tail wrapped cleverly around the slender wooden column. The drapes were of fine muslin – in natural daylight they would, I thought, have been white. It was a beautiful bed. And he didn't need to tell me for me to know that it was Mia's.

"I have something for you," Uncle Tom declared, in a sudden change of direction. "Though in truth they are not really mine to give. Still, I think Mia would like you to have them." He made to stand up again out of the chair. Then, with a small, involuntary cry, his arm gave way beneath him. In an instant I was there beside him, my inhibitions abandoned on the other side of the room.

"Does it hurt?" I asked him anxiously. "Can I help?" I touched his arm tentatively.

His head was bowed and I noticed how thin and sparse his hair was compared to Pod's. When he looked up his eyes were full of tears. Had I thought for an instant, I might perhaps have behaved differently. But, as Lizzie constantly grinned, that wasn't my way. Kneeling up beside the chair, I threw my arms around my sad Uncle Tom.

I felt his shoulders shaking underneath my embrace and I held on tighter as if I could squeeze the sadness out of him with willing it. And then I was afraid I might be hurting him and so I relaxed back a little and took his hand instead. With the other hand he took a handkerchief out of his pocket – we always teased Pod that he was the only man alive who carried a pocket handkerchief – and pressed it, for a moment, to his face.

"I am sorry, carina," he said huskily, "it has been so long, I have forgotten how to be."

"What can I do?" I asked him earnestly. "Should I fetch Giuliana?"

Though it was small and wry, the smile lit up his whole face. Suddenly he was no longer an old man and for the first time I could see that he was my father's brother. "No thank you!" he chuckled. And I grinned too.

"The journals are in the box over there," he said, pointing shakily to the wall opposite. "Would you bring them to me?"

I stood up and collected the battered, shoebox-sized box from the top of the small bookshelf. On the lid was inscribed in large hand-written letters: *'ART THINGS'*. Placing it onto his lap, I was about to sit down on the floor beside him when I caught sight of the large shuttered window. I looked back at Uncle Tom. For an instant he hesitated, then nodded his consent. The windows creaked begrudgingly as I opened them just far enough to allow me to push back the shutters. I leant out and fastened them one by one to the wall, lest they too should show their discontent by slamming shut at the first opportunity.

My eyes ached a little at their sudden liberation from the gloaming, but it wasn't until I drew back into the room that I was conscious of the transformation. Uncle Tom sat blinking in the dazzling light. A myriad cobwebs billowed out from beam to beam on the playful wind. The muslin drapes, yellow-tinged with age, fluttered coquettishly against the bedposts, and where before the room had been painted in a subtle palette of innumerable greens now it was a riot of colour. The ivory bedspread was bejewelled with tiny red rosebuds. The rug on the floor at Uncle Tom's feet was rich with the colours of the Raj, deep reds and plums and golds that drew the light down into themselves so that they seemed almost alive with colour. The walls were not merely painted, but were hung with fabric, a wine-red silk, that reflected back the radiant light with its own glorious sheen. It was a room not of the 'real' world but of the land of fairytale, of knights on white chargers, unicorns, far-eastern princes with brocade coats and half-moon swords – and, I thought sadly, of a beautiful maiden, a damsel in distress, imprisoned for all eternity in her ivory tower... My imagination feasted indulgently on the extraordinary scene.

'Hello Mia,' I whispered inside my head. 'If you are ready to tell your story, I am ready to listen...'

Disturbing the dust as little as possible, I made myself comfortable on the thickly piled rug. From the top of the box, Uncle Tom drew out two

193

books. Each was similarly, and beautifully, bound in a striking combination of chocolate brown leather and the most decorative 'marbled' paper. But it was what was inside that took my breath away. As he had handed me the first without a word, I had sensed my uncle's eager anticipation of my response. And I was not to disappoint him. Alternately looking down at a page and then back up at Uncle Tom's now-shining eyes in wonderment, I was, at first, lost for words. The book was filled with the most exquisite pictures, page after page of watercolours and pen-and-ink drawings. Seed-pods and flowers, grasses, mosses, tree-bark and buds – the natural world reproduced in the tiniest detail, so that I could almost smell the blowsy rose, touch the wrinkled bark, feel the feathery dandelion seed tickling across my cheek.

"Are they Mia's?" My voice was hardly more than a breath. I had seen so many works of art at the gallery over the years and knew enough to recognise that these were quite extraordinary. Uncle Tom nodded simply but I could tell that he was pleased, even proud, at my response. He handed me the second book. Though this time I felt I was more prepared for what lay within, still the contents made me gasp. Here it was the animate world – butterflies, moths, tiny lizards seeming almost to squirm off the page, grumpy old toads, leaf-green caterpillars – that flew, wriggled and crawled their way through the sheets of ivory vellum. Each illustration was a thing to marvel at, providing innumerable new insights into the miraculous world around me. Surely, with so much life teeming inside it, the very book might, at any moment, scurry off into the undergrowth!

"She had a gift." Again I sensed a pride in his recognition of Mia's remarkable talent. I nodded my agreement, still struggling to find the words. "They should be seen," I managed finally. "Not hidden away up here like this."

And Uncle Tom replied that since they now belonged to me, their fate was in my hands. I pictured each of the individual images mounted and framed. Could there be an exhibition? I wondered excitedly. At the gallery? 'Life' by Amelia-Anne Beresford Linnel, it could be called – with printed postcards as invitations and posters to show to full effect the beauty of her work. How I longed to show Pod! And then it occurred to me.

"Does my father know?" I asked. "About these, I mean, and how extraordinary they are?" I felt suddenly deflated. My consciousness of the sadness of it all came stealing back in with the thought of my father.

And then Uncle Tom took me back with him thirty-three years to when the books were new and their pristine pages could only have dreamt of the part they were to play in such beauty. She had been twelve years old when she went into hiding from the world, overcome by fear and shame. What, I wondered sorrowfully, could she possibly have done for shame to entreat her to hide away from the vibrant, miraculous world that she loved so much? Uncle Tom didn't tell me. But he did tell me of his daily pilgrimage to the lordly peacock door that stood sentry between them. It was God's world beyond her window, she said. And God would not want her anymore. But she couldn't let go entirely. So he brought God's world to her, little by little. "Bring me something new," she had whispered through the keyhole. And he would leave it for her; the fragrant rose, the silver-green olive spray, the reedy grasses that only minutes before had been whispering on the wind. He caught tiny insects in clear glass jars, rescued toads from the high-sided swimming pool beyond the terrace and abducted fat caterpillars that still clung tenaciously to their hole-y leaf – to inspire her pen and fuel her needy spirit with life. Whilst Giuliana brought her food to sustain her frail little body, he brought her the world to nourish her fragile soul.

For almost three years they had fought to free her from the dark. Until one day her whisper never came and he knew that the battle was over. They buried Mia still wrapped in the shroud of guilt and shame that had smothered her. They talked in hushed voices about forgiveness and sin. When all the time it was they who danced with the demons. And he knew that he would never forgive them.

Then he had finished telling me and we were both crying and I hugged those books close to my own, so-alive body and loved her. My eyes were full of tears so I didn't see it coming and, when it came to me, it was like a stab in my heart. My father had left her, shut away up here without the light! He had gone to France to paint mountains and beaches whilst his little sister was dying inside. And, in some way, knowing that was every bit as unbearable as knowing she had died, and my tears flowed still more freely as I tried to understand.

"Don't blame him." Uncle Tom's voice was gentle and calm. How had he known the colour of my thoughts? "I have spent too long in anger, looking for someone to blame. It threatened to take us all, the dark, and it is no wonder we could not see our way."

Then I knew that I had still not reached the heart. But I was afraid to know and so I gave my faith back to my father and, for now, dried my eyes. We sat there quietly together, my Uncle Tom and I, sharing our sadness. How much time went by I couldn't say – ten minutes, maybe more – until he reminded me that they would be missing me downstairs before long. I had almost forgotten that there was a living world down there, with a breakfast table, jam pots, milk and cheese.

He gestured then to the piles of paper scattered about the floor, some half-hidden beneath the bedstead, others slightly torn or crumpled where an inadvertent footstep had caught them unawares. "Would you read them for me, *carina*? They were written for her, long ago. Perhaps, you and I together, little by little, can finally set her free..."

I picked up the pile nearest to me. '*The Kingdom of Celador*' I read aloud. My heart quickened. "Are they fairy-tales?" I asked.

"To us they were real," he answered, tired now. "Will you gather them now while I sleep and take them with you?" He settled back in his chair and closed his eyes. Silently, I set about collecting together the papers, careful to distinguish between each separate batch. Amongst the loose leaves I spotted a leather bound journal – more stories? I marvelled, already amazed by the reams of hand-written pages full of magic. I let the book fall open and began to read...

Chapter Forty-Seven

'*The temperature in the car was almost overwhelming,*' I read. '*Mother would turn awkwardly and glance back at us all now and again as we squirmed uncomfortably on the hot seats, our bare legs repeatedly sticking and unsticking to the malevolent black vinyl. The anxiety on her face, we knew, was as much a warning to us not to irritate our already irascible father as concern for our well-being in the increasingly insufferable heat. We needed no added inducement to avoid inflaming him further. Fear was enough.*'

I glanced across at Uncle Tom. His head was lolled sleepily to one side. Almost despite myself I turned back to the book.

'*The journey from home to London was always a forlorn one. Two days trapped 'en famille' in such a confined space was never going to be fun but on that occasion our spirits were as low as they could go. Though how often we had felt that that was so only to find that our capacity for joylessness had only just begun to be tapped...*

To add to the usual tensions, Father had had news from the gallery concerning an important sale – the little we knew of the situation we gleaned from our nightly vigils listening on the staircase – and clearly the news was not good...'

As I read, the walls of the room seemed to draw in around me. And then I was there with them inside the peculiar little car, with the tensions and the heat, and I knew that I had to discover where we were going.

'*It always took a good few days to make the 1000-or-so mile journey in our small, aged Fiat. At nightfall we would pull in at a small roadside 'auberge' – a number along the way were, by now, regular stopping points. We would look out for familiar sights and sounds as we forged our way across the ever-changing landscape. We marvelled silently at the endless horizon beyond the sea at Cannes, the rust red rock of the Esterel mountains, the undulating fields of sunflowers laid out in vast blankets along the roadside and, as we did so, sent our spirits out of the cramped, suffocating car to wade in the bubbling brook beside the mill, to dance*

197

in the heavily scented fields of lavender, to feast on the ripe plums that hung plump and succulent from their too-spindly trees...Then it was back across the grey and grimy sea to England, calling back our spirits to be locked close inside our tight little hearts once more for fear of the Demons lurking in the shadows that loomed around the next corner...

This time, though, progress was even slower than usual. The acrid smell of burnt rubber, at first a mere tickle in the nose, was becoming increasingly difficult to ignore. Every so often father would pull over to the side of the road and 'rest' the 'straining clutch' whilst he got out of the car and paced back and forth, drawing, tight-lipped, on yet another cigarette. Finally, not long after Aix, where the road became ever steeper, the 'straining clutch', like our father, reached breaking point. As we all tumbled out onto the grassy bank, our happy lungs celebrating their reprieve from the intense, choking confinement of the car it was clear that this, for now, was the end of the road...

For us, the opportunity to stretch our legs was a welcome one. We filled our gasping lungs with honey-scented air, running and scrambling over ancient granite rocks as though with each step we were leaving him behind forever. Until the farmhand passed by along the twisty-twiney track, peered hopelessly beneath our bonnet and bundled us all into his rickety old trailer for the three or four miles to the farmhouse across the way. And there we feasted on still-warm bread, honey and cheese and the knowledge that our father was going on to England by train without us, so for seven long days we would be free...

Later, as the rumbling old tractor disappeared down the lane carrying our father off and away, to us it was a magic carpet, borne on the wings of all that is right and good... He was gone and never to return and where there had been fear and pain there would forever-after be joy and celebration... The late evening sun cast a warm-blush light over all and we knew that this golden land was enchanted and that we would never leave. The kingdom, I told them, was called 'Celador', but to all who lived there it was 'Cielolino' – 'little heaven' – and, from that moment on, all of our old world was shrivelled and burnt to dust. Here there would forever be flowers beneath our feet. Flowers that were really stars that God planted deep down in the earth when the world began, so that there would always be light in the darkness and no-one need ever be afraid.'

For an instant, I forgot how to breathe. How did he know about the flowers, the flowers deep down in the earth that were really stars?! It was my father who had told me. Once upon a time. How they were so far down that even when we dug over our little vegetable plot to plant the onions or when I pressed my finger far down into the soft rich soil to bury the first bean of that year's crop, even that was not far down deep enough... But if I closed my eyes tightly I could see them shining oh so brightly in the deep dark earth beneath my feet and forever when I walked there would always be the flowers, and a lightness in my step and beauty in my heart...

And all at once I realised how I *really* knew about the flowers and that I had known Uncle Tom all along. But I'd never really known about the dark.

'My name,' the journal went on, 'henceforth was Leo, like the lion, and I was a strong and invincible knight who guarded the palace gates which were built of spun sugar in a more intricate and lovely design than you can possibly imagine...

'I,' Paul announced in a deep, measured voice, 'am Olivier, right-hand man to the king; respected throughout the land for my wisdom and my noble spirit. And you,' he told Mia, 'are the beautiful and mysterious Princess Katia. I am honoured to be at your service.'

Our little sister performed a shaky half-pirouette, a balletic spin that she practised rigorously at every given opportunity. When she was a prima-ballerina, she would say, she would travel the world and so delicately fleeting would each appearance be that no-one (she didn't need to tell us who she really meant) would ever be able to find her.

'No', she replied resolutely, 'I am Mirabelle and I live in a little house in the woods and all the animals and birds are my friends. And when I eat my breakfast the squirrels sit at the doorway and eat beechnuts that they have found in the wood beneath the trees. And when I carry out my washing the swifts swoop down with a long, green vine in their beaks and wind it between the apple trees so that I can hang out my dresses in the sunshine. And when I want to look my best the butterflies that dance around the garden settle in my hair and look pretty...And when...'

'Alright, alright,' I laughed and then we all laughed and we realised that we hadn't forgotten how and that in this new world the only law was that you had to laugh until your sides ached for at least an hour a day. 'You are Mirabelle...'

And perhaps I should have guessed, long before she told me all those years later, that, for our new, golden world she chose a name she thought was like 'Miracle'...'

I was aware of the smooth rise and fall of my chest with each slow, expansive breath. Regular, instinctive, almost hypnotic. And altogether separate from me. My mind, where, after all that I had seen and heard, I might have expected turmoil and disarray, was strangely calm, even peaceful. As if there was so much that there was nothing. The eye of the storm. Then I must have stood up, because the book was there neatly on the table by the bed and I was walking towards the door. Under my arm was a large bundle of old papers. My hand was reaching out...

"Amelia-Anne." I turned, surprised. His head was bowed and his eyes, I think, were still closed, but the words were clear and resolute.

"Tell your father I am sorry..."

Chapter Forty-Eight

It must have been because I was still with Mia that I wasn't really there at the breakfast table that morning. I watched it all from a distance – the milk jug roaming up and down the table, Bacchus curled up peaceably at Jamie's feet (he really does have a miraculous way with animals) – and Lizzie's shining eyes as she read and re-read to herself the letter from Ben. From afar, I was glad for her. First thing each morning she wheeled hopefully out to the large metal post-box that was built into a brick column a short way down the drive. Despite her aching, until now the box had always been empty; save, that is, for its resident lizard, Lucius Maximus, (Jamie had been doing Roman history shortly before we left). The post, Pod would remind her sympathetically, took at least three days from England, so she mustn't be disappointed. And she would count the hours until tomorrow... Well, Lucius must have had a big surprise that morning as, for the first time in thirty years, Giuliana said, a letter had undoubtedly arrived! In fact, were it even simply bound, this letter might reasonably be described as a tome. Poor Lucius must have thought the sky was falling in. Still, Lizzie was delighted and that was what really mattered.

A fortuitous side-effect of all this excitement was that nobody thought to ask me why I was late down to table. And Lizzie was much too distracted to even raise a quizzical eyebrow at me about my absence when she woke. So the other world went on around me whilst I attempted to make sense of the one inside my head. Gradually the surreal feeling of calm was being replaced by a disconcerting volley of incoherent thoughts. How much I had to understand before I could even begin to reconcile myself to what I had learned. I tried to lay down the implications of Tom's words, both written and spoken, in an ordered and objective way. For once I attempted to put Rationality before Emotion. It was, I told myself firmly, a question of fitting together all the pieces. And I tried not to hear the other voice that whispered 'all you really want to do is cry'.

About one thing there could be no doubt. At the heart of the darkness stood Grandpa Beresford-Linnel. As Tom had described their journey across France, the fear and hatred of his father had been almost palpable. I recalled Pod's anger and defiance at the mere mention of his name. I thought too about the way in which his childhood had remained for so long a secret, even from his own family. And I imagined the pain. And then, too soon, I felt Emotion welling up behind my eyes, so I sent it back deep-down inside until I could afford to set it free. And Mia, was her fear of her father really so great that she had chosen to die over dancing through the living world she loved so much? For that was what it was, I knew now. A choice. And how much more than death there was in suicide.

My heart ached. Emotion was very close at hand. I thought of my love for Pod. Of my certainty of his love for me and my knowledge that both would go on forever. Was there anything that he could do or say to me that would change that surety?

And then, like a ghastly spectre it rose up out of the dark and the confusion. And I remembered the haunted eyes of the mad, sad Lucius Pomeroy and I knew that he knew too.

I hardly heard the crash as my chair fell away behind me. And then I was out of the door and running and running as if, like little Mia as she 'whirled', I could leave the 'knowing' far behind me.

My father found me much later at the old tennis court, because it was a place that I knew would understand sadness. Its red-brown surface had long-ago been abandoned to a state of disrepair that, when I had first discovered it on our arrival, I had thought romantic. That evening it was simply sad. The disused net sagged despondently, yearning for the sound of animated laughter and the amiably inane 'poc' 'poc' 'poc' of the tennis balls that once fuelled its spirit. And I drew on its yearning to help me cry. Then, as the pain, along with the light, began to fade, I knew that it was a place for ghosts, not for the living, and that just for a while I hadn't been sure where I belonged. And, as my father appeared across the meadow to take me home, I was already standing up to meet him – and to take his hand...

We were many hours together that night, Pod and I, in the little 'salotino' that had become our confidant and friend. It wasn't something that was talked about then, he said quietly. Not like now. So that meant that it didn't happen. Like drug abuse, depression or sex before marriage. 'Paedophilia'. When he said the word we couldn't look at it – or at each other. It hung there in the space between us. A fancy term for something so terrible and base.

Where the boys were concerned, he had not so much raped their bodies as their minds, forcing them to be complicit in scenes so unnatural that, when they were finally alone, they got down on their knees and prayed that they might be blinded when they woke.

I thought I had been carrying 'the knowing' with me all day, but somehow it was very different having it confirmed. And by my father. Tall, strong, invincible Pod – how difficult it was to even imagine him being a small, vulnerable child, let alone suffering such terrible abuse at the hands of someone who ought only to have loved him. I struggled hard with the grotesque images that I could not keep from rising up out of the darkest receses of my imagination. My head resisted merging the two Paul Beresford-Linnels, the adult and the vulnerable child, into the one that was Pod. So they stayed separate. But they were both there beside me in the room.

They had made a pact then, the three of them – Paul, Tom and Mia – that they would never speak of it. In the real world there was nowhere for them to run. So instead they would find a place inside to send the demons and create another land that was far beyond their reach. And Tom discovered Celador so that they always had somewhere to run to; even when the door was locked and, either through force or fear, their legs were pinned down beneath them.

Just listening to Pod's tale, I found myself longing to run there too – to the land where there was always light in the darkness and no-one need ever be afraid.

He was a monster, I said, Grandpa Beresford-Linnel. And Pod nodded sadly. But sometimes, he confessed, he hated Nonna Sofia even more. For knowing and standing idly by. At his words, new horrors entered the room, to flit and screech about our heads. She knew! A monster was living in her house, little by little devouring her children, body and soul, and she did nothing! And that was even more incomprehensible than the thing itself, and my mind reeled and my hand reached out for Pod to know that he was still there.

And Lucius? I asked then, needing to know. Pod bowed his head and rested his face in his hands. One day their father had been careless, he said. And shy, good-hearted Lucius Pomeroy had stumbled in on a scene so terrible that drip by drip it would bleed away his sanity. He did try to save them. But instead it cost him his reputation and his life. The priest arrived the following morning. Grandpa Beresford-Linnel and Nonna

203

Sofia smiled graciously and told him, 'in confidence, of course', all about Lucius and their suspicions that he had 'unlawful desires' for their little Mia. Even in their 'sorrow' and 'distress', they were, as always, the epitome of respectability and charm. What chance did a young, impoverished tutor stand against such a bastion of propriety and softly-spoken moral principle? And the priest drew his breath and took their hands sympathetically – whilst the children cried behind their 'best-behaviour-faces' and knew that if even God was fooled then they could never be free...

Pod had told Nathalie, he said then. Through the night, after he had forbidden me to see Uncle Tom. He knew me too well to imagine that I would leave things at that and, somewhere buried beneath his shame, he knew that it was time to stop running. Even more than the shame, it was the guilt that he had worn, like a hair-shirt, for almost thirty years. A guilt born, as he saw it, out of the cowardice that led him to abandon his younger brother and sister to their fate. He did not need Tom's anger to bring home to him the selfishness of his flight all those years ago. Nathalie understood, he said, that this was really just the beginning. That the healing would be long and arduous, may even take a lifetime. But they would do it together. And I was glad to know that they had shared it.

For a while then, we just sat, my father and I. The night was quiet and still. Rather than harbouring the demons, the dark beyond our window was keeping benevolent guard. The cool air still carried the scent of honey and roses when I slipped easily from my chair to be at Pod's feet. My head and forearms rested on his knees; his hand lay gently on my hair. When it came, the knock at the door was low and rhythmic. Two short raps and a long one. And by the time Uncle Tom had touched Pod's hand I was already slipping softly out of the room...

Chapter Forty-Nine

It was nearly two months before I was able to tell Alessandro. We were sitting together in the shadow of the broad shelf of granite that marked the highest point of the hillside, in the hope of some reprieve from the intense, sticky August heat. Now and then we raised our sun-flushed faces to the welcome breeze that wafted beneath the stone. In the weeks since that night when Pod and Uncle Tom finally stepped out of the shadows, I had wanted often to share it with him. At first it was the horror that had held me back. Then, following on at its grotesque heels, came the shame. I struggled hard, then, to reconcile myself not merely to the monstrosity itself but to the fact that it was born and harboured within my own family.

Alessandro's disgust was only to be expected. The vehemence of his anger took me by surprise. 'From four years old...' he had muttered over and over in his fury. And the thought of such innocence lost was beyond bearing. But I think it was only as he swept up little Aisling in his arms and held on to her and her giggling vulnerability with all his might that it fully 'hit home'. I cried then, as he stroked my hair, so hard that my whole body shook with the grief and the pain. And this time, when the crying was over, something deep-down was changed. When I looked inside me, the shame was gone. Though the horror, I suspected, would stay with me for always, the past was no longer looming large and terrible over all. As I breathed in deep of the soft, warm air, I was breathing in 'today' instead of 'yesterday'.

And there was so much, I saw then, to celebrate about today. 'La Casa Cieca' had truly opened its eyes to the world. And how it loved what it saw! As Alessandro, Aisling and I made our way back across the hillside to my family and my home, I found my pace quickening with my heart. And then I was running, faster and faster until I was breathless and laughing. It was Uncle Tom I saw first, sitting in the dappled shade beneath a vast, ancient pine, paper and pen in hand and a broad smile on his face.

"It's almost finished!" he called out delightedly across the meadow, his waving hand clutching a single page that gleamed white and dazzling where it caught the midday sun. The play, we had decided, would be a comedy, with a generous sprinkling of magic and fairytale. Like 'Midsummer Night's Dream' I had declared excitedly and Uncle Tom had chuckled and said modestly that he would do his best to oblige. The antique puppet theatre was almost under new management. Through my afternoons at Theo's emporium I had paid off more than two thirds of the, much reduced, price that was finally agreed. It had already been decided that we would invite its original owner, the Contessa Borodini to our debut performance. Theo had agreed to collect her from the crumbling house in the Perugian hills – and I rather suspected he was looking forward to it.

The wonderful old shop had almost become a second home for Lizzie, Jamie and me. We had, he said, 'moved mountains'. For Jamie the mere fact of the rummaging was incentive enough and he had leapt gleefully upon the challenge of designing a spreadsheet and catalogue for the gallery stock. Secretly, however, Pod had agreed with Theo that he would match whatever Jamie earned euro for euro to contribute towards the high-spec mountain bike that, in the absence of wings or a vintage Aston Martin, no secret agent should be without. For Lizzie – plaster cast off and raring to go – the rewards were more cerebral. She was exchanging her hours for those of the wizard himself, who, it transpired, when he wasn't taming unicorns, was a much respected expert in Etruscan history. To cap it all, Ben was arriving the following week for the remainder of the summer. So you see we were, all in our different ways, very happy.

And perhaps none more so than our extraordinary parents. As I watched them that day crossing the parched late-summer field hand in hand, I wondered how I could ever have doubted their love for each other. Though I knew they had a long road to travel down when it came to Pod's putting the past to rest, I had no doubt that together they would make the journey. Knowing that he was simultaneously having to come to terms with his brother's increasing frailty and ill-health was unbearably poignant for us all. Still, though it might have seemed that time was not on their side, each precious week spent reunited with Tom would, I knew, stay with my father for always.

But for now we are all together on that sunny lawn. That's me, Apricot, over there beneath the pine trees with the freckles and the wide grin. Lizzie and Jamie are running out of the house to announce lunch. Bacchus the goat skips closely alongside. And our Uncle Tom surveys the happy world around him, smiling in the knowledge that at long last his house has become a home.

Epilogue

Still now I pass by Uncle Tom's tree most days, though *Castel di Sopra* is no longer officially my home. After we were married, Alessandro and I, we moved into one of the old farm-workers cottages on the Pittini hillside. Alex set to fixing the roof, whilst I cleared a sunny patch of the tiny walled plot to grow tomatoes and *zuccini* and a row of fat broad beans.

The walk from there to our 'castle' – no-one will ever call it 'blind' again – is a happy one, calling back those early days and reminding me of the progress we have made in the ten years since. The two farms, ours and the Pittini, are managed together now, with Alessandro and his father at the helm and Pod – with Jamie when he's home from university – learning all the time. Our olive oil won a local prize last year and with each passing season the vineyard shows more flourish.

Will she love it all as I do, my little Mia, who kicks and squirms inside even as she hears her name? How much I will have to show and tell her as the past continues to relinquish its lessons and the future calls us brightly on...

For now, though, I will bring my story to a close, with a recollection more about beginnings than about the end. Still, it is, for me, an inextricable part of that extraordinary summer and I hope that in its telling, I will leave you with a sense, if not that what we learned then was a good thing, then at least the knowledge that without the darkness the light would never shine so bright...

It was just over a year after you left us there in the meadow that the parcel arrived at our door. We had returned to Paultons Square, Pod and I, just for a while. Pod was in the process of interviewing candidates for the role of manager at Beresford's. To the immense delight of all, he had decided to hand over the reins of the gallery in the interests of 'my family and my heritage'. Work had already begun on the immense task of restoring the *Castel di Sopra* estate to its former glory. Nature, we knew, would set its own pace where the neglected vines and olive trees were concerned, but we were already seeing things springing to new life.

It was early October and whilst Italy lounged lackadaisically in the last lazy days of summer, in England autumn had well and truly blustered his way onto the scene. I sat on the broad window seat looking out on the world that used to be my home. The rain ran in impatient rivulets down the pane. As if in a desperate bid for my attention, the trees in the square were waving wildly up at me in the wind. For me there had always been something melancholy about this season of the year – a sense that the earth was in perpetual mourning for a golden time that would never come again. And now too it was about Uncle Tom.

It had been almost a year before that we had buried him. The first leaves were beginning to fall, spiralling skittishly down onto the narrow coffin as they laid him to rest. Though we had known that he was dying, it still took us by surprise. In those final hazy days of summer we had thought we were invincible – that in our 'togetherness' we could take on the world. But death, as Mrs Rainier said, as I sat at her feet as of old and told her a tale of secrets and revelations, darkness and light, 'will have his way'.

And I nodded sagely and was still no closer to understanding why some of us have a whole lifetime and others only a few chapters. All I knew for sure was that however much of my story I got to live, I would make it a good one.

Which, when I think about it, was really why I was there, packing my trunk for the first day of the university term. Actually I was re-packing my trunk, hoping that the third time around everything would be infinitely smaller so that I might be able to shut the lid. I recall wondering, as I crammed one wellington boot into the last available space, how the ancient mariners had managed it. At least I was only away for three months – they, on the other hand, had to bear in mind not just the first few weeks at sea but the subsequent ten years shipwrecked on a desert island. Well, there was nothing for it. If it rained I would have to hop.

I was just wondering how I was going to convey the trunk down the numerous flights of stairs, when Pod called up to my room. Had I seen the parcel? he was inquiring, rather too nonchalantly to be convincing.

Recklessly abandoning all my worldly goods, I thundered down to the entrance hall. And there it was. Whilst there's no doubt that, in comparison to the string-wrapped brown paper parcel, the humble 'jiffy bag' is somewhat lacking in the 'magical intrigue' department, this one did have my name on it, in florid hand-written script, which went a long way to compensating for its otherwise prosaic appearance. Who could be sending me a parcel? And how did they know I would be there? I tore excitedly across the 'easy-access' strip.

If I told you that it was from Uncle Tom would you be as surprised as I was? Perhaps if I explain, as I learned from the letter that accompanied the slim leather-bound book, that he had started writing 'The Fairy-Tale' for me the day that he and I first made our stand together against the demons, you will, like me, be able to follow its path from pen to publication. I had reminded him, he said, that though it is sometimes hard to see the light in the deep-down dark, it is always there waiting. And you will understand why it made me cry when he told me that I had been the key to opening the door and setting Mia free... free...

THE WINDOW OF FAR AND WIDE

BY TOM BERESFORD-LINNEL
ILLUSTRATED
BY P.O.D. BERESFORD-LINNEL

THE WINDOW OF FAR AND WIDE

It wasn't so much that the peacock spoke to her that took Mia by surprise but that he had found her at all. Her attic bedroom was too far and away from the Real World and no-one before had managed to break the spell. And oh! how strange, the little round-paned window that might have been his only entrance remained resolutely shut, its veil of cobwebs whispering still of the lost years and of the spiders who were her only companions.

But then of course, she reasoned (in so far as you can reason about enchantment, which this happened to be), peacocks aren't from the Real World and they have a magic all their own…

And they do have surprisingly big feet.

From Mia's perspective, lying, as she was, on her tummy under the mighty oak bed, the peacock might have been all feet if it wasn't for the astonishing sweep of tail feathers that followed them, casting, as they did so, myriad particles of dust up into the shaft of light that shone soft but triumphant through the circular glass; (though perhaps if she had asked him he might have told her it was only the magic

shimmering in his wake...). As she watched, the Light and the Tail admired each other immensely, each luxuriating in the other's otherworldly beauty. And in doing so they enhanced still further their own glory: each colour in the mighty tail, with the Light's caress, was not one but infinite – purple, green, gold and every nuance in between. And the Light, with the feathers to woo, was still more a magician of wonders, a conjuror of miracles...

Mia's thirsty soul, so long shut up in a small dark box and thus denied the awe and wonder that are its sustenance, drank in the scene before her. She wriggled a little further out from under the bed, her curiosity getting the better of her fears. With each wriggle she was rewarded with another inch or two of the peacock's magnificent form and, with such a shimmering prize, became still bolder... As such when he spoke again this time, it was to a small, white face that peeped out from beneath the deep red fringe of the overhanging bedspread.

"Hello Mia," he repeated, in a strange honking tone, quite undeserving of its handsome speaker. Mia's eyes, already large and dark, widened further.

"I am here at the bidding of the wind," he told her.

And Mia nodded. She knew the wind well. Each day as he passed by, this way or that, he tapped his greeting on the small round window by prior arrangement with the ancient creeper that fingered out across its pane.

"And of the rain," he went on, "who drums your tale onto the grand glass roof of the conservatory below your room, and whispers of your sadness in the leaves of the stately beeches in the grounds beyond."

Mia nodded again.

"And of the sunlight," the peacock continued, "who longs to venture beyond the narrow sphere of this tiny pane, to press further into the shadows and show them the warmth and joy that light can bring…"

And as he spoke, of these, her friends, Mia became emboldened.

"But why did you come?" she asked of him, her voice thin and small, as if it had almost forgotten how to be.

"Because there have been too many years lost," he answered. "It is time that the spell be broken. The Real World is waiting for you and I have been sent to show you the way back…"

With this Mia's eyes narrowed and she shrank back a little into the shadows, now so familiar as to have become her refuge…

Some minutes passed in silence before, from the safety of her hiding place, she spoke again; "This is My World." she said, for so long ago was the spell cast that she could remember no other. And she did not know why she felt afraid.

"We will show you another," he replied gently, as he understood her fears. "The one that lies beyond your window. The one where the sky goes on forever and anything is possible. The one in which you truly belong."

The kindness in his voice drew Mia out a little

further once more. And she felt a strange kind of yearning from deep inside.

"But I cannot leave this room," she said aloud, as much to herself as to her visitor. "The enchantment is ancient and powerful and this is all I know." But even as she spoke, the yearning grew stronger, and whispered 'half-rememberings' of another world, long since lost, danced somewhere just beyond her reasoning.

"We will weave you a window, a 'Window of Far and Wide'... he answered her. "I and the friends who have for so long looked in at your window and willed you to be free once more. And through that Window the Real World will come to you. Its glory and its shadows, its wonders and its trials will fill this sad and lonely room with Living until your spirit is dancing and your heart is strong and you are ready to find your own place in the life beyond these walls..."

And with that the mighty bird did not stay for an answer but rose up as if by magic (which of course it was) to the little round window that we have spoken

of before. Taking the small iron handle in his curved silver beak he craned his long neck, and with a sudden jolt the hinge gave way, happy after so many years to stretch his stiff old joints. And as the window opened wide so the room breathed deep and long of the air that flooded joyously inside. And Mia wondered at its teasing caress as it buffeted, warm and soft, against her cheek and coaxed a smile where none had been for more years than she could remember…

The peacock saw the smile and held it close in his breast and knew that the magic was truly beginning. Then, even before that smile had faded, he conjured the next of his miracles. Through the window came the birds, flitting and dancing on the breeze that was still finding new, uncharted places into which to breath its life. One by one they came, willing and eager to be a part of the enchantment that would see Mia back in the lush green beauty of their world once more.

So overwhelmed were Mia's long-dimmed senses by the sights and sounds before her that, at first, she was afraid and even uttered a tiny cry, part astonishment, part fear and part wonder. And the peacock heard the wonder in her cry and knew that the magic was truly beginning…

And, in case there might be any doubt in that, behind each of the birds, held fast in their tiny beaks, stretched what to Mia looked like the most delicate, slender threads. Some were so pale and fine as to be visible only when the Light touched upon their radiant beauty, others were stronger looking, either in colour or form, but all were accompanied by an aura of white-gold that spoke graciously of a higher world than ours...

As the birds began a strange and intricate dance above her head, their fluttering wings stirring the air about her until Mia's heart, roused to emotions it had long-ago resigned itself to forget, danced and fluttered with them, so she asked of the Peacock:

"What do they do as they dance and swoop?"

"They are weaving your Window," he answered her. "The Window that will show you the way back. Though the threads that they weave are blessed by a higher power each of them is born of the Real World, each alone is precious but together, intricately bound, they are beyond price."

At some point during this exchange, though she could not tell you when it happened if you asked her, Mia found herself sliding out of the shadows beneath the bed and sitting cross-legged at its foot, all the better to observe the activity around her. Her face with new-found animation turned upwards and, from deep inside her dark eyes, shone with a tentative remembering of being alive.

"And that one?" she asked him of a particularly beautiful thread as it spun overhead. "What is it that gleams so golden and bright?"

"That is Joy," he answered her, "and it is beautiful indeed. But it shines so particularly bright as it is entwined with Goodness which gives Joy a purity and intensity that it cannot attain alone."

"The thread beside them, carried by the orange-beaked blackbird," he went on, "is Truth."

Mia looked up at the strong, vibrant thread that snaked confidently in and out of those around it, seeming to lend its own light to others as it went.

"There are many indistinct threads that pose as Truth," the peacock warned as she marvelled, "though once you have seen it in its purest form you can never mistake it."

Mia found herself resolving to know always the difference between Truth and its shadowy counterfeits.

Then: "The blue," she said, pointing to another shining strand, "of that one is just like the blue of the sky." And as she spoke she felt, just for a moment, less afraid of the vast canopy of blue that she knew went on forever, up and beyond the small round patch that peeped in through her attic window. "And this one (she reached up irresistibly to touch the gleaming thread as it passed above her head) is the bright new-green of the first spring leaves on the vine outside my window."

"But what is that one?" she asked, a small frown creasing across her forehead as she considered a coarse, dark yarn that contrasted so blackly with the light, luminous threads she had so far seen.

"Well," the peacock informed her, "the blue thread

is Honour and the yellow-green of spring buds unfurled is Wonder. The gleaming amethyst threads beneath the attic beams are Awe and the shimmering silver are tiny slivers of Miracle, all strong, precious and beautiful. But the black thread has an equally important role to play in the Real World, though it may not be pleasing to the eye or uplifting for the spirit. The black thread is Despair and without it or those similarly drear strands, Pain, Suffering, Sadness and Misery, the other threads would not shine so true and bright. Only when they are all inextricably bound is their true glory revealed, and it is only through that glory that the human soul can set out on its journey towards the Higher Realm..."

And Mia took his words down deep inside and pondered them and knew that as she did so something within her was changing...

All about her was life and colour, movement and song. Mia's long-neglected spirit could not fail to be moved and, almost despite itself (so long had it known only fear and mistrust), it sat up and shook itself like a dog shaking water droplets from its shaggy coat, irresistibly drawn into this new, animated world.

THE WINDOW OF FAR AND WIDE

But still the legacy of the evil spell remained, even as her spirit rejoiced, so Mia found herself bound by the ties of the terrible enchantment. That awful day now so long ago – was it years or months? time had no meaning in the realm of the enchanted – when the world outside was shut out and the very thought of its vast Unknown would forever fill Mia with dread and fear, still loomed large and ominous over all. Though she could no longer recall the moment or the nature of its casting, the Spell had permeated so deeply that it had taken her head and heart and made them its own. As its dark magic stole again across her heart, so the very instincts that drew her into the colourful scene around her made her wary and chill. Shuddering, she withdrew a little into the familiar 'safety' of the shadows, uncurling her crossed legs and sliding them back behind her under the mighty oak bed.

And it was then that she noticed them. The spiders, her day and night companions who, even when she could not see them, were always at her side, reassuring Mia that she was never truly alone. Dancing a strange and intricate dance, they went

about their task with diligence and purpose. But what, Mia wondered aloud, is it that they are setting about with such resolve?

"Ah," the peacock smiled, as much to himself as to Mia, as he was secretly glad that Fear had not completely routed Curiosity, "if we are to break this enchantment then their role is perhaps the most important of all..."

"The thread which they weave is Hope and without it the spell can never be broken. Though it is strong, it is extremely fine and it takes weavers of immense skill and sensitivity to spin its gossamer form."

"But I cannot see anything," Mia responded. "Where is the thread that they will set about weaving?"

"Ah," the peacock smiled again, "therein lies the magic. To touch Hope you must first believe hard enough that it is there. Only then is its true beauty and power revealed to you. Unless you give yourself up to Belief and to her sister, Faith, this most miraculous of all threads will remain invisible to you."

Mia found herself longing to see this mysterious thing, about which she had heard but had herself never seen.

"What does it look like?" she asked, feeling that if she knew what she was looking for her chances of finding Hope might be the greater.

"Its hue is more light than colour," the peacock told her, "and it is unique to itself. Perhaps it is only the early morning sunlight, when filtered through a soft summer mist, with all the promise of a glorious day before it, which comes close to emulating its beauty – but there is nothing truly like your first glimpse of Hope to fill your world with light..."

And then Mia knew that Hope was what she had for so long been missing. And she knew that more than anything she wanted to find it for herself; but she did not know how to begin the search.

"Can you help me to find Hope?" she asked her new friend, for she felt the power of his magic shimmering all around her.

"I can take you on a journey," he replied, almost

before she had finished her question. "On the way, if your heart is open and your head is wise, you will learn many things and perhaps you will find what you are looking for. In understanding what it is that you are missing you have already taken your first step along the road..."

Then, as Mia watched, the smallest of the birds, a tiny wren, flew down from the rafters where she and her companions had been so busily weaving. She hovered daintily before the peacock and, though she spoke in music not in words, Mia found that she could understand what passed between them.

"We are almost ready," she sang. "The Window is finished and is eager to find its place."

And as she looked up, Mia caught her breath. High in the eaves of her ancient attic room hung the most glorious cloth of all imagining. Shimmering with light and, indeed, seeming to tug eagerly at the constraint of the myriad birds who held it tight, the Window of Far and Wide was all colours and no colour, intangible and yet as real as the world that it was about to bring to her.

The peacock smiled inside and nodded his approval. With his wing he gestured to the little birds above.

"Guide it carefully," he advised, "its placing is a critical part of the magic."

At his words the birds began their descent, as steadily as the vital, animated cloth would allow. Mia watched in wonderment.

"They are hovering over my bed," she whispered in awe.

"The Window will form a canopy," explained the peacock, "draped over the four posts which rise up from the corners of your bedstead. As you lie in bed, so you can look up and out of this dark and shuttered world and into the life that is waiting for you. What is required of you on the journey that follows is courage and heart and the wisdom to know that there is more to living than existence. Without your part, the Enchantment cannot be broken and the chance for your spirit to be truly free will be lost forever."

Though she was afraid at his words, for the prospect

of leaving her dark, wood-panelled world filled her with as much dread as that of losing the opportunity to escape it forever, Mia held them solemnly in her heart.

"I will do my part," she whispered, and, as if to reinforce her promise, she clambered up onto the lumpy old mattress and looked up between the bedposts at the attic roof above. But then, all of a sudden, it wasn't the ancient beamed ceiling that looked back at her.

At first, so unexpected was the sight that confronted her, Mia pulled urgently at the heavy bedspread, covering her eyes. Her head pounded with what she had seen and, though her eyes were tight shut, still light and colour danced before them, zigzagging disconcertingly across her inner dark.

In an explosion of colour and life, the Window had found its place. And as it did so it took on its ultimate form. What greeted Mia was no longer a shimmering ream of cloth but a vast and open window, the scene beyond which was still more dazzling and remarkable to the eyes of a small girl who had forgotten what it

was like to live...

How do you begin to describe The World when you are seeing its wonders as if for the very first time? Well, in that instant Mia, body and soul, was one with the light, the dark, the blue and the gold; with the running stream, the highest mountain, the tiny celandine and the mightiest oak. Mia belonged.

As she opened her eyes so The World looked back at her and acknowledged her belonging.

"Hold tight," the peacock smiled. "We have a lot of World to see."

Then, with a rush, like a sudden wind in a thousand beeches, Mia found herself hurtling through the sky, the fat white clouds strung out long and thin in her wake. Though she still felt the soft old mattress beneath her (how could that be?), The Window had caught her up in its magic and before she could take a breath her spirit was flying like a bird, up and beyond her fears to freedom...

She raced over hills and valleys, mountains and glittering streams. She marvelled at snowy peaks,

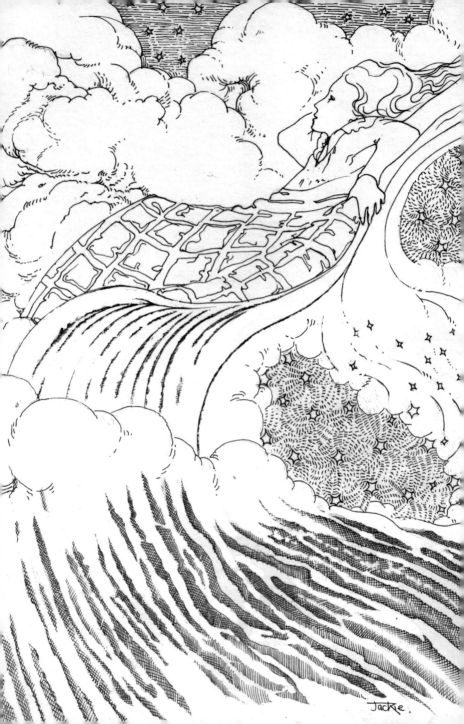

never-ending rivers that snaked their sinewy way round all that stood in their path, drank in the green, green, green of the vast grassy plains, dotted here and there with puffs of creamy-white that might have been sheep. She rejoiced in the crisp, fresh air that cooled her cheeks but fired her heart and discovered its scent, faint but distinct and ever-changing. And as the journey progressed, Mia fancied that if she closed her eyes she could tell you whether she traversed, in that instant, mountain or plain, ocean or desert, just by the scent that hung on the wind...

So her eyes were wide, her nose twitched with curiosity, and her ears, so long attuned only to the sound of her own breathing, learnt to find sound where there almost was none and to wonder at the hushed, rhythmic breaths of the sea on the shore, the deep roar of the icy waterfall, the pure, clear voice of the lark soaring high above the moors and the rough, grating crack of the barking deer.

And all the time she was a thousand miles away and still at home. Beneath her was the familiar bedspread, to her right and across a bit, the old wooden washstand, and yet her spirit was a hundred

miles distant, a thousand, then two...

And then there was something new in the air, something thick and exotic and strange and Mia's eyes and nose and ears saw and smelt and heard and questioned.

"This is Maurya," the peacock explained in answer to her unasked question, from his place beside her at the foot of the bed, "and she has much to teach one who is ready to learn."

So Mia bowed her head to the East, giving up her head to her wisdom and her body to the intense, moist heat which took her up into itself until she was altogether one with all around her, diffused wholly into the sultry air. Light, colour, sound and smells permeated similarly throughout her being, too extreme to be fully comprehended and thus experienced purely for what they were. If she had but known it, Mia smelt the warm Monsoon rains as they rushed down the dusty streets. She smelt the herbs and spices of the market place and in the same breath the putrid, rotting stench of meat and fish, their age not yet masked by the golden tamarind, cumin, saffron

and coriander seed that would become their culinary saviour. And she smelt the life that teemed through every street, thronging at the market, sitting on rugs of red, gold, blue, the women draped and swathed in endless reams of cloth that shouted colour from every fibre, challenging for supremacy the brightly painted lorries that flitted ostentatiously by.

And yet even such intensity of colour was subordinate to the sounds that were inextricable from the dense warm air. From all sides, it seemed, Mia was assailed by a million jabbering voices, holding forth their excitement in a strange and unintelligible tongue. And Mia reeled and was overcome and the peacock saw this and knew that it was an important part of her journey. And as he carried her beyond the city, beyond the chaos and the noise, beyond the poverty and the stench to the mountains of Karashim he knew too that soon it would be clear whether the Enchantment could ever truly be broken.

Then, as the haunting strains of the world lifting its soul up to God echoed out across the vast flat lake, Mia wept. She cried for Maurya, her palaces and her poverty, her glory and her squalor, her joy

and her suffering. She cried for humanity, for the old and the young, the empty and the fulfilled, the cruel and the kind. And she cried for Mia, for the fear and the trust, for the loneliness and the belonging, for the despair and the hope – and for an innocence that was lost too soon, too soon...

And the peacock knew that it was time to go home.

In an instant the Window was a gleaming cloth once more and Mia found herself once again lying on her back and looking up at its ethereal beauty. Just as before the journey began.

Except things weren't just as before. For Mia was changed. Her cheeks were flushed, rosy with life. Her eyes sparkled and danced and her heart beat firm and steady in her breast. As if by magic (which of course it was), her arms and legs were strong and limber and, when she tried to stand, her gait was as steady as her gaze.

And the cloth too, now that she really looked at it, was different. "That exquisite border," she asked of her feathered friend, pointing upwards to a filigree of the most sublime and delicate lace work, more light than colour, that bordered the cloth, "why did I not see that before?"

And at that the peacock knew that his work was done. As suddenly as he had appeared, he was gone.

And as Mia reached up and touched the spider's delicate tracery, she knew that what she saw was Hope and that the Enchantment was broken. As she looked about her she saw that Hope gleamed from every beam, stretched across her little round window pane, bridged the smooth, round bedposts and that the once dark room was filled with a heavenly light.

And, as she reached out to open the heavy oak door, ready to greet The World that was waiting, Mia smiled...

The End

between
angels &
demons

Emma Bowes Romanelli

BETWEEN ANGELS & DEMONS

Emma Bowes Romanelli's first book, 'Between Angels and Demons' – 'a moving and unexpectedly funny' (Daily Telegraph) account of her battle with leukaemia – was published in 2004 (978 0954 4011 6 0 £7.99). Illustrated by Jackie Astbury.

"I should have died at 19…

When I was eighteen I had it all. I sailed through my A-levels, out of the school gates and across the Atlantic to America, arms outstretched to greet the world that was waiting.

Three months later they told me I was dying …

This is the story about a year in my life; an extraordinary year. It is a little about dying, a whole lot about living and, I hope, something about what it is to be eighteen and know all the answers and to be nineteen and to realise that you have only just begun to understand the question."

"Emma's endearing humour shines through the pages of this inspirational and moving book." – The Duchess of York

"Emma's wonderfully positive view on life is extraordinarily uplifting … a source of strength, comfort and hope to many people who are facing their own tests." – Gary Lineker

"Read it and, if your back is ever pressed against the wall of life, read it again; it could fill you with fight when you might just need it." – Sir Jimmy Savile OBE

A PERCENTAGE OF ALL PROCEEDS DONATED TO
THE TEENAGE CANCER TRUST

BETWEEN ANGELS & DEMONS

"This amazing story, written so eloquently by this exceptionally talented young woman, embodies so much of the spirit of what Teenage Cancer Trust is trying to achieve. Emma is a born fighter who has battled against her illness and the effects of its treatment. Through the tapestry of her words she sends a positive message to us all about what really are the important things in life. This book is a good read in its own right, not just because of its subject matter. But the compelling combination of the two is what really sets it apart.

And to top all that Emma has decided to donate a very significant percentage of the proceeds from the book to Teenage Cancer Trust so that youngsters in the future can benefit from improved services and treatment. This donation will enable us to develop more units around the country that are specifically geared towards teenagers. Environments that whilst providing the best possible care also include computers, PlayStations, social facilities and are geared especially to the needs of young people. It will also help us to deliver our associated support services for families and our education and awareness programme in schools and universities throughout the country, (www.teencancer.org).

Thank you Emma for your selfless generosity."

Simon Davies
Chief Executive Officer
Teenage Cancer Trust

Emma is currently living in Tuscany with her husband, Lorenzo, and is concentrating full-time on her writing.